Misconceptions

Pride and Prejudice:
A Conclusion

Misconceptions

Pride and Prejudice:
A Conclusion

Doris Nieves

To order additional copies of this book, contact:
Xlibris Corporation
1-888-795-4274
www.Xlibris.com
Orders@Xlibris.com
75544

Dedicated to Rosemary

and

all my family

Preface

Lady Catherine traveled to Dover where she arranged to stay the month with her old friend Lord Carrington, an aristocrat of reputation, large fortune and property. Her return to Greenfield Castle rekindled deep seated memories of a time long past. These two families, the Carringtons and the de Bourghs, once enjoyed very close associations. Their friendship remained strong for many years until the death of Lord Carrington's revered wife, Lady Stephanie.

"Lord Carrington, I am very happy to see you again. It has been many years since we have seen each other. Reviewing your grounds, seeing them much like before, helps me remember when my late husband, Sir Louis, was your particular friend. We had some wonderful times together," said Lady Catherine provoking memories in Lord Carrington.

"I am happy to see you as well, Lady Catherine. Your visit is welcome as I preserve the cherished memory of Sir Louis as well. Time does go by quickly," said Lord Carrington seated in his favorite chair. He peered at Lady Catherine through clouded squinting eyes. "I trust all has been well for you and Anne?"

"We have remained fortunate. Anne has grown to be a lovely young lady. I am very proud of her. Rosings is all arranged to be inherited by her someday as I do not believe in estates being entailed away from the female bloodline," she answered. "How is your son, Matthew?"

"You would find Daniel in fine health if he were here," he answered. "He is a devoted son. When my daughter Kristine married and began to keep her own house, I would have been alone but Daniel would not have it and returned upon his graduation from Cambridge to supervise my care as my health has been failing steadily. He remained so committed that I fear he would lead a lonely life and never experience the love I was so fortunate to have with Lady Stephanie. You do not find him here because I urged him out into the world in search of a most worthy wife."

With great interest Lady Catherine asked, "And how successful has he been?"

"As it stands now, my son remains unattached. He does not have the same sense of urgency I do. But he is wise to be selective and choose someone who will fit in with his character and routine. I want his happiness but am so afraid he will not marry in my lifetime. I can't rest in peace without having this matter settled." Lady Catherine could see how troubled he became and was pleased to be of service to him.

"I understand you Lord Carrington. It seems that we are in a similar situation. I am worried for my Anne as well. Similar to Daniel, she is dedicated to remaining at home with me. I am put out that, in the event of my death, Anne will have the security of Rosings but remain quite alone."

"It is disheartening," agreed Lord Carrington, "but it was my understanding that you were fortunate to have contracted your daughter to marriage since childhood. You had written me yourself. Has that changed?"

"You are speaking of Anne's long standing engagement to Mr Darcy. It has been broken for some time and since then he has married quite beneath him, I must say. But at the moment I am only thinking of Anne's happiness. She is a steady girl who needs nothing else in life but to find suitable companionship. Maybe someone like your Daniel." Lord Carrington sat back in his seat to contemplate the matter. A discomforting silence followed as she sat waiting for his response.

A servant soon entered rolling in a tea cart. To keep the setting intimate Lady Catherine served the tea and helped Lord Carrington with his portions. After a short intermission, concluding with the consuming of cakes, Lady Catherine spoke out again.

"Lord Carrington, it may be possible that you and I have worried needlessly. If you are agreeable to arranging a marriage between your son, Daniel, and my daughter, Anne, we can secure a bright future for both and rest in peace."

"Lady Catherine, I have given it some thought and believe it would please me tremendously. I have no objections to following the long established custom of arrangements and if you can assure me of Miss de Bourgh's compliance, I shall take on the difficult task of writing Daniel," he said coming to life at the negotiations.

"I guarantee you, she will accept his proposal," smiled Lady Catherine. "The two are well suited."

"Then it is agreed," he said slapping his arthritic hands on his knees from the sheer delight of it.

"Yes, Lord Carrington, it is," she affirmed.

"We must arrange for a meeting," he said excitedly.

"They will both be attending Miss Georgiana Darcy's engagement ball. I have seen the guest list and recall seeing his name. They will certainly have the opportunity to meet there as I have no doubt that your son will ask my daughter to dance. I shall write Anne to make her aware and arrange for a close relation to seek him out and make the proper introductions. Rest assured, they will naturally appeal to each other," said Lady Catherine with the satisfaction of knowing that her daughter was so instructed days ago before Mr Darcy escorted her to Pemberley.

"Then we shall both correspond. There is no need to take chances with these things. Please hand me a quill from the escritoire. I will write directly. He is in London and I can reach him there before he moves on."

Lady Catherine was more than happy to fulfill his wish and handed him some writing paper and quill. She held his ink well patiently as he wrote:

Dearest Son,

I have news for you that may put both our minds at peace and complete your quest for a bride sooner than expected. It has come to my knowledge that you have an invitation to Miss Darcy's ball at Pemberley. You must forfeit any other plans and accept it. On the occasion of your attending the ball, you will make the acquaintance of a young lady equal to your rank and situation in life. You are to befriend her as it has been arranged that one of her closest relatives will seek you out and make proper introductions. She will specifically be awaiting your offer to dance. You must request the first two to exhibit significant interest and validate her as the one in question. If you are pleased with her, as I cannot see that you will not be for her father was an especially cherished friend of mine, you have my every blessing to marry. Take your time. Know her well. Do not worry for me as I am with good company and in good health for the time being. I await your return as planned, with wife in hand as I remain hopeful. Your father.

Lord Mathew Carrington

Chapter 1

"Papa, my aunt Philips only wants me to help her entertain! Our old friends Captain Carter and Mr Denny will be there, not to mention Colonel Forster. You remember them!" urged Kitty in a futile attempt to persuade Mr Bennet. She wanted her father's permission to assist her aunt Philips in the first among many socials for the newly transferred officers.

"I have met Mr Wickham too! That did not stop your sister Lydia from scandalously eloping. Let the regiment find entertainment at Mrs Philips without you," contested Mr Bennet standing firm.

"But my aunt cannot host all of our soldiers adequately without me! If I don't help her, they may abandon her hospitality as they did Mrs Watson's the last time they were stationed in town! For the sake of my aunt's reputation, I am obliged to go!" argued Kitty.

"I release you from any obligation put upon you by her to amuse our militia. Your aunt Philips has a good head for entertaining, as no one else can offer. She does her part and it is very much talked about. For our part, we shall make record of it. As for the officers, they must suffer her diversions without the benefit of you. If they are not thoroughly entertained because of your absence, they may make their way to Clarke's library for a quick pick me up!" he suggested carelessly putting an end to the debate.

"I don't see why I must constantly pay for what Lydia did!" cried Kitty stomping her feet convinced her father could not be swayed.

Dejected, she looked at her older sister Mary for a sign of empathy but saw that she would not stir from her book. Mary, who always assumed a more serious state of mind, had no particular love for officers. She could never be enlisted to help when it came to engaging the soldiers in town. Kitty needed the benefit of her mother's advocacy as Mrs Bennet would certainly induct Mr Bennet's consent despite any objections. Dissatisfied with her failed attempts, Kitty determined it wiser to sit, albeit discontentedly, until her mother could come to her aid.

"What did Lydia do?" inquired Mrs Bennet happily as she appeared at the door animated by the mention of her most favored daughter. She entered the parlor with Mr and Mrs Philips, cheerfully escorting them to the couch.

"Mama, Papa says I may not go to my aunt Philips to assist with the officers! Its Lydia again! Shall he never forget what Lydia did!" protested Kitty desperately appropriating her mother's alliance.

"What is there to forget?" stated Mrs Bennet with confusion. "Lydia saw an opportunity and used it to her advantage. She did very well for herself, I must say," endorsed Mrs Bennet, proud of Lydia's willful stunt.

"It was fortunate indeed, Mrs Bennet," said Mr Bennet. "The matter was patched up with relative ease," he said trying to remain composed. "We managed to suffer only temporary disgrace and as a reward, we pay the debts the Wickhams accumulate wherever they go, not only with merchants but also those Wickham imposes upon his friends!"

"Oh, Mr Bennet, no one recalls such insignificant details—especially his friends!" Brushing away Mr Bennet's comments, she turned to Mrs Philips for support. Mr Philips placed a cautious hand on his wife to prevent her from becoming involved in her sister's affairs. Mrs Philips, who would have much to say in the defense of any officer, was eager to draw herself into the conversation but Mr Philips' gesture left her to check herself and respond with a complacent nod of the head.

"Ahh, yes, our little community has focused on someone else's troubles for the time being. What would the world be without a regular dose of gossip and of scandal? After all," continued Mr Bennet in quick wit, "what do we live for if not to be the subject of folly for our neighbors and they ours in their turn." Mrs Bennet chuckled, amused by his philosophy of the nature of gossip. She thought he was putting a lighter edge on the conversation and allowed herself to feel at ease until he included, "With you at the helm, Mrs Bennet, I always trusted our prospects would oblige them satisfactorily but our Lydia has exceeded even those expectations. We could not have been bestowed with a more puerile child than she."

"What are you saying?" defended Mrs Bennet as the dialogue took an acute turn for the worse. She would never tolerate anyone belittling her youngest daughter. "Lydia has every bit of maturity and intelligence as I do!"

"If it is your intention that I debate you on that premise, fear not, for I have long ago come to the conclusion that you, and all my girls, with the exception of Lizzy, lack equally in those quarters. It has been the cause of my affliction for many years now," taunted Mr Bennet.

"Any man would consider himself fortunate to have such fine girls. You should not hesitate to count yourself as such," advised Mrs Bennet with airs.

"It is true, Mrs Bennet. Since childhood I have thought I should like to be surrounded by women in my later years and those aspirations have been realized," he said coaxing her into agreement. "Alas, destiny has looked upon me with a satirical eye and fulfilled my dreams to no doubt, warn my sex against any such desires. So goes the life of man . . ." Mr Bennet spent many years needling his wife with a unique blend of sarcasm and reserve. He never tired of her stupefied, flustered reactions and his company was by now accustomed to it.

"Do not think your meaning is lost with me! This is entirely your fault! You need not remain so surrounded if the girls could venture out beyond our mundane assemblies. It is not from my lack of trying that Kitty and Mary remain unmarried," she explained. "A little cooperation from you and we can successfully arrange to marry them off as well. Only then can you retire in peace with just me to confront around the house," she said in attempt to console him.

"Happy thought indeed," retorted Mr Bennet.

"Well then, my parties are just what are needed!" exclaimed Mrs Philips deciding Mr Bennet's response was an approval for her acquiring Kitty's assistance. Her renewed attempts were the stimulus Mrs Bennet and Kitty needed to proceed dauntlessly with their objectives for the night of the party. Mrs Bennet and Kitty eagerly clamored around Mrs Philips as she reviewed their agenda. "Kitty shall have her choice of the finest officers!" planned Mrs Philips as the women stood over her. "It is only right that she meet with them before the other young ladies of the neighborhood do!" Mrs Bennet was pleased with her sister's point of view as she and Kitty smiled in blissful agreement. "Goodness knows, those other girls show no restrain. They are already flowing into town in great clusters," continued Mrs Philips. "Why, I have recently found out that Mrs Watson is attempting to host a social for our officers the very next evening after mine. She tried, but could not persuade them to forfeit my invitation as was her original intention. She had to settle for the following night, so as not to lose any more time I presume. And she promises there shall be countless young misses there! You are aware, of course, that she alone has nieces enough to capture all of our soldiers!" she said in irritation. Sharing Mrs Bennet's concern for competition, she found Mrs Watson too predatory for her own good.

"Those eager, desperate girls!" belittled Mrs Bennet. "Kitty deserves to have first choice after all the time she spent with them during their last visit here. And Mary would have first choice as well, if she had the good sense to develop an interest in her own future," reproached Mrs Bennet employing charitable compassion from her sister. Mary, who had been sitting, reading quietly by the fire, willfully ignored her mother's comments as was her practice. Officers would never be subject to her fancy as she was not subject to theirs. It had been her experience that officers were not the type of intellectuals she preferred. She thought them too frivolous, wanting only to dance and be entertained, and would not allow herself to become involved in her mother's exploits by accompanying Kitty to Mrs Philips' tedious socials. Instead she found much satisfaction in the company of a good book.

"All of Herefordshire should proceed as they will without so much as a care from us," contended Mr Bennet acerbically. "I wish them all the best of luck but I will not allow anyone to take cruel advantage of my family's credulous simplicity again. I do not wish to spoil your amusements but Kitty shall not fall subject to your notions anymore than I should have allowed Lydia."

"How can you speak so ill of us?" challenged Mrs Bennet.

"I do not speak ill of anyone. The facts are as I have stated," he said firmly dismissing her rebuke.

Mrs Philips sat in disappointment. She could not believe all her planning and expectations were so easily dismissed. "Mr Bennet, I assure you that Mr Philips will interview the officer of her choice before any attachment forms," she said struggling to secure Kitty's attendance. Mrs Philips depended on Kitty's youth, vigor and beauty to supply the officers with an endless amount of pleasurable distractions. She knew that Kitty would shine and single handedly upstage Mrs Watson's homely nieces. Kitty was a vital part of her operation and she could not set forth a successful campaign to defeat Mrs Watson without her. "Wouldn't you, Mr Philips?" she asked anxiously. Mr Philip was caught completely off guard by what his wife offered and took a short time to compose himself from the very addition of his name to the conversation.

"With the greatest pleasure," confirmed Mr Philips while clearing his throat uneasily. He could not, after all, refuse the charge. He lived with the guilt of acting unwisely three years ago when the officers were there last and could not help but assume some of the responsibility for Lydia's elopement. He did not want to promote an alliance between the remaining Bennet girls and the militia as much as Mr Bennet, but did not think it necessary to argue the point with his wife at this very moment. In his quest to promote peace in the Bennet house, Mr Philips thought it better to comply with Mrs Philips, trusting that Mr Bennet would keep the entire affair under control.

"Mrs Philips, your suggestion is admirable and I thank Mr Philips for volunteering," said Mr Bennet as Mr Philips squirmed about. "I have the utmost trust that both of you will take every precaution necessary in preventing a recurrence of past events. Nevertheless, I need not impose my responsibilities upon you," he said generously. Turning to Kitty he said, "My final response to you is a resounding 'No' and that is the last I shall speak of it!" Kitty wailed as Mrs Bennet thought hard on how to make her next attempt. "If you will forgive me," added Mr Bennet resolutely, "I shall take a few minutes to skim through the afternoon post." Bringing the conversation to an abrupt end, he left the parlor to make his way to the library. Mr Philips thought Mr Bennet's response was a capitol maneuver and was relieved to consider the subject closed.

"Mr Bennet, you take every opportunity to vex me!" snapped Mrs Bennet as he closed the door behind him.

Mr Bennet enjoyed taking refuge in the library. He sat there regularly to pass the time of day with very little contemplation on his family's affairs. Coming to terms that his women were the extreme opposite of his gentility and self control he was resigned to allow his wife to lead herself and their daughters wherever their antics took them, keeping his distance until imposed upon, as he was today.

"Mama, I shall remain an old maid for the rest of my life because of Lydia! It's not fair!" cried Kitty. She was tired of living in Longbourn and wanted desperately to marry and see the world as her other sisters had.

"Do not worry so, Kitty," comforted Mrs Bennet. "At least you have the good sense to scout around for a husband when the opportunity presents itself. I admire your every attempt, unlike Mary who has no interest at all," she said calling everyone's attention to Mary who adjusted her seat and refocused her attentions on her book. "Her nose is always in a book. Her whole approach is wrong!" she continued without restraint. "You alone have the proper attitude, Kitty, and it shall not be as difficult to find you a husband as it will be to find one for her," said Mrs Bennet in a hopelessly tiresome manner. Taking a moment to think over the situation, Mrs Bennet continued, "But Meryton has been so desolate since the militia abandoned us to our little assemblies. The same faces again and again. There are just no prospects for us here without new faces!"

At the brutal mention of her poor prospects, Mary felt obliged to come to her own defense. After all, it was not entirely true that she had no interest. She just gave up trying. Having no claim to being the prettiest or most accomplished, Mary compensated for the lack thereof by taking refuge in professing to be the most knowledgeable. She buried herself in books and cited passages at every opportunity in attempt to stimulate conversation, which had the adverse effect of social alienation. No longer yielding to visions of marriage, Mary said with an air of confidence, "I never found a companion as companionable as solitude." She stood holding her head proudly while she searched through her books by the window.

Mrs Bennet and Kitty never appreciated her philosophical views and were exasperated by Mary's indifference at a time like this. Frustrated, Kitty poked at the fire as Mrs Bennet turned to the Philipses rolling her eyes in disapproval, wishing she had not heard Mary speak at all.

"Oh, Sister," moaned Mrs Bennet, "how is it to be believed that now, at a time when Kitty could break free from the dependency of our small assemblies, Mr Bennet is bent on keeping her to the house!?! He will be her ruin!"

The sisters became quickly absorbed in a furious conversation which involved, among other things, Mrs Watson's pitifully deficient parties. Kitty was distracted as she heard the mention of her name but did not trouble to investigate. Her mind was preoccupied with the sullen disappointment of her father's final decree. Mr Philips sat in repose twiddling his thumbs as he would not join in the conversation. Mr Bennet soon returned holding an open letter in his hand, looking rather pleased with himself. Mr Philips was particularly relieved to see him again eager for some stimulation.

"Mr Bennet! All is well I trust," began Mr Philips opening up the conversation giving Mr Bennet the floor.

"All is not well and you know it, Mr Philips," blustered Mrs Bennet, riled at the sight of her neglectful husband. "What man would leave his daughters with no chance of procuring some security, especially when one of them is so willing? Well, never you mind, Mr Bennet. Mrs

Philips and I have derived an alternate plan." Exhilarated by their newly contrived scheme, Mrs Bennet felt confident enough to deliver their latest strategy. "We shall strive to make the name of Miss Catherine Bennet known to our officers through happy rumor and conjecture, saying that Kitty is sought after by every man that comes to Longbourn and cannot be compared to by any one of the other ladies in Meryton. The Watson girls shall be mentioned there as comparison," she said with Mrs Philips agreeing every step of the way. "We shall promote her beyond their every expectation and they will come knocking at our door seeking her out. Then, for all purposes, she could not refuse to meet them and must go out to satisfy their curiosity as they will refuse to leave without it!" concluded Mrs Bennet with devious delight. Mrs Philips was equally satisfied with their scheme as their audience stood silent in astonishment.

"Mrs Bennet, I urge you, inasmuch as there is glory in the unspoken word, proper speech should be stored up for something of a more cognitive nature," declared Mr Bennet disturbed by his wife's thought processes. "In any case nothing of the sort that you conspire to will happen."

"But you see Mr Bennet that is where you are mistaken. No one can stop the power of a rumor traveling full speed for as you are fully aware, even whispers can be heard a county away. The very allure will bring every curious eligible young bachelor to her door before the door of anyone else. Is that not so Mrs Philips?" Mrs Philips took a moment to analyze the curiously inquiring looks of unsettling disbelief on everyone's faces. She thought quickly on how to amend their plans to gain the family's approval. However, before she could speak, Mr Philips prevented her response with a look of mortification and asked, "Is that what you two were about!?! Must there be a scheme afoot every time you assemble!?! Mr Bennet has enough to handle without your menacing interference!" In haste to terminate their visit Mr Philips stood and announced their sudden need to leave.

"You may proceed with your plan as you wish, Mrs Bennet, and when the regulars come knocking at the door, send them away for

Kitty shall not be here. She will be leaving Hertfordshire to go directly into the society of her sister, Mrs Bingley, in London," he announced unperturbed. "She writes that the winter there is particularly confining for one in her condition. Her sisters, by marriage, are not society enough and she would enjoy having one of her own sisters there to keep her company. You see, they are already expecting you!" he said handing the letter to Kitty with much satisfaction. Kitty's response was slow and unsure as she took the letter.

"Kitty!" exclaimed Mrs Bennet in ecstasy; her scope completely redirected, "This is wonderful for you! You must go ahead of us for we have given Jane an adequate amount of time to get her household together, as we have Lizzy, and it shall not be considered improper to begin your visits. You cannot imagine the opportunities for you there in London. The exposure, the encounters, and the clothes! Be sure to call upon your aunt Gardiner for guidance where that is concerned. She is up to the minute in fashion and the styles alter so quickly these days." She stopped and thought aloud. "It is not too late to alert her with this evening's post. She will be sure to procure a proper gown for Pemberley that Hertfordshire would not have offered," she said happily to her sister. Mrs Philips failed to appreciate Mrs Bennet's sudden abandon but knew very well she would not be able to infiltrate the Bennets' joint convictions and mustered an adequately agreeable look.

"How good it was of Jane to think of you, Kitty," suggested Mrs Bennet. "She is not expecting for at least two more months and could very well use your diversions. Her condition will work to your benefit, as it shall also free up your time for shopping and tailoring before going out to the many social events London affords. Lovely thoughtful Jane," rejoiced Mrs Bennet thinking about her eldest and most considerate daughter. "Expecting a child in just one year of marriage! She does know her duty!"

Mr Philips smiled approvingly toward Mr Bennet and congratulated Mrs Bennet on the success of her daughter's removal to better pastures. On their way out he said, "We should say our farewells to you, Kitty. Give our best wishes and regards to the Bingleys. Mrs Philips and I shall visit them and their new addition when they return home to Netherfield. As for us, we shall have our hands full with the militia until then," he said cheerfully rushing his wife to the door. Mrs Philips swallowed her resentment and thought about Kitty's excursion.

"She should leave soon. I think the weather has let up temporarily," noted Mrs Philips looking toward the sky. Expressing their desires for Kitty's safe journey, they exited the house to find their way home by the light of the late afternoon sun. Mrs Bennet turned from the door and anxiously called to her servant.

"Hill! Make haste, Hill!" she said with a sudden need for urgency. "You would think Kitty's boxes have already been packed!" She worried about the weather as she scouted about for Hill. She did not want anything to prevent the promising sojourn. Hill quickly appeared at the bottom of the steps as Mrs Bennet approached to inform her of Kitty's good fortune. "Kitty is to begin her visits to Mr and Mrs Bingley in London. If we get started with her packing tonight, she should be able to get an early start by morning outwitting any possible snowfall." While Mrs Bennet consumed herself with instructing Hill, Mr Bennet discussed the journey with Kitty.

"It will be lonely while you travel Kitty, and the cold weather does not help. The scenery shall be very dull," noted Mr Bennet. "I hope you are up to it!" Mrs Bennet overheard him and swiftly defied his concern.

"Of course she is up to it!" Mrs Bennet dismissed Hill to her task. "Mr Peters shall drive you in the carriage all the way to London but remember to order it to return instantly since you would not need the horses," she instructed Kitty. "Let sweet Jane know we shall arrive in time to see the baby as soon as we hear it is delivered. She is well aware that I am having new garments made up for my travels. After all, a mother of two wealthy daughters cannot travel in worn costumes!" she announced proudly. Cheerfully turning to Mr Bennet, she said with satisfaction, "Mr Bennet, what a fortunate accommodation! Isn't it just what I have been trying to tell you? We have such wonderful daughters!"

"As you say, Mrs Bennet," conceded Mr Bennet, "but wonderful was never my contention." Taking no account of Mr Bennet, Mrs Bennet giggled in delightful anticipation of Kitty's new exploits.

"Come Kitty, we must look through your threads to see what can be salvaged for your trip. You must only wear your very finest so as to be prepared for incidental meetings. Be sure to have Jane arrange as many as she can!" she urged. "I cannot stress enough how significant chance meetings can be. They have been known to make a greater impact than proper introductions more times than I can say," she advised as they ascended the stairs to Kitty's room.

Mrs Bennet, preoccupied with supervising Hill, did not revive any of the previous discussion pertaining to Mrs Philips' social. She could not see that Kitty did not appreciate the compromise she had to make in traveling to London, abandoning the occasion she had most looked forward to in meeting her fine men of uniform, right there in Meryton. Kitty knew she would be deprived of numerous accounts of adventures and gallantries that were exchanged by the officers when they were at ease enjoying their rest and relaxation. She remembered being thoroughly amused by their tales and was disheartened to realize that she would miss out on the opportunity to enjoy them once again. The prospect of leaving Hertfordshire removed all hopes of her ever seeing them as she did not know when she or they would return.

As always, unable to champion her own causes successfully, she was left to accept the fact that once her mother was settled on a matter, she had no choice but to reconcile herself to it and realize that London's metropolitan lifestyle should provide her with a variety of novelties and diversions which, to say the least, promised to be a source of unprecedented enjoyment.

In the meantime, Mr Bennet remained downstairs with Mary. "That went very well, don't you think, Mary?" he said striking up a conversation.

"Impeccable timing I would say," replied Mary approvingly.

"Precisely!" returned Mr Bennet happily. "Thanks to your uncle Philips' forewarning me of the 'Meryton invasion' and our wives' ambitions, I was cognizant of what Kitty would request even before herself. Concluding that London should prove to be the distraction she needed, I wrote Jane, who was agreeable to my plans and provided me with an open invitation last month to present as I saw fit, at the proper time, requesting Kitty's presence in a way that could not be refused," he said flaunting his carefully laid plan. "We must stay a step ahead, Mary, and if you will excuse me, I shall now write Mrs Bingley and inform her that Kitty is on her way." Having said his piece, he sported a smile and turned contentedly for the library leaving Mary in the parlor to return to her book.

Chapter 2

The long journey prompted Kitty to realize how glad she was to be in London. She became anxious to see the Bingleys again. The roads were not easy and made the ride wearisome and rough going. As she looked out of the carriage window she enjoyed viewing the many novelties London possessed. It was vastly different from country life in Meryton. The numerous carriages and the vigorous activity by the population would have been greatly curtailed by March's unrelenting weather.

The city's buildings were tightly lined in rows so uniformly it was difficult for her to distinguish one from another. It took some time for Mr Peters to locate the correct building as he pulled up close to the sidewalks of Grosvenor Place.

Her carriage was met by her new brother, Mr Charles Bingley, a handsome gentleman of five thousand pounds a year, whose countenance was easy and personality kind and amiable. Mr Bingley was genuinely happy to see Kitty and welcomed her wholeheartedly. As for Kitty, she was naturally at ease around her favorite brother in law.

"How do you do, Kitty? I am very pleased to see you have arrived safely. I hope your ride has been smooth and tolerable. The weather is so unpredictable and the roads are not what they should be this winter," greeted Mr Bingley as he helped her from the carriage.

"It was very comfortable, thank you," replied Kitty relieved to have finally arrived. "I am as well as you see!" she answered with a smile.

She decided she would make the most of her situation and accepted his hospitality with overtures of her happiness in being there.

"Your sister Jane shall be particularly comforted by your visit," related Mr Bingley trying to look as little distressed as possible. He looked to his feet in order to avoid Kitty's eyes as he was aware his demeanor was easily read. "I must tell you, we did not want to worry your family needlessly, but we have been having quite a start. With the weather so harsh and her condition so delicate, Jane has recently come down with a case of pneumonia. It has kept her bedridden a fortnight. Her family way only complicates the matter," he said as his voice gave way to his concern. Realizing Kitty should not be so hastily burdened by their troubles, he put a lighter tone on the conversation saying, "My sisters, Caroline and Mrs Hurst, along with Mr Hurst, are here to help. They have been magnificent in keeping house for us. Miss Bingley and Mrs Hurst have gone out of their way to command the servants, prepare the menus and do all they can. However, Jane shall be especially pleased to have you here as well. We anticipated your visit for some time now and are most grateful for your arrival." They walked up the front steps and advanced into the corridor where Mr Bingley ordered a servant to show Kitty to her room and help her settle in. Kitty, however, would not agree to go. She had, instead, an eagerness to see her sister right away.

"You are most accommodating, Mr Bingley, to consider my comfort with all that must be worrying you but I implore you to take me to Jane right away. I could not be more alarmed than when you, who knows my sister's condition, are so apprehensive. I will not be at ease until I, myself, see how she is," urged Kitty. Jane's illnesses were never a light matter. The slightest cough would often erupt into an intense, more complicated affliction and confine her to bed for prolonged periods of time. Pneumonia would certainly take its toll on her and her baby.

Mr Bingley understood her distress and obliged Kitty without opposition. Inclined to share more news with her he explained, "I have hired a physician who came highly recommended. He is a prodigy in the medical field. 'On the cutting edge' they say. His name is Dr Alexander

Kindrel. He has been working round the clock with Mrs Bingley this past week. She is not out of danger yet but the doctor says, with proper care, she and the baby will be made right again."

They arrived at the Bingley bedchamber and quietly entered the room. The sight of Jane so helplessly ill made Kitty rush to her side. She could not recall ever seeing her sister look so grave. "Jane, how are you feeling?" she asked putting her hand upon her forehead. "Mama and Papa planned to arrive in time for the birth of your child but I shall write hastily and have them come sooner," she said. Jane shook her head in disagreement. Her weakness was clearly visible.

"Please do not worry our parents, Kitty," appealed Jane scarcely audible. She mustered all her strength to appear improved in health. Smiling assuredly Jane explained, "Dr Kindrel is very experienced and has treated pneumonia many times over. He is a knowledgeable man and I have the fullest confidence in him. Just the same, Kitty, I am very glad you are here. Your presence will be a solace to me," said Jane, who even in illness thought of the feelings of others.

"Indeed, Kitty," confirmed Mr Bingley stepping forward to relieve his wife of her overexertion, "as I have said, we have with us the most reputable of physicians. We feel quite fortunate to have acquired him. Do not feel you must concern your parents; it is Jane's special wish. Your sister, Mrs Darcy, has not been informed either. She is happily employed with entertaining Lord Watney. Jane does not wish to distress or distract her from her own duties. As you know, Lizzy would drop everything in Derbyshire and form a pilgrimage to London as she has done in the past. Word has it Miss Darcy and Lord Watney are engaged and the pleasurable task of forming wedding plans are being discussed as we speak. Jane would not have those preparations disturbed for the world. You can understand how distressful it would be for her to dampen their spirits with her hardships. I have honored her request and trust you will as well," concluded Mr Bingley now sitting beside his wife.

"Well then," insisted Kitty yielding to their wishes, "you shall have it your own way but you must involve me in your care, Jane. I assure you I will not have it any other way. I will have my things put away and return immediately," said Kitty as she departed without waiting for an answer. Jane gave Mr Bingley an encouraging smile before she turned to fall asleep. Mr Bingley remained temporarily and observed her beauty, still evident in spite of her illness, before getting up to leave the room.

Kitty returned in good time to find Jane sleeping soundly. There she encountered Dr Kindrel. He was searching through an unusual wooden medical box that could only have been fashioned by himself as it was obvious to have had a previous life as a portable wine chest. His clothes were neat and clean but not in the style worn by the fashionable young men of the day giving the impression that he was not naturally bred a gentleman.

Far from the typical stout, dank, musty doctor she was used to in Meryton he was young and slim. His features were pleasing and his general appearance was a symbol of health as he stood when she came in. His bright eyes met hers with warmth and welcome as he introduced himself saying, "You must be Miss Catherine Bennet. I am Dr Kindrel. It is a pleasure to meet you. I was informed of your visit and of your desire to help. Mrs Bingley is asleep for now so I shall use this time to inform you on her treatment and acquaint you with your new duties. Miss Bingley and Mrs Hurst have had servants care for Mrs Bingley until now," he said in a businesslike manner as he turned to carefully place his bottles into their assigned slots. "They do their best, I suppose, but I do have my hands filled with them. The sisters employ the servants to apply outdated practices based on old wives tales, totally ignoring my orders," he said shaking his head annoyed with their incessant defiance. "I am constantly undoing their applications to set Mrs Bingley right again. Mr Bingley does what he can but is not adept as either nurse or director. Yet all I really need from him is to prevent his sisters from treating Mrs Bingley outside of my authorizations!" He continued placing scales alongside his potions as he spoke. Reconsidering, he took a deep breath and brazenly concluded, "Sadly, he is inept at that as well." Kitty was surprised to hear someone speak so critically of the Bingleys but she knew he was right. Mr Bingley was too easily persuaded by his friends and family alike. It was his greatest flaw. 'The servants shall steal them blind,' she recalled her father once saying of him and Jane. "They are quite a team, those two ladies," continued Dr Kindrel. "Poor Mr Bingley is no match. It seems he is too complacent and cannot control them."

The sisters, although polite and urbane, were generally disengaged. Their indifference was flagrant with blatant detachment. They were too self absorbed to be less than distant to Jane who they resented for interfering with their social engagements through illness. As they were reluctantly involved, they performed their duties as they deemed appropriate remaining hands off, sending the servants to provide for Jane's care. Fortunately, regardless of their attitude, Mrs Bingley remained unaffected. Her thoughts were on her husband who remained vigilant awaiting Jane's full recovery.

Turning his thoughts to Kitty he added, "If you are up to it, you shall be the first in the family to give direct care. I am glad to work with someone who will nurse Mrs Bingley with consideration and sensitivity above and beyond the call of duty. Empathetic as I believe you to be, you should prove to be of great assistance to me and, in return, ensure Mrs Bingley's swift recovery."

"It will be as you say," assured Kitty. "She will be well attended and it shall be no other way but your own. My sister Jane has an excellent nature and is kindness and goodness to everyone. She should not be neglected by her family and should never have to go through any illness poorly cared for. I am also frightened for her baby," she said honestly. "There is nothing I wouldn't do."

Kitty's care for Jane was the most serious occupation she had undertaken in all of her nineteen years. Keeping the intelligence from the rest of the family was less consolatory for her than Jane realized. Kitty knew only too well what the risks involved. The last time she was a confidante, nothing but trouble came from it. She could not help but recall the dilemma she put her family in when she did not expose Lydia's plans for elopement. It had repercussions beyond her imagination causing potential ruin and humiliation to the entire family. At that time, there was nothing she could do to alter the situation and, should her care for Jane fail, her silence would again be a cause for great alarm to her innocent family. It was a weighty burden to carry. Therefore, in this case, since she could not betray her confidence, she would work diligently to improve the situation. She would be both nurse and confidante, twenty four hours a day, seven days a week. The thought of socializing, shopping and the touring of London was altogether forfeited since there was not any form of deprivation she would not undergo for the return of Jane's health.

*   *   *

As expected, Kitty was true to her convictions. Dr Kindrel was impressed with her diligence. He enjoyed watching Mrs Bingley receive the tenderness of Kitty's care as she vigilantly wiped Jane's forehead. He observed how she shooed the servants away with remedies not his own and found adoration in how she lay with her sister to provide added warmth when covers alone would not do. It was a sight sadly lacking before Kitty arrived. Proving to be every bit the proficient nurse, caring for two lives in one, gave Kitty a new sense of responsibility that helped her mature rapidly as Jane's health improved. Working earnestly, with persistence and tenacity, filling the void with deftness and delicacy, Kitty made herself a credit to her family and Dr Kindrel was charmed.

On occasion, Kitty read to Jane to lull her to sleep. When Jane would not have it, Kitty provided Jane with news from home which Jane readily absorbed. Kitty was especially gifted at mimicking Mary, the Philipses and her parents. The impersonations were humorous and thoroughly enjoyed as Kitty mercilessly presented her family in their purest, unadulterated form. Their whimsical mannerisms and combatant speeches were abundantly comical and Jane could not object to Kitty's most accurate portrayals. Dr Kindrel was amused by her accounts as well. He liked the sound of her family, eccentric as they seemed. He appreciated people with personality, preferring the pleasures of their lively spirited company to the conventional vanity of the arrogant predictable gentility.

As Jane convalesced, Kitty found she had more time to herself and roamed throughout the house for a change of venue. Hearing the sound of familiar voices, she was lured to the drawing room. Discovering the door ajar, she stood outside contemplating whether to enter into the ongoing scene. Miss Bingley's voice was the most distinguishable as Kitty overheard her protest how severely crippled their social lives were by Jane's untimely sickness.

"To think of us so indisposed! It is all Jane's fault we are in this predicament! It is disgraceful that we cannot host dinner parties as we should! By the time she is recovered, all of society would have moved on to new acquaintances without us," scoffed Miss Bingley who was particularly worried. The lack of social functions would seriously handicap her odds of finding a husband while she still had a respectable chance.

"Without a doubt, it is extremely inconsiderate of her to take to her bed at the height of the season. The injustice is most severe to you, Caroline, with Charles suspending all entertainments until Jane is restored to full health," added Mrs Hurst to increase the tension. "How can you possibly impress the gentlemen if you cannot attend parties or reciprocate invitations by hosting diversions of your own. You shall certainly be looked over!" warned Mrs Hurst glancing at her husband for reinforcement. Mr Hurst nodded in agreement as he adjusted his seat cushion.

"And I am not getting any younger! I cannot and will not wait another year. I will be considered too old before long!" cried Miss Bingley worried that the last of her youth was passing before her. Allowing a moment to pass before regaining her composure, she altered the tone of the conversation adding, "In any event, we can count our blessings that Miss Catherine came to London to care for Mrs Bingley. Their kind should care for their own and I, for one, am glad for it. It was a dreary job!" Mrs Hurst agreed shuttering at the thought of caring for Jane.

"And what about that dismal Dr Kindrel!" remarked Caroline seeking to belittle yet another human being remotely involved in her predicament. "What good is hiring a medical man if he is not to bleed the patient? He should bleed her and be done with it," she said with indifference. "Charles thinks because he lived among savages that he knows more than the average doctor. I cannot see how anyone would trust their health to a man whose background is so controversial. I think his reputation grows from the novelty of his life's experiences and nothing more. As for me, I shall remain faithful to treatments tried and true."

"There is also a lot to say for home remedies," agreed Mrs Hurst. "If the servants were allowed to continue following our instructions, I cannot imagine that Jane would not have experienced a more rapid recovery but Charles insists," she said with fatigue. Mr Hurst took his cushions and moved to another couch where he lay down to take a nap.

"Well, we should use it all to our advantage," plotted Mrs Hurst. "It justifies us in every case, to be out in assembly when a sister is watched over so thoroughly. After all, when it is said and done, who would beg to differ, for what more can we do for Jane that her own sister and a professional man could?" she asked. Having heard enough, Kitty turned away disheartened. Realizing that they cared nothing for Jane's well being was sufficient for preventing her from ever desiring their company.

Strolling aimlessly around the house she came upon the ladies' agenda propped up against the wall on a brightly polished lowboy. She quietly thumbed through it amazed to discover their calendar filled from dusk to dawn with theaters, readings, teas and shopping appointments. 'How could they even entertain the thought that they are lost to society when they are out in it every day!' she wondered. 'They give little consideration to Jane's constitution and think selfishly of themselves and their reputations. Hateful, malicious people! And what do they mean by speaking so ill of Dr Kindrel who is so caring and considerate. Jane would not be improving if not for him! They would have certainly kept her in danger. I should be mortified that Jane is obliged to associate with them, but Mr Bingley is very much worth it.' Desiring to return to good company again, Kitty returned to Jane's bedside, determined to nurture her sister with even more devotion than ever before.

It was not long before Jane began to exhibit signs of significant improvement. Caroline and Mrs Hurst would come in to visit on occasion with Kitty and Charles faithfully at Jane's side. Caroline towered over Mrs Bingley as she and Mrs Hurst stood, as usual, at the foot of the bed.

"Mrs Bingley, we are exceedingly happy to see you much improved," exclaimed Mrs Hurst.

"You are kind to be so concerned," said Jane. "I cannot thank you enough for running the house for Mr Bingley in my absence. I should apologize that I never got around to hiring a proper housekeeper for our London home. You have done me a great service. I should like to show my gratitude any way I can." Kitty rolled her eyes and gave way to an audible moan. She hoped Jane would perceive their neglect and in turn reject them as they have rejected her but realized it would be unlike Jane to doubt anyone's sincerity.

"We want nothing, of course, Mrs Bingley," said Mrs Hurst appealing to Jane's compassion. "At least nothing for myself and Mr Hurst, however, when I think of Caroline selflessly missing out on the splendors of any number of social engagements, it makes me very sad indeed. I cannot but think that something should be done for her."

"Louisa, what are you talking about? Please do not worry our sister in law with such trivial matters at a time like this. What is a little sacrifice for the family?" asked Caroline.

"For heaven's sakes, you must not deprive yourself of your pleasures on my account. It cannot be. I will not have it! It will not do Mr Bingley!" Jane was noticeably distressed. "What can we do to correct our dilemma?" she asked her husband.

"They should name it and it will be done," complied Mr Bingley eager to do their bidding. Kitty did not appreciate his lack of insight. She listened intently to hear what would come of their manipulations.

"I wonder if we may take this opportunity to extend a few invitations to a handful of friends that may provide some stimulating amusements and distractions for Caroline. Just four to five of our closest acquaintances. Of course, if it is too much for you . . ." professed Mrs Hurst addressing Jane.

"It should be bigger than that! Caroline is partial to playing hostess at parties and that is what she should have," interrupted Mr Bingley, whose generosity took him to extremes. "That should do the trick!"

Mrs Hurst and Caroline were visibly delighted by the suggestion. They could not refrain from glancing at each other for the success of their scheme. It was more than they hoped for. Jane was a bit overwhelmed by the extravagant suggestion but did not want to disappoint anyone or reverse Mr Bingley. Reluctantly, she acquiesced and looked at him with an approving smile. Mr Bingley was about to give a final consent when Kitty abruptly spoke up.

"A party would be just the thing when Jane is fully improved but for now the noise and activity may prove too harrowing for someone recuperating with child," she said. Applying directly to Mr Bingley, Kitty urged, "You would not want to do anything that might distract Jane when she is beginning to do so well, would you? There must be another way to make amends, at least until your son or daughter arrives and Jane is back on her feet."

"Yes, of course! You are right!" he quickly reconsidered, "How careless of me to place Jane under additional stress! In light of Kitty's most prudent suggestion, we should first consider Jane's requirements. The occasion should be less eventful. I declare that you should host a card playing party. You can still accomplish the goal of inviting all the guests you desire and maintain some quietude just the same. Yes, that is a splendid solution!" he said to Jane with complete satisfaction. "And you will continue to have your way with the servants to help you any way they can," he offered Mrs Hurst. Jane was very pleased with the idea of an innocuous card game. The sisters, disappointed, forced a smile of gratitude.

"Why Miss Catherine, you have such foresight," complimented Mrs Hurst as agreeably as she could. "A party was more than we would ever have conceived ourselves with Jane not yet fully recovered to help plan it. Surely a humble card game would be more than generous. Are you certain it would not disturb you Jane?" she added with sarcasm.

"No, not at all. I don't see why everyone feels they must stay confined because of me. It would give me great pleasure to know you are happy yourselves. You deserve it," she said to Caroline. "Kitty, I know you will enjoy the change since you have been my constant companion and deserve the diversions now that I am out of danger." Mrs Hurst and Caroline were aghast. They had no intention of presenting Kitty to their guests and were only too relieved when Kitty answered, "I am no card player and would not do honor to the game. My place is here with you Jane. I prefer it and shall not think to reverse myself until you are completely restored." Jane was about to insist that Kitty share in the party when she was suddenly cut off by the voice of Dr Kindrel.

"Please excuse my interference," he interrupted as he stood up from a chair in the corner. "Mrs Bingley needs to rest if she is to regain her strength. If you would be so kind to allow her to sleep . . . ," he ordered. Kitty was very pleased with his timely request and readily rose to open the door to show the ladies out. Satisfied to conclude their visit with Kitty's refusal to join the game, the sisters quickly gave their thanks and well wishes. Kitty glanced appreciatively at Dr Kindrel, who met her eyes obligingly.

With the formalities of applying for permission behind them, Mrs Hurst and Caroline wasted no time at making the best out of the rest of the season. Their card game party was a great success and proved all the motivation they needed to assume the full role of Mistress of the House. Receiving no objections from Mr Bingley, who could not see the slow takeover, the sisters assumed a free hand hosting lavish dinner parties and copious socials. For Caroline and Mrs Hurst, all was made well again.

As expected, Kitty received no gracious invitations to their parties. Never forgiving her for interfering with the possibility of an elaborate party Mrs Hurst would remind her that she should not want to be taken away from Jane for such insignificant affairs. Dr Kindrel was invited with the same hypocrisy and having had enough of the sisters' condescension he would decline as well. Mr Bingley would have never approved of his sister's behavior but was so preoccupied with Jane that he did not take notice of it.

In any case, Dr Kindrel preferred to dine where he was amicably included. He, Kitty and Mr and Mrs Bingley delighted in each other's company and became fast friends. The doctor was easy to talk to. His straightforward attitude lightened the atmosphere and promoted the suspension of formality. Their discussions made mention of everything from Jane's health to life's absurdities. As they grew increasingly comfortable, the subject of Pemberley and Miss Darcy's wedding plans were revealed. Jane pulled out a letter recently received from Lizzy and shared a portion of it with them. Lizzy had written:

Dear Jane,

The wedding is set for August, as Miss Darcy and Lord Watney have generously offered to wait until you and your new baby can travel, but do not wait so long if you can travel sooner. We look forward to spending as much time with the baby as possible. As you know our closest friends and family members are to arrive a fortnight earlier so as to make the most of our time together.I have invited Mary to Pemberley early this spring. Besides desiring her to share in our excitement, her organizational skills shall be of great assistance as there is much to be done in preparation. We expect her to arrive soon. I wish I could have seen Mama's face when she acquired the intelligence of Miss Darcy's engagement ball! It was more than she had expected when she was to visit this summer. Mary should have much to say as to Mama's delight for I have little doubt she did not make a big deal of it to all her friends and neighbors. Poor Papa! He will not hear the end of it for these next few months.

Lizzy

Kitty, taking the subject of marriage one step further, took the liberty to mention how envious she was of her sister Lydia's marriage to a military man. "I wish it was I who was marrying! When I think of Lydia and how she will travel with the militia for the rest of her life . . ." she said in a blissful dream. "Every day I envision such happiness for myself. I cannot wait for my handsome redcoat to come for me!"

"Kitty!" admonished Jane. "It is true that Lydia is happy with her situation but that doesn't make it right for you!" Jane could not allow Kitty to revive her desires to attach herself to an officer. It would defeat every purpose for her visit to London.

"But Jane, a man in regimentals is absolutely breathtaking," sighed Kitty shamelessly forgetting herself in front of the doctor.

"Army life cannot be relied upon to provide a steady means of happiness," warned Jane. "Do not forget that Mr Wickham lost his position and remained unmade when they transferred to Newcastle. It was such a long time before his friends came through with his Ensign's commission and that took a great deal of monies to purchase! To date, he has never been able to properly establish himself to go any higher," disciplined Jane hoping the conversation would be quickly dropped. "Besides, Papa would never approve since he adamantly opposes your association with officers and shall never budge!"

"Miss Bennet," asked Dr Kindrel with newly found interest, "Has no mere civilian a chance to win your heart? I could not imagine you refusing the hand of a worthy man because he is not in uniform."

"Well, it is my preference," she insisted not caring what Jane thought of her inclinations.

Mr and Mrs Bingley became extremely uncomfortable with the topic of conversation. It was beyond decorum. Mrs Bingley gave Kitty a look of disapproval while Dr Kindrel, deep in thought, did not notice. He was getting an intimate view of Kitty that he did not attribute to her before and it caught him off guard. He spent many weeks studying her character and her bias for soldiers was unforeseen. Mr Bingley, seeing Jane unhappy, found the need for adjustment and quickly changed the topic. He redirected the conversation toward Dr Kindrel, urging him for information on his family instead. To everyone's surprise Dr Kindrel recited a history beyond anticipation. It made Kitty grow more curious of him than ever before.

His story began with his parents, both missionaries, who traveled to America to preach to the native population. Mr and Mrs Kindrel gained the trust of the Algonquin tribe and lived among them peacefully. His father preached while his mother moved among the people learning, among many things, their healing ways until they were forced to flee because of the wars. It was a great feat for his family to get to the coast near Canada, where his father, seeing no other means of transport, put them aboard a whaling ship to return to Great Britain. He promised to return within the year. "I was but five years old," he said continuing his story. His father never returned. He and his mother received word through the church that his father died of the smallpox. It left his mother to fend for them both but she would not remarry. Utilizing the skills acquired in America, she became a midwife eventually treating an increasing number of illnesses for the indigent with great success. "After apprenticing with my mother, I was accepted into the University and here I am today. I have become quite the itinerate worker, never settling in one place, tirelessly travelling throughout Great Britain wherever the need, but it is my calling and I enjoy it," ended Dr Kindrel putting a lighter note on it.

The Bingleys listened intently. Kitty was in awe of his experiences in this curious place, America and was saddened by the hardships he and his mother endured upon their return. 'Who cannot favor this man, so experienced, dedicated and sincere? He is engaging and has no pretense when he speaks. His ease and humility deserve merit. He is to be esteemed and I am very pleased to have made his acquaintance,' she thought delighted in the evenings he spent at home with them, in her company.

Jane recuperated steadily as the days flitted by and Kitty soon found time to visit her aunt and uncle Gardiner in Gracechurch Street. Mrs Bennet had indeed written and arranged for Mrs Gardiner to take Kitty to the best warehouses. Both casual and elegant gowns were designed and tailored to Kitty along with one exceptionally elaborate gown for the ball at Pemberley.

Dr Kindrel found free time too and took on more patients as his schedule allowed. He took every opportunity to escort Kitty to Gracechurch Street as it was located in Cheapside where he had many appointments to keep as well. She accepted his offer with absolute delight. His presence always put her in good spirits and she looked forward to their little excursions. Kitty would listen in earnest to him talk of his visions for the future of medicine while Dr Kindrel would, in turn, listen to everything Kitty would say, captured by any subject she cared to share. She spoke of her family, balls and the militia and they both talked about Caroline and Mrs Hurst.

Dr Kindrel admired Kitty more and more each day. He thought her every bit as beautiful as her sister, Jane, and was especially fond of her bold, lively spirit and delightful sense of humor. He cherished Kitty and, for the first time in his life, experienced a wondrous feeling of rapture as he discovered that he was very much in love.

Meanwhile, Jane recovered completely and gave birth to two beautiful babies, one boy and one girl respectively named Charles and Elizabeth, marking the end of the good doctor's services with grateful goodbyes.

Dr Kindrel left with many regrets. Possessing no fortune to speak of and no steady residence to call home he would not risk disclosing his true feelings for Kitty. He felt she deserved more than promises and could not in good conscience engage her to him, a man of dreams and expectations with nothing of substance to offer. As he left he was, however, determined to find his way to her again.

*   *   *

The Bennets arrived in Grovesnor Place the day after Dr Kindrel's departure. They were jubilant and thoroughly amused by the presentation of their two lovely grandchildren lying content on either side of Jane.

"Twins, Mr Bennet!" exclaimed Mrs Bennet clasping her hands with joy. "Jane is such a dutiful wife!" She picked up her granddaughter to observe her more closely. "Oh, Jane, young Elizabeth is as beautiful as you were when you were a baby." She weighed the child in her arms and said, "I estimate about five pounds of pure elegance!"

"Let us not forget young Master Charles, Mrs Bennet," chimed in Mr Bennet becoming the proud grandfather. He touched the infant's tiny hand with his index finger so as not to disturb him as he lay comfortably with his mother. Young Charles got a hold of Mr Bennet's finger and would not let go. "He has a mighty, mighty grip and is as stealth as a young man should be. I predict he will handle his women with a stronger hand than I or your Mr Bingley, Jane."

Mr Bennet was delighted with having a grandson. It redeemed the guilt he endured from not supplying a son for the security of his own family. Young Charles would provide the assurance the next generation needed and Mr Bennet took great comfort in it.

"It is a job well done, isn't it Mr Bennet?" commented Mrs Bennet seeing the joy in her husband's face. Turning to Jane, she went on to say, "You certainly are blessed Jane. Not everyone can boast of twins! I must write Mrs Philips right away to make Mrs Long aware of your twins. That Mrs Long," she sneered, "Always smug about her one grandson. Such a teeny little thing he is and she assuming Jane would have nothing but girls since that was all I was able to accomplish!" Collecting herself, she returned to lauding over Jane's success saying, "Jane, you have done well, one daughter to lavish in fineries and one son to manage it all. You have outdone all our neighbors at Longbourn and supplied me with infinite delight!"

"All is well enough, Mrs Bennet," said Mr Bennet jauntily, "and I trust Mrs Philips will do justice by you and promise all our neighbors that Jane intends to secure Netherfield with a half dozen more children before reaching their fifth anniversary," exaggerated Mr Bennet in jest as Mrs Bennet reeled in laughter.

Mr Bingley entered the room excitedly stating, "I have been about the city inquiring as to the reliability of the route toward Pemberley.

I am glad to report that the weather ahead warrants good conditions perfect for traveling. The roads promise to be dry and firm within a few weeks. Therefore we can surmise that, as long as Jane does not compromise her health or that of the babies, we shall make it to Miss Darcy's ball after all!"

"What do you mean 'after all'? Jane is fit and the children are as strong as any. Mr Bennet said so himself!" advocated Mrs Bennet. "With the nurses, there should be no reason to miss the ball!" She dismissed Mr Bingley's statement and diverted the conversation to something more substantial. "You have no idea of the gowns we have had made Jane. When you are up and about, I will display them for you. But you must allow us to rummage through your jewels. Kitty needs a bauble or two to perfect the look of her attire and so do I. I would wear my own jewels but none will look as good as one of your pieces would, though I am sure not to find the design I'm looking for among your treasures either." She paused in deep thought before saying, "Just the same, I am exceedingly excited! A ball of that caliber is just the exposure my Kitty and Mary need." Happily scanning the room to encourage everyone to share in her joy, she came across Mr Bingley standing by attentively. "Not go indeed! Who can afford to miss this occasion when we all know we cannot depend on Mr Bennet to find a means to expose our daughters.

"Mrs Bennet's discretion has never been a strong point," interrupted Mr Bennet by way of a reprieve to Mr Bingley. "If you will excuse me, I will find my way to your library," he said as he kissed Jane on the forehead, took a quick glance at the children and made his way out the door.

The house was coming to life all at once for Kitty. Since the arrival of the babies and Mr and Mrs Bennet, London took on a new perspective. Mr and Mrs Hurst and Caroline were seldom seen at Grovesnor Place these days and their absence brought immense satisfaction to Kitty as she thought she could finally enjoy her visit with peace of mind, at least for the next few weeks before they would all go to Pemberley.

Chapter 3

Pemberley was a majestic estate happily situated in one of the finest lands in all of Derbyshire. It displayed a great variety of grounds that extended for miles. Every prospect captured the spectator with matchless beauty. Nearby woods stood eminent as they framed a portion of the hills that sloped softly beyond the rear of the house. Nature, with its pristine rivers, streams and sparkling lakes provided a reliable source of water that maintained a large assortment of wildlife, as well as provided a source of pleasure for its residents. Widely reputed as being incomparable in elegance and beauty, Pemberley continued to put most other estates to shame by the equal resplendence that was contained within its walls through the blissful union of Mr and Mrs Darcy.

Their sister, Miss Georgiana Darcy, a young lady of eighteen, was recently engaged to her cousin Lord Benjamin Watney, the eldest son of the late Earl Watney. Lord Watney, a renowned man of large estate and fortune, resided in the West Indies for the last six years. He owned the sugar markets and many other foreign investments which he managed himself. Upon his return to Derbyshire, he met Georgiana and courted her for a full six months before he proposed and she accepted. As the up and coming marriage promised to be one of true affection everyone turned their attentions to the preparations leading to the ceremony itself.

The advent of spring along with the pending ball signaled a vast transformation at Pemberley. The housekeeper was busy replacing heavy winter tapestries, draperies and the like with lighter, fresher silks and satins in addition to freshening up the guestrooms for the affair. Menus and itineraries were planned, orchestras hired and entertainment was prearranged.

Early each morning Mr Darcy surveyed the grounds to make arrangements and preparations with the groundskeeper as Mrs Darcy conspired with the head gardener for flowers. When Mr Darcy was unexpectedly summoned to visit his aunt Lady Catherine de Bourgh, Elizabeth and Mary took every opportunity to dote on Georgiana.

The women ran out eagerly to meet each of their guests as familar carriages approached daily. Miss Anne de Bourgh and her nurse Mrs Jenkinson were among the first to arrive as they were safely escorted to Pemberley by Mr Darcy. As they disembarked, Mr Darcy pulled Lizzy aside for a brief tete a tete. Lizzy took his arm as he escorted her into the house leaving Georgiana and her company cheerfully engrossed in conversation which discussed the prospect of seeing Lady Catherine in the near future.

"Why hasn't Lady Catherine come as well? I did not think she would miss it for the world. Has she not forgiven us, even on this great occasion?" asked Lizzy.

"She has an uncompromiseable schedule," said Mr Darcy regrettably.

"So there is a glimmer of hope," remarked Lizzy laughing in jest. She looked forward to reconciliation but quickly realized Lady Catherine would not have it. "Why did she summon you so urgently at a time like this?"

"Of all people, I was called upon to secure the introduction of Miss de Bourgh to a Mr Carrington, which she added to the guest list," he said grimacing at the displeasure of his charge. His obligation, though seemingly innocent, was particularly dissatisfying for him. He turned to glance at the feeble Miss de Bourgh with increased apprehension. Her pale, thin frame and sickly manner were not strong winning points while her quietude provided no clue as to her mental abilities. He wished he would have eschewed the disagreeable role of matchmaker, as his instincts dictated, but he was compelled to honor the request in attempt to make amends and pacify Lady Catherine.

"Now that is news!" she said with delighted fascination. "I find it safe to say she does not know your reputation for matchmaking. And, for your part, one would think you have learned your lesson in remaining out of the path of potential lovers!" taunted Elizabeth. "As I see it, you stand with two points against you. First, you do not converse easily with those you do not know, and you do not know Mr Carrington and secondly, all of your romantic campaigns have fallen victim to your generosity. In short, they were greatly mishandled. I hate to be hard on you, my very own husband, but there you have it." She laughed in amusement. He too saw the irony and was enlightened by the humor of it.

"You are right Elizabeth. I knew she put too much on me but I had no choice. You know very well I did not accept it with open arms."

*　　*　　*

Miss de Bourgh was, of course, welcomed with cheerfulness and great fondness. For someone so delicate, she felt unusually well and was genuinely happy to be there. It was her first excursion without Lady Catherine and she and Mrs Jenkinson settled in nicely.

Lord Watney, the Bingleys, the Bennets and the Collinses soon followed making the essential party complete. To the Collins' delight, Daniel, Mr Collins' youngest brother, was met with Georgiana's immediate approval as it was arranged by Lady Catherine herself that he was to become the pastor at North Courtlandt, Georgiana's new home in Birmingham.

Initially, the guests busied themselves with a variety of interests and occupations. Mr Bennet claimed Pemberley's library while Lizzy and the ladies agonized over last minute gala arrangements. Mr Darcy, Mr Bingley and Lord Watney rode as every opportunity afforded while Mary preferred the company of Daniel and Miss de Bourgh leaving Mr Collins to make his own way from day to day.

On one particular occasion, while strolling down a corridor, Mr Collins heard the tender cries of babies coming from the parlor. He entered and found Mrs Bennet fretfully cradling young Elizabeth with one hand while trying to quiet Charles with the other.

"Mr Collins, you have appeared at a most opportune time! While the nurses have gone to prepare for the children's feeding I thought I could care for them myself until their return but as you see, my hands are well employed and I am in need of your assistance. Do take Charles into your arms and rock him while I embrace Elizabeth. They are so fidgety with hunger," appealed Mrs Bennet.

"With pleasure, Mrs Bennet. I have a way with children, if I do say so myself," volunteered Mr Collins taking Master Charles into his arms.

"Is that so? Then I am surprised you have none of your own, Mr Collins," she said striking up a conversation. "You have been married to Charlotte much longer than my Jane and she has already bestowed the world with these two precious gifts."

"Mrs Bennet, it is my humble opinion, and that of the Great Lady Catherine de Bourgh, that although Mrs Collins and I are well suited at Hunsford Parsonage, it would be best to wait until we attain optimal stability at Longbourn before we bring children of our own into this world," he explained referring to his future possession of Longbourn.

"Optimal stability at Longbourn? Mr Collins! Longbourn is entailed to you, we are well aware of that," she shrieked in a quick burst of temperament, "but if you are implying that you are waiting to see my Mr Bennet in the grave so you can move into Longbourn before you have children, let me inform you, you have a long time to wait as I am not through with my husband yet?" The babies began to cry out harder than before.

"Mrs Bennet," began Mr Collins trying to calm both her and the babies, "let me assure you, I am not prematurely placing Mr Bennet in the grave. It is only that Lady Catherine has instructed Mrs Collins and me on the benefits of raising a child in a home of our own. 'Fixed surroundings rear a secure child,' she said. It is more beneficial than having them grow attached to a surrounding in Hunsford Parsonage that they will someday leave," he clarified, satisfied that he had effectively explained his position.

"Mr Collins, I will not spoil this sweet moment by having you expel me out of Longbourn and remove my Mr Bennet from the face of this happy earth," she said collecting herself for the benefit of the children. "It is not for my sake that I take offense. I will not be wanting. I need not worry as to where I shall go. Lord knows that three of my daughters are married and two of them particularly well. I will be welcomed wherever I go, but to direct Mr Bennet six feet under for your gain is more than I can endure." Having had enough and feeling an attack of nerves coming on, Mrs Bennet instructed, "Please be so good as to place Mr Bennet's grandchild gently back in the layette. It was much more efficacious when I handled the babies myself. From this point on, I can manage without the advantage of your assistance." Mrs Bennet's eyes were filled with fury as she stood motionless, ready to attack if he would so much as hesitate. Mr Collins considered it wise to comply with her wishes in order to prevent any further provocation.

Anxious to leave, Mr Collins bowed humbly to exit quickly. "I apologize for any distress I may have caused you, Mrs Bennet. It was not ill meant." He reached down to carefully place the child back in his layette when Master Charles unexpectedly broke water. Mr Collins felt the warm moisture soak into his vest and run down his pant leg. Concealing a sneer, he forced a smile and merely said, "Lovely child," as he wiped his hands on his coat. Exiting, forgoing another bow he left.

"Well done Charles," encouraged Mrs Bennet petting her grandson with one hand while cradling Elizabeth with the other much as before.

In short time the nurses returned allowing Mrs Bennet to retire to her bedchamber. Her nerves were fluttering and she needed a respite. When she got to her room, she spotted a tiny parcel lying on the bed. At first she was inclined to toss it aside and tend to it later but at second glance she noticed it had a card secured to it from Mr Bennet's hand. As she perused it, it simply read, 'Mrs Bennet.' Curious, she tore it open.

Inside laid the rich intense sparkle of green emeralds linked all in a row. It was a delightful surprise. Moreover, it was precisely the necklace she was hoping to wear with her newly designed ball gown. A felicitous joy overtook her nervous condition as she ran out of the room giggling and shrieking toward Pemberley library where Mr Bennet remained confined.

Reaching the door, she swung it open abruptly exclaiming, "Husband, you are the most wonderful man in the world! I knew you loved me much too much to have me seen in a borrowed necklace." Admiring the necklace anew, she went on saying, "you took me by complete surprise. I am dazed!" Mr Bennet, fixed in his chair, scarcely peered up at her from behind the desk. Despite his genuine amusement, he resolved to restrict his reaction to keep her at bay.

"You deserve it," he said acknowledging her gratitude in a business-like manner. "You worked hard to be where you are today. I must admit I have begun to see you in a new light. The string is the least I can do," he said casually. He maintained an air of indifference in the hope that she would take her leave.

"And you let me search and worry for a fashionable solution these past weeks knowing full well Jane's necklaces would never do," she teased gliding behind his seat flinging her arms around him to kiss him on his head. She draped her necklace around his neck sharing her excitement with him as he sat stoically, beginning to feel largely inconvenienced. "It must have cost a small fortune but we can economize to the bare essentials once all the girls are married to make up for it," she said joyfully kissing him twice more.

"Mrs Bennet, that is enough! You have made me fully aware of your appreciation and may leave me be now," he said removing the necklace from his neck and releasing himself from her embrace. "Let me loose," he demanded. Mrs Bennet took no offense from his actions. Instead, she ran playfully around to the front of his chair and promptly sat on his lap. "Is there no way to make you leave short of showing you the door?" he asked returning to his old self.

"Oh you are a parodist," she snickered marveling over her necklace as she adjusted herself on his lap for a comfortable prolonged stay.

*   *   *

Georgiana played masterfully that evening as she impressed her fiancé with the crisp clear melodic sound of the pianoforte. Lizzy and Mary took their turns at performing as well. Although they were not as dexterous as Georgiana no one noticed as a good time was had by all.

Kitty requested an Irish jig to entice the crowd to dance. Everyone rose to reel with their partners and danced until the late evening hours. It was a delightful preview of what was to come on the night of the ball.

Daniel danced graciously with Mary and Kitty while Miss de Bourgh, despite the gentlemen's offers, steadfastly refused to dance. She chose instead to observe the dances with Mrs Jenkinson fixed at her side. Daniel glanced at her with every new tune and eventually became curious at her lack of interaction. He considered Miss de Bourgh an accomplished young lady and assumed that every polished lady was inclined to dance. If Miss de Bourgh did not participate, something had to be amiss. His inquisitiveness got the better of him and when he danced with Mary next he voiced his concern for her. "It distresses me so to see Miss de Bourgh so separated and uninvolved. I hope she is well."

"Maybe we should sit with her. She may simply not wish to dance tonight but instead desire someone to talk to," she suggested. Daniel gave her a staggering look of disbelief. Seeing him so affected she continued saying, "It may be difficult for you to believe but not everyone enjoys dancing!"

"Those words should never be put together. Why, I believe the blessed advent of music was specifically designed to promote unison in civilized society through dance. Surely a lack of desire to dance could not be the case. I am certain it is not intentional since every well cultured woman dances!" he exclaimed as they removed themselves from the dance floor to sit with Miss de Bourgh. "Miss de Bourgh," began Daniel addressing Anne, "Miss Bennet is of the opinion that you may not enjoy dancing and I say every young lady enjoys dancing including you! Will you settle the matter for us?"

"I have been known to enjoy dancing very much but I have given it up with my childhood. We do not dance at Rosings. Poetry recitals, arias and other performances are how we entertain our time. Mother says physical activities are not for me and has always restricted them," explained Miss de Bourgh with more timidity than she cared to possess. Confined to the select company of Rosings, she was not accustomed to unsolicited questions.

Mrs Jenkinson saw Miss de Bourgh was vulnerable to Daniel and Mary's opinions and reinforced Anne's comments with an affirmative nod of her head placing a protective hand on Miss de Bourgh's elbow. Mrs Jenkinson, an elderly nurse, invested the remainder of her life to Miss de Bourgh's care and did not think it in her interest to have Miss de Bourgh gain independence through the enticements of these intrusive outsiders.

"But are you to dance at the ball?" inquired Mary who never missed a ball or the occasion to dance.

"Yes, I will but only the dances Mother has obliged me to," she responded in her quiet manner.

"But how can you be assured of your talents if you do not practice?" probed Mary a little further. "You will be at a great disadvantage!"

The music paused as Kitty searched for another arrangement. Seizing the opportunity, in the hope that he could entice Miss de Bourgh, Daniel interrupted. "This would be an ideal time for you to increase your flair and finesse," he said. "For your pleasure, Miss de Bourgh, please allow me escort you to the dance floor when the music recommences. After all you are among friends and fair cousins," urged Daniel offering his hand good naturedly. He was well intentioned and wanted to accommodate her.

"I couldn't. Not right now," she answered shrinking away. "I shall dance at the ball—just once. That is enough for me," she said reluctantly. Although she saw the logic in their remarks she felt very much put upon. Desiring the issue resolved, Miss de Bourgh looked away nervously.

It was obvious she wanted the conversation dropped. Mrs Jenkinson embraced her for comfort but Daniel would not give up.

"Miss de Bourgh, as a man of the cloth, I am concerned for anyone who does not take advantage of the gifts we have here on Earth. Every man of consequence has discovered that 'Heaven is under our feet as well as above our heads'." Mary turned to look at him with delight. She knew that quote well. He continued, "You should dance the nights away, as it is the right of your class but, for now, with the music so inviting, Miss Bennet and I shall leave you to think the matter over."

"Daniel is correct. There is a lot of amusement to be had in the art of dancing but you must partake of it if you want to have fun. Once enjoyed, no other substitute will do. You should give it some thought, Miss de Bourgh," advised Mary supporting Daniel's efforts.

"Miss Bennet," said Daniel, seeing Miss de Bourgh unsure as to how to respond, "the music has resumed. Let us rejoin the recreation." Mary readily accepted Daniel's invitation leaving Miss de Bourgh to review her position.

"You quoted Thoreau," confirmed Mary taking a turn around Daniel in step with the music.

"Yes, I did. Are you a fan of his work?" asked Daniel impressed by her literary knowledge.

"I am," answered Mary discovering a common interest.

"Actually, I read everything that comes my way. I must say, I have become an avid reader as you never know where your next bit of useful information will come from," insisted Daniel taking her hand as the music demanded.

"I enjoy the company of books as well," said Mary suddenly realizing she was, at long last, in the presence of a man who might find her as provocative as she was suddenly finding him. "They are filled with so much information and provide infinite knowledge suitable for every occasion."

Daniel was impressed. "When I read, it is not for the mere pleasure of it but it is to expand the mind," he explained finding himself developing an ardent interest in her. "I am not a seasoned traveler yet I need to know the world I live in and the way men think. It helps when you are trying to reach a flock with scriptural knowledge," he said with a pause. "In this case, I am curious to know what advice you would have for a lady in Miss de Bourgh's situation. I am not convinced that she does not enjoy dancing," said Daniel exhibiting high regard for Mary's opinion. "How would you reason with her?"

"Is it not possible that we should accept her as she is and not necessarily advise her to anything?" said Mary feeling they would not be able to persuade her to any such thing. "After all, you might be aware that Socrates advised people all the time and was poisoned for his troubles. Should we not be wiser to remain out of her affairs?"

"Miss Bennet, please do not think of me as imposing," he said eliminating the perverse notion that he lacked discretion. "Lady Catherine de Bourgh was so kind as to secure a commission for me with Miss Georgiana Darcy, without my requesting it of her. I was merely visiting my brother when she opened her heart to my troubles and found a way for me. I must repay her in whatever capacity confronts me. As a holy man I am bound to do as Proverbs orders me to, 'not hold back good from those to whom it is owing, when it happens to be in the power of my hand.' It is a duty I must fulfill. I involve you only because I feel you would be a credit to the cause and a perceptive accomplice. Intelligent as you are, you may aid me in persuading her. 'There is a frustrating of plans where there is no confidential talk, but in the multitude of counselors there is accomplishment,'" he quoted. "I think if we take counsel in each other we may come up with a solution to help this misguided ewe," he added persuasively.

Mary was quickly won over thinking, 'He has need of me and has mistaken my comments as contrary to his cause. I do not want to seem difficult as he has chosen well.' She pushed up her glasses and wore a studious expression hoping to disguise her unsalvageable submission. Daniel looked upon her with admiration. The prospect of helping Miss de Bourgh with Mary's assistance was very gratifying. "If you would be so generous as to council me in my plight, I ask you again, have you any advice for enticing our Miss de Bourgh?" questioned Daniel making one more attempt.

"I think words of advice are not enough," she finally offered. "We have attempted that much. Perhaps for now, we should set the example and show her how delighted two people can be while consumed in the activity," she suggested. Mary was happy to be conspiring with him since at Longbourn her advice was never so appreciated.

"That is a brilliant beginning, Miss Bennet. 'Actions speak louder than words'," he agreed. With that she and Daniel hopped about the floor with overzealous buoyancy and exhilaration, exchanging philosophies and remaining in each other's company with unending interest.

By evening's end, Mary found herself totally enchanted by Daniel. His interests, his personality and selflessness captivated her as his appreciation of her good company and analysis brought her hopes of him, someday, returning her affections.

Chapter 4

The ball was still more than a week away and no other guests were expected until one day prior. The families took full advantage of the warm summer weather and kept themselves thoroughly entertained with quoits and croquet. Of those activities, croquet became a quick favorite. Teams of all kinds were formed to keep the interest level high and create a sense of competition in the game. Everyone tried their hand at the skill and engaged themselves for hours. To her credit, Miss de Bourgh made her attempts as well.

Dampening the spirit of the games, Mrs Jenkinson pulled her away and insisted she sit it out as her health was at risk. Daniel noticed Miss de Bourgh's look of defeat. His suspicions that she wanted more out of life rang true and he again called Mary to his side. "It is not pleasurable for me to see Miss de Bourgh left out. She cannot be happy with a life so uneventful. It is our duty to get her more involved."

"It appears to me that Miss de Bourgh does not have the opportunity to increase her skills at any activity with a guardian like that," noted Mary with accuracy. She could not understand Mrs Jenkinson's constant patronization of Miss de Bourgh.

"I agree one hundred percent. Just look at her. Miss de Bourgh follows the game at the edge of her seat. I am confident she would like to join in again, but her nurse is reprehensively protective," resolved Daniel. "I have employed the greater part of my leisure to giving the matter considerable thought. I fear Mrs Jenkinson's actions are more of a detriment than a benefit. Observe how the destitute Miss de Bourgh is made to play the invalid when in truth she is not! I declare that Miss de Bourgh should be involved with life's pleasures but does not allow herself the experience. Is that your analysis Miss Bennet?"

"Your observation is not challenged by me," agreed Mary staring at Anne with an analytical eye. "It is obvious she yearns for more. Her demeanor shows compliance with the act of solitude but her eyes tell a different story. She is holding herself back with unsettled restraint. There should be an intervention before she falls too deep."

That was all Daniel needed to hear. He faced Mary, encouraged by her astuteness and without resignation said, "Miss Bennet, I have already made you aware that I am indebted to Her Ladyship the Great Catherine de Bourgh and could think of no other restitution than to come to the assistance of her daughter in her time of need. If you, Miss Bennet, on your secrecy, should like to solicit your humanity in an innocent scheme I have devised, in proper context with our convictions to unburden Miss de Bourgh from herself, I shall be infinitely grateful." Mary, knowing very well she would come to his aid for whatever he asked, looked at him devotedly. She would not deny him.

He detected her excellent insight had caused her to assent and continued his contrivance without a moment's hesitation. "The dilemma stands as such: Miss de Bourgh is to dance at the ball but cannot possibly be as nimble as the other ladies if she is depending on skills acquired in childhood. She is destined to perform poorly without the constancy of practice and her nurse, we agree, is a hindrance to that effect. In short I have come to the conclusion that we must remove the nurse and retrain the patient."

"However do you mean to accomplish it?" inquired Mary. "How can anyone come between this most devoted nurse and loyal patient? Furthermore, how would this involve me?"

"We should take it upon ourselves and our influence to make it possible for circumstances to allow Miss de Bourgh to practice her dancing with us in private. It is a simple harmless ploy that will only serve to benefit Miss de Bourgh and allow her to enjoy herself a little more. In fact, there is nothing but good intention behind it. Can I count on your help, Miss Bennet?"

"Of course! Miss de Bourgh deserves the best out of life, as anyone does. But how am I to help you?"

"First, you can help me convince her of it. Secondly, you can play the pianoforte for us while Miss de Bourgh and I dance, and although I do not condone deception, you can also look out for Mrs Jenkinson and help devise a distraction. There is an abundance for you to do!"

"I suppose 'he who dares nothing hopes for nothing . . .'" shrugged Mary in submissive compliance hoping this little endeavor would commit him to her evermore.

Daniel was in high spirit as he had accurately suspected he could trust in Mary. "Let us then review, Miss Bennet, how will you approach her?"

"But this was your idea!" she said stunned to learn she was to initiate the commission.

"Yes, but on second thought, it may be better to present the offer woman to woman. She is partial to you. You are a favorite to her here." he explained.

"You have obtained her good opinion as well as I. It does not seem likely that I alone can secure her compliance. We will tell her together," insisted Mary who had no talent for artifice. Submitting to her argument, they joined Miss de Bourgh for a cold refreshing drink.

Mrs Jenkinson remained dutifully with Miss de Bourgh and gave no signs of retiring until an unexpected opportunity finally arose. Both the pitcher and Miss de Bourgh's glass were empty. Daniel cunningly suggested to Mrs Jenkinson that Miss de Bourgh should not remain out in the heat without a cooling beverage. With no servant readily available, he urged Mrs Jenkinson to enter the mansion and arrange for a refill.

As soon as the nurse stepped away, the coconspirators presented Miss de Bourgh with their plan. The proposition of private lessons was so adeptly delivered that Miss de Bourgh welcomed their assistance and accepted their kindness. She was impressed with their devoted interest in her and considered them very good friends indeed.

"I have been thinking over what Miss Bennet said about preparedness yesterday. I tried it alone in my room and began to realize you were right. I was, in fact, out of tune and should have joined in the dancing when I had the opportunity. I deeply regret it now. I will like to perform with increased confidence and courage. I will do as you say and arrange for Mrs Jenkinson to run some errands for me and avoid her intrusion." She smiled from the very thought of being without Mrs Jenkinson and happily inquired, "Where are we to practice?"

"I know just the place for it." volunteered Mary. "There is a room past the gallery of family portraits where my sister Lizzy's portrait is now displayed next to Mr Darcy's. Miss Darcy used to practice the pianoforte there when she was a child. About three years ago, it was replaced with a new one that was a gift to Miss Darcy from Mr Darcy. Of late, she is too preoccupied with His Lordship and all the arrangements for the wedding to make use of it. We should meet there daily after lunch when everyone goes their separate ways." The plans were agreed upon and they were to begin the very next day as there was no time to waste.

*   *   *

As planned, the trio met daily. The room was secluded and equipped with a pianoforte as expected and Mrs Jenkinson was distracted by fabricated errands.

To no one's surprise, the rehearsals proved vital to Miss de Bourgh's dancing abilities. Her steps were terribly awkward. She had difficulty distinguishing the appropriate sequences to the right variation of music. In addition, her coordination and agility were in desperate need of improvement.

Since Miss de Bourgh did not possess a talent for the pianoforte, Mary and Daniel went through the dance steps slowly humming the melody. They pointed out the distinct differences in every step with skill and intelligence, encouraging Miss de Bourgh to hum along as well to get a better sense of the rhythm.

Increasing in confidence and familiarity with this daily drill, Mary was suddenly compelled to impress Daniel with her vocal skills and sang a few songs. It was not the most inspiring of sounds but her tenacity was encouraging and soon the others sang along with as much reserve. It was an enjoyable experience for each of them, as it was unusual that no one interrupted their song in the name of goodwill and harmony. They indulged in their boisterousness as they delighted in the spontaneity of the moment. Miss de Bourgh was growing especially content. She had not felt such happiness since her youth.

Days before the ball, Miss de Bourgh was dancing as graceful and as assured as any lady of quality and proper upbringing. If this evening was to be filled with dancing, she would have no reservations in debuting her newly polished skills. Holding her head erect, floating gracefully through her moves, Miss de Bourgh absorbed herself in the music as she and Daniel practiced on thoroughly engrossed.

Deeply entranced, she could not hear the rattle of the door knob that gave Daniel a start. He was fearful that their lessons would be found out when they were so close to its completion. He looked at Mary in alarm and she quickly stopped playing. They both ran toward the door leaving Miss de Bourgh in mid step. As Daniel turned in haste to prevent the intrusion, his leg became entangled in her's. Their ankles locked and Miss de Bourgh fell as he tripped over her. Before she knew it, she was on the floor howling with pain. Mary let out a wail as the door flew open.

"Miss de Bourgh! Are you alright?" exclaimed Daniel as Mrs Jenkinson came rushing in.

"Are you all right Miss?" cried Mrs Jenkinson in horror.

Sprawled on the floor, unable to move her leg, Miss de Bourgh could not answer clearly. Her pangs of pain were more than she could bare and she fainted. Daniel and Mary looked on in dismay. Their faces turned pale as Mrs Jenkinson gave orders to "get a doctor right away!"

As Mary raced down the gallery, she could feel the eyes of every family portrait looking down on her. She glanced up as she passed Lizzy's portrait wondering, 'what would Lizzy think? How could it have gone so wrong?' Finally, she found Lizzy with Kitty and Georgiana in the private sitting room embroidering initials on handkerchiefs.

"Lizzy!" exclaimed Mary as she burst breathlessly into the room, "Miss Anne de Bourgh has had a terrible accident! We need a doctor right away!" The ladies immediately threw down their work making themselves available to help in any way they could.

"Kitty, order a servant to town for Dr Bodley, then inform Mr Darcy. Come with me Georgiana," instructed Lizzy. "Take us to her Mary."

Mary explained the incident as they approached the distant room. Mr Darcy emerged with Mr Bennet and three servants just as the ladies arrived. They entered the room together to find Miss de Bourgh still lying in pain on the floor. Mrs Jenkinson glanced up at them as she patted Anne's hand to maintain her consciousness.

"Let me see," said Mr Darcy taking control of the situation. Lightly touching her ankle, Miss de Bourgh screamed in agonizing pain. "It is swelling terribly." He turned to the servants. "Carry Miss de Bourgh gently to her room. Bring some cold soaks for her ankle. Mrs Jenkinson shall apply them to reduce the swelling until the doctor comes. He will examine her and tell us what more needs to be done." The servants acted upon his orders with all speed and carried Miss de Bourgh to her quarters as supervised by Mrs Jenkinson. Once they parted, Mr Darcy asked Lizzy, "How did this happen?" Everyone turned from Mary to Daniel prevailing upon them to answer. Lizzy thought it best that she set the pace of it by initiating the explanation.

"It was a harmless folly," she began in her most calming manner. "Miss de Bourgh, Mary and Daniel were dancing privately and tripped over each other."

"We were practicing for the ball. Daniel and I only meant to help her improve her dancing skills. She was coming along so well before this happened!" explained Mary realizing they could not detract detection and had to answer for themselves.

"Please believe that our intentions were true and did not lack merit," apologized Daniel. "Who could think that such honorable workings would produce an unprofitable conclusion?"

"The hazards of a good deed," declared Mr Bennet. "There has never been more damage done than by people who think they're doing the right thing." Lizzy gave her father a reprimanding stare hoping to discourage him from sharing his thoughts at a moment like this. She took her husband's arm and separated him from the group.

"It doesn't seem to be broken," admitted Mr Darcy in private, "but we cannot take any chances. We must hear it from the doctor. Either way, this complicates things. To think my only consolation throughout this weighty ordeal was the knowledge that all I had to do was to arrange for an introductory dance between Anne and Mr Carrington. How am I to fulfill my promise now?"

"This is a wretched set of events," remarked Lizzy excessively sorry. "The odds are stacking against you."

*   *   *

Dr Bodley diagnosed the injury as, "a sprain which will improve with elevation of the leg and cold compresses. I'm afraid Miss de Bourgh should remain immobile to allow for a speedy recovery. She should not do anymore dancing for a while. I will return the morning of the ball to see how she improved." He turned and left the room for further discussion with Mr Darcy.

Lizzy and Georgiana stayed long enough to see to Miss de Bourgh's comfort. After satisfying her needs they left the room allowing her to rest. Mrs Jenkinson remained at Anne's side to apply her nursing skills. Mary and Daniel came to visit the patient with guilt and apologies, feeling their actions were reprehensible. They should not have tried to deceive. After all, there was no one at Pembereley that would not have understood Miss de Bourgh's plight and no one who would not have respected their privacy. Mrs Jenkinson was their only threat and she should have been confronted from the start instead of sent away on fraudulent errands.

"Please, Miss de Bourgh," began Daniel in contrition, "accept our apologies for advising you to participate in such foolishness on our part. It was an inane and fallacious act from which I cannot, in good conscious, ask to be absolved. The scheme should have never been attempted and for that I, alone, am to be held fully accountable. Miss Bennet only desired to help you as much as I did. I assure you, her intentions were all well and good. This is a tragedy no one could have foreseen, but it was my fault just the same. I should have never involved you or anyone in anything that had to do with deceit."

"It is an unhappy turn of events," sighed Miss de Bourgh. "What will Mother say!?!"

'What would my brother say!?!' Daniel wondered. 'He was so proud of me just two weeks ago. I am afraid I have not only lost favor in his eyes but may have caused him to lose favor with Lady Catherine.' He shuttered at the thought of her resolve. 'This may cost me North Courtlandt Parsonage and him Hunsford Parsonage. Oh, divine irony! Are we both to live a nominal existence from this day forward?'

Daniel was completely disheartened and felt altogether defeated. "We would like to keep you company Miss de Bourgh if you will have us," he offered humbly. "It is your decision as you may have it your way without censure from us."

"I would very much enjoy your company. It was really no one's fault. I was so completely turned around and was on the floor so quickly, I am still unsure as to how it happened but it was fun while it lasted. I have not experienced such pleasures in a very long time," she admitted. "On the other hand, I am sorry I put the ball at risk for myself. Mother and I had high expectations."

"Please be assured Daniel and I would never have attempted any feat that would have resulted in your unhappiness," consoled Mary. "We will sit the ball out with you as well if you cannot attend." Daniel nodded in agreement. It was the least they could do.

"Do not feel compelled to remain with me during the ball. Upon further contemplation, I must admit, I do not know how I like my situation. In one respect the anxiety of performing may be completely eliminated and the relief of it is very soothing. Yet, on the next respect, it will not be to my advantage to return home without holding true to my agenda. So much of my future may have depended upon that one night. I will use this time to figure out my true sentiment."

Her gentle forgiveness in light of her deepening insecurity increased the gravity Daniel and Mary felt for their failed attempts. It was a solemn time for them as they took consolation in the constancy of each other's company.

*   *   *

Mr Collins, paralyzed with shock after hearing of the fall, was to become as much a patient as Miss de Bourgh. The knowledge that his brother, the very object of his benefactress's humanity, had caused the injury of her only daughter was inconsolable. He was so overcome that he could not gather his wits to inform Her Ladyship in his next correspondence.

"How can I write to Her Ladyship with the intelligence that my brother, in whom she showed such charity, had the poor judgement to incapacitate Miss de Bourgh," he confided in Charlotte with anxiety.

"Why don't you wait these next few days to see how well she improves? I can see no sense in alarming Lady Catherine needlessly. After all, we possess only half the story. It is all injury and no cure. The doctor will return soon. You will have a full account by then," advised Charlotte with the voice of reason. "You can defer that much time. It might save Lady Catherine unnecessary distress and any good news might vindicate your brother." Mr Collins conceded with grave doubt. Remaining insensibly distraught, he allowed Charlotte to do the thinking for him.

In the days that passed Mr Collins and Charlotte visited Miss de Bourgh twice daily. Mr Collins vowed to remain unforgiving of his foolish brother and cousin until Miss de Bourgh was fully recovered. Until then, whenever the opportunity arose, Mr Collins gave Daniel and Mary unrelenting looks of scorn, making Mrs Jenkinson as pleased as she could be.

Chapter 5

G uests were beginning to arrive at Pemberley for their overnight stay before the gala. Among them were Col Fitzwilliam on a furlough from the military, Miss Caroline Bingley, Mr and Mrs Hurst and Mr Carrington, who arrived with an unexpected guest.

After Mr Carrington's introduction to the Darcys and the proper appreciation expressed for the extension of an additional invitation, the introductions were advanced to the Bingleys. Jane recognized the visitor immediately.

"Dr Kindrel! It is a pleasant surprise to see you again!" she exclaimed cheerfully.

"Yes, indeed" added Mr Bingley eagerly. "We are very glad to see you. I was completely unaware of your knowing the Darcys."

"I confess, I cannot say I am so familiar with the Darcys above what I recall from your reference in London. However, when I was graciously invited to Pemberley by Mr Carrington, I could not refuse," stated the doctor happily. "I remembered you mentioned you were going to Pemberley and am extremely pleased that my recollection was correct. Is Miss Catherine here?" he asked trying not to sound too eager.

"She is out in the parks. I am confident she will be delighted to know you are among us once again. You will be able to see her tonight at dinner," said Jane with sincerity, "after all, you must be tired from your journey. We can speak later. Mr Bingley will escort you to your room since he was just going to look in on the children." Dr Kindrel followed

Mr Bingley as instructed but would have much more preferred to have had his bag brought in while he walked about the park.

That evening, Jane looked in on Kitty to share the intelligence that an old friend would be joining them for dinner tonight. "Who could it be? When I glanced at the guest list there weren't any names I cared to recognize. Tell me Jane! It's cruel to make me guess," she inquired enthusiastically, anxious for anything new and exciting. Jane could not withhold the information from Kitty any longer.

"It is Dr Kindrel! He certainly does get around. He has come here by invitation," explained Jane. "His friend Mr Carrington solicited one for him."

"Dr Kindrel! I am glad to hear it. I will thank Mr Carrington for inviting him when we meet," replied Kitty with unconventional celerity. She dressed quickly and made it down before any of the other guests, hoping to get a chance to review the seating arrangements with Lizzy. If Lizzy was amenable, she might arrange for Dr Kindrel to be seated next to her.

Fortunately, Lizzy was found in the dining area giving attention to last minute details. Kitty stood back and viewed the table to admire it before she asked, "Lizzy, would you be very upset if I asked you to move the seating around a bit? I would very much like to sit next to Dr Kindrel, if it is at all possible."

"You are in luck, Kitty. I just came down to make some changes. Sadly, Miss de Bourgh will not be dining with us tonight. She has an impenetrable notion that she should not be seen in less than perfect health and feels her limping would draw unwanted attention to her. I suggested she be seated early and leave the table last, but she would not make compromises. There was no manner of persuasion that would convince her. The de Bourghs do hold to their convictions. You can take her place between Mr Carrington and Dr Kindrel. That would please you wouldn't it?"

"I could not ask for better," she said gratefully. "I did want to get acquainted with Mr Carrington as well. Tonight will be a wonderful evening!"

Indeed, dinner was sensational. It was served in the banquet hall as a prelude to the soiree that was to come. Fine china and linens complimented the colors of the ornamental stuccoes and light blue walls. The candelabrum and wall sconces created an inviting aura of serenity as the guests conversed with great anticipation of the ball. Dr Kindrel leaned toward Kitty to express his joyful guilt in manipulating the invitation to Pemberley.

"I was very self conscious, almost ill at ease, accepting the gracious invitation to the Darcy home. But I have no regrets. I am glad I've come."

"Dr Kindrel, you must never feel you are a stranger. We are old friends now. By all means, put your mind at ease. I assure you the Bingleys and I are very pleased to have you here. If I didn't think you were otherwise too occupied to be distracted, I would have obtained an invitation for you from my sister, Mrs Darcy, while we were still in London. I wish I would have done so now just the same."

"Actually my being here at all is the result of a surprising turn of events. I was caring for a friend of Mr Carrington from his days at Cambridge. Mr Carrington happened to have visited on a day I was asked to share in the dinner. He explained to his friend that he had to leave to Derbyshire post haste. When he mentioned the name of Pemberley and the Darcys, I could not help but inquire as to the rest of the family. He was not familiar with any of you and kindly asked me to come along as he was in the mood for company and thought I might be able to enlighten him as to the nature of the family he was to meet. Naturally, Miss Catherine, I had nothing but perfection to dispatch."

"I am glad it happened that way. I do not know what we would have done in London without you. For certain, those walks to Gracechurch Street would not have been half as pleasurable. I think we should do our best to maintain our friendship."

"The memory of your association has remained with me these past few months as well," he said showing the first signs of timidity Kitty has ever observed in him. "Miss Catherine, in the spirit of the ball, which encompasses everyone tonight, I would like to ask if you would be so kind to allocate the first dance for me or any dance you may have available tomorrow so that I may look forward to dancing with you."

"I have not reserved any dances thus far and would like very much to designate the first to you."

With that established, Dr Kindrel and Kitty cheerfully discussed a number of topics almost exclusively throughout dinner. Only the occasional chat with Mr Carrington tore them apart. Charlotte motioned for Lizzy to take notice before everyone's conversation was interrupted by the suggestion of a toast by Mr Collins.

Well wishes for the future bride and groom were resonated through out the dining room and the party soon broke for after dinner refreshments. The men and women rose to file into their separate lounges.

Mr Darcy showed the men to the billiard room while Lizzy escorted the women to the large formal sitting room she rarely occupied. Her private sitting room was far less pretentious and prettily fitted up to exhibit a more relaxed atmosphere. However, as the occasion called for the need to impress, extravagance had to be displayed.

Caroline and Mrs Hurst avoided the Bennet women with polite diplomacy. They formed an intimate group among old acquaintances while Kitty, Jane, Charlotte and Lizzy mingled about until they eventually formed a small group of their own.

"Mama had a gown made for me that is so elegant, I hardly know myself in it. It makes me unsure and pretentious. Having Dr Kindrel there will help me feel much more at ease. His presence is an unexpected pleasure, Charlotte. You will like him. In his own way he is above the rest. Isn't he Jane?" said Kitty in eager readiness to share her opinion of him.

"For an enterprising learned man, he is modest and unaffected with himself and his achievements," confirmed Jane glancing at Lizzy. It was a pleasure to see Kitty in these unusually high spirits. "I believe it to be attributed to his humble upbringing," she concluded.

The men could be heard exiting the billiard room and heading leisurely toward the ladies. They were just about to join the women when Mrs Bennet suggested that Kitty and Mary retire for the night.

"You two would benefit greatly from a good night's sleep. You should retire to your rooms before the men arrive or you will be here all night," she said ushering them out the door. Kitty protested strongly.

"There can be no harm in staying up as long as the others since we will be equal in form," she remarked comparing herself to the other women.

"I do not care about the rest. My only consideration is your fate tomorrow. Let the other ladies fend for themselves," she retorted still ushering them out.

"Mother!" declared Kitty resisting in protest.

"Do not mope so, Kitty. There is no one of particular consequence for you here tonight and you will appreciate the extra rest. You will have the edge by being well restored as some guests will arrive in the early afternoon to rest before the ball. You don't know who they may be. Go straight to bed Mary. You can use all the help you can get as well." Mary did not wish to leave either and put a defiant scowl on her face. Mrs Bennet scooped up her daughters from behind one last time and forced them out the door with little regard for tact and good manners.

Caroline and Mrs Hurst gave a look of disdain for the ever expected outlandish behavior of the Bennet family. They would have much to contribute in the circulation of their reputation if it would not stain them as well.

Charlotte would not let the incident affect Lizzy and Jane. They were always embarrassed by their mother's outlandish behavior in public as Mrs Bennet could not be controlled. Instead, Charlotte turned her friend's attention to another, more pleasant subject. "I think Kitty has developed an interest in Dr Kindrel," she whispered as things settled down again.

"Oh, I don't think so," said Jane with caution. She remembered how platonic their friendship was and thought everyone could be misreading their camaraderie. "We have thought of him as a fast acquaintance when we met him this season in London. We spent many weeks in his steady company," she said wishing to protect the concealment of her illness. "Kitty never exhibited anything more than friendship toward him. It would be hard to conceive that her image of him could alter so dramatically."

"She does light up at his mere presence," challenged Charlotte not accepting her explanation.

"I warn you to beware, Jane. I wouldn't dismiss Charlotte's intuition so readily if I were you. She has an eye for budding romances," defended Lizzy with a smile. "She detected Mr Darcy's attraction to me even before I did! She is very observant." Not quite convinced herself, Lizzy determined to keep an eye out for any future signs of romance.

Caroline Bingley kept an eye out for romance too. Not for Dr Kindrel but for Mr Carrington. She had been predisposed to form an interest in him since she heard of him at St James Court this past winter. She already knew he was in possession of his father's estates and wealth and, tonight, she was equally impressed with what she saw of him. He was a slender man, not excessively handsome but of noticeable fine manners and upbringing. Happily, his height was tall enough even for a woman of her stature. With all these promising attributes, she determined he had, indeed, everything she could desire.

Intent on forming an immediate acquaintance she and Mrs Hurst lost no time employing Mr Hurst to make the proper introductions at the very first opportunity. Accepting his assignment with great reluctance, Mr Hurst displayed no urgency to enact the meeting. He preferred instead to stand by the array of cakes to nibble on one or two. Miss Bingley stood conveniently by in complete preparation for the introduction to Mr Carrington when she saw him moving in her direction. As he came closer, Mr Hurst, not caring enough to take advantage of the opportunity, continued to snack. Mrs Hurst tried to nudge him into making his moves but it was all to no avail.

After letting several opportunities slip by without Mr Hurst applying himself, Caroline walked away offended by her brother in law's indolence and proceeded to mingle with the larger crowd in the hopes of meeting him through the auspices of others.

Mrs Hurst pulled her husband into a corner and reproached him on his negligence. Provoked into action, he hurried off to Mr Carrington and immediately offered to acquaint him with his wife.

"Mr Carrington, I have been assigned, by powers untold, to initiate an introduction between yourself and my wife. Would you be so kind as to allow me to make the formal presentations?" Curious as to who should specifically want to make his acquaintance, Mr Carrington readily accepted. Directing him over to Mrs Hurst, Mr Hurst made the long awaited overtures.

"Mr Carrington, allow me to present my wife, Mrs Hurst," he said with all the enthusiasm he could command.

"A pleasure to meet you Mrs Hurst," said Mr Carrington bowing with style. She glanced toward Mr Hurst with approval as he turned away in disinterest to win his way back to the puddings.

"I am very pleased to make your acquaintance, Mr Carrington," began Mrs Hurst sweetly. "I have often heard your name mentioned and had no face to go with it."

"I hope it does not disappoint you, Mrs Hurst," he said in good humor.

"Not at all, it is just that you have been a mystery to us. We knew you were traveling when we did not see you in London."

"My lady, I have been in London just prior to my arrival here and though I have spent much of the later season seeing to an old sick friend, I have not kept myself hidden away. I have partaken in all the sophistication London has to offer by way of entertainment. An exhausting occupation I must say. I was most content to sit out half the season," he said jokingly.

"Well then, I am not surprised we have not met. We too were occupied with the most unfortunate business of caring for our brother's wife Mrs Bingley during our stay there. She was unwell and in the most adverse of circumstances with the babies. It was all we could do to pull her through. We were fortunate to have Dr Kindrel enter the scene and direct us with his expertise," she said knowing full well that they arrived together.

"Then you are to be admired, Mrs Hurst. Dr Kindrel does have superior skill. If he used your assistance, it was a tribute to you and your abilities," he remarked in earnest.

"Thank you. I certainly have learned an abundance from him but fortunately we have no use for such knowledge as there is no illness with in my family. It was all for Mrs Bingley."

"I am always taken by the strength and devotion family tragedies can muster in us. It must have been very trying."

"There is nothing I would not do for our brother's wife, however, do not think that I have undertaken the task alone. My sister, Miss Bingley, was equally involved," she said as she finally caught Caroline's attention and motioned for her to join them. "You have not been introduced and I am quite intent on it. Caroline, it is my pleasure to introduce you to the honorable Mr Carrington."

"How do you do sir," she said humbly as they bowed in acknowledgement of one another.

"I do hate to be so forward, Mr Carrington, but we are all family here and I would like to be certain that you will have the greatest experience tomorrow. Therefore, if I may be so bold as to inquire if you have a full complement of engagements for tomorrow's event for it occurs to me that, as destiny would have it, Caroline has only a few dances left available. The first two purposely being among them, as they are not to be bestowed on just anyone."

Her direct approach was not lost to Mr Carrington who was actively seeking his connection to the mysterious lady his father was so highly impressed with. He quickly surmised that Mrs Hurst might be functioning under the guise of their predetermined directives. However, the failure of seeing anything that should affect him to act impulsively in Caroline's features brought him to the conclusion that he should proceed with caution. At once he decided to put them to the test before committing himself any further as he did not want to give away the first dance erroneously.

"If you would allow me first to say that I believe your father, Mr Bingley and my father, Lord Carrington, were particular friends. If this is the case, I would like you to know that my father remembers him fondly," interviewed Mr Carrington verifying his contact.

"Yes, he and Lord Carrington were good friends. They traveled in the same circles," assumed Caroline candidly, "however, our beloved father has been taken from us for some time now."

Using this communication as a valid confirmation of his father's instructions, Mr Carrington assumed he had indeed made the proper connection. "Please forgive me for bringing up sad memories. We must talk of other things," he suggested putting any reservations to rest.

Mrs Hurst could not determine why he would digress from her offer and swiftly pursued it once again. "Yes. We should not be so grave. The ball is a far better topic for discussion."

"I agree wholeheartedly," he said turning to give Caroline his full attention. "Miss Bingley, your sister, and my father, will have it no other way but that we are to reserve the first two dances tomorrow for each other. If you would accept my offer, I will be honored to share the dances with you."

"Mr Carrington, I do accept and look forward to it as it will make me very happy," she said agreeably. Mrs Hurst stood proud of her accomplishment and considered Mr Carrington the gentleman she bargained for while Caroline basked in the good fortune of attaining his attentions.

Mr Carrington remained in the company of Caroline and Mrs Hurst the evening through. He was intent on furthering his acquaintance with Caroline to pursue the possibility of fulfilling his father's request. The ladies were elated with his constant applications. By the time the evening was through Caroline had thoroughly established herself with Mr Carrington.

Chapter 6

The following morning, Miss de Bourgh received a satisfactory bill of health from Dr Bodley. "I suggest that she select her dances wisely. Too much dancing will encourage the swelling to return. Either way, her ankle should remain well wrapped," he suggested to Mr Darcy. Miss de Bourgh was delighted she was able to attend the ball after all. Where her trepidations were once true she had now come to the conclusion that she would be very pleased to attend and was looking forward to dancing once more. In the best of spirits she ordered a servant to lay out her dress and make the proper preparations for her evening's attire.

Mr Collins, eager for the news, was spying about in the corridor awaiting the doctor's removal. As Dr Bodley and Mr Darcy left Miss de Bourgh's room, he and Charlotte took the liberty to knock on her door. Mr Collins needed to inform Miss de Bourgh that he was under duress to compose a letter to Her Ladyship about the incident and came seeking the outcome of the doctor's report to complete the details.

"Please, allow us to inquire as to your health, Miss de Bourgh. We have resolved that although we will attend the ball, so as not to offend Miss Darcy, we will not like it one bit if you do not go. It is beyond our ability to enjoy ourselves when one as deserving as you should be so vastly disappointed," volunteered Mr Collins as he peered onto her injured ankle.

"Mr Collins, I am grateful for your loyalty but you do not need to feel compelled to share in my pain. I have received an acceptable bill of health and will attend after all," she declared appreciating his concern.

Charlotte detected her joy and thought it would be wise to inquire as to the urgency Anne might feel in relating the good news to her mother. "Have you written the good Lady Catherine as to your improvements, Miss de Bourgh?"

"I have not written Mother at all about the incident. I was hoping for a full recovery in attempt to avoid relating this circumstance to her at all until I can do it face to face. As for your correspondence, I know you will not tell Mother either if I request it."

"Please Miss de Bourgh," pleaded Mr Collins apprehensively, "allow me to correspond with Her Ladyship as to your injury for she has asked me to keep her fully informed of every occurrence and I must remain loyal to my duty." Charlotte thought him foolish to insist on delivering the potentially disturbing dispatch.

"Mr Collins, we should honor Miss de Bourgh's desire to keep her mother from such dismal tidings when she is not near to help. Miss de Bourgh would like to tell her in her own time," said Charlotte playing the agreeable mediator.

"You are wise, Mrs Collins. I would like to forget the past and look forward to tonight. Most of all, I would like for Mother to think I am well off despite her absence. I have considered the matter well behind me, even non-existent." Anne did not want her mother to think of her as 'impetuous' or 'thoughtless' as she has so often heard her say of others. She insisted that she was in good spirits and thought well enough of Mary and Daniel to desire the incident put behind them. Mrs Jenkinson, under protest, had already vowed to keep it to herself. Charlotte sided with Miss de Bourgh and agreed that they both do not want to disappoint her mother, leaving Mr Collins to surrender his own judgment.

"There is not a more considerate, wiser, devoted daughter than you, Miss de Bourgh, who with all you have endured, would not cause her mother the consequence of unnecessary burdens," he said lauding over her. This resolution saved face for everyone involved. Mr Collins would write to Lady Catherine giving her an account, in good conscience, that all was well and that Miss de Bourgh spent her days quietly reading under the unvarying company and watchful eye of Mrs Jenkinson.

Daniel and Mary entered the room as the Collinses filed out. Mr Collins, not wanting to relieve them of their anguish prematurely, continued to look at them accusingly as they crossed paths. Charlotte, on the other hand, gave them a broad smile.

Needless to say, Daniel and Mary were ecstatic that Miss de Bourgh would join them that night. It meant their rehearsals were not for naught as they were now essentially validated. When Miss de Bourgh mentioned she would not inform Lady Catherine about the event, Daniel and Mary sighed a breath of relief. They greatly appreciated the acquittal and thought of Miss de Bourgh as a truely considerate trusting friend. Mary happily offered to help Miss de Bourgh dress for the evening in addition to the help provided by the parlor maid. Miss de Bourgh gratefully accepted.

*   *   *

With the evening fast approaching, Mrs Bennet entered Kitty's room fully dressed in an intricately patterned deep green satin gown. Her new emeralds sparkled brilliantly with every move and focused the attention on her cheerful face. Her beauty excelled and she looked exquisite. Her energy was contagious as she was overflowing with vigor and excitement from the optimistic suspense in what the evening had in store for her eligible daughters.

"Mama, you look beautiful," commented Kitty with jubilant sincerity. Her mother made some turns to lavish in the attention. "Your jewels suit your attire so well. Papa does have great taste."

"I have been describing it to him in full detail ever since you left us at Longbourn," she confessed. "I knew just what I needed and just how to get it. I only made it seem as if he selected it but it was as per my instructions," she said with glee. "Men like to feel they are functioning out of their own accord. Remember, the greater the bounty if we allow them to think it." Changing the conversation ever so slightly, she said,

"Now this is a very important night for you of all people. It is the moment I have dreamed of for all my girls and tonight you will have the benefit of my labor. You must look your very best for you are sure to have your pick of eligible rich suitors, after all, your sister is the hostess, and they must all dance with you. Don't accept any dances from anyone over marriage-able age. You would only be wasting your time. Of course, that excludes dancing with your brothers Mr Darcy and Mr Bingley," she added, "since each of them have the potential of delivering you into the hands of another man of fortune. The wealthier your partners are the more other wealthy men will want to dance with you."

"Yes, Mama," answered Kitty complaisantly.

Mrs Bennet looked around the room and inspected Kitty's garments and frills. She found her elaborately beaded gown on the bed.

"Your costume is the most flattering gown that could have ever been made. My sister Mrs Gardiner does have exceptional taste. I am glad we spared no expense. The dividend will make it worth it. Jane's adornments really bring it together nicely too. You are fortunate to have sisters who have married so well and soon you will have fine jewels of your own." Realizing that Kitty was running late she inquired with sudden agitation as to the whereabouts of the hairdresser. "Why does she take so long?"

"She is on her way, Mama," explained Kitty trying to calm her mother down. "She is with Mary."

"Mary!" she screeched in disbelief. "Why would she see Mary first? Mary doesn't care how her hair looks. She intends to spend her time prior to the ball fussing over Miss de Bourgh instead of caring for herself. I have quite given up on her. She will go nowhere tonight. I will retrieve the hairdresser and have her come to you at once. Get your dress on, child. You won't want to mess your hair once it is done," instructed Mrs Bennet as she exited the room in haste making her way to Mary.

Coincidentally, the hairdresser was in the corridor on her way to Kitty. "I suppose Miss Bennet is through with her hair styling. Do move briskly. Miss Catherine is waiting for you," she stated with urgency. "Is Miss Bennet still in her room?"

"Miss Bennet may be found in her room for the moment but she was going to Miss de Bourgh's room directly."

Mrs Bennet proceeded to Mary's room to check on her progress. Mary was already dressed in a subtle pale gown with delicate lace trim made especially for the occasion. It was not as dazzling as Kitty's but represented a quiet elegance befitting Mary. Her own gold link chain necklace hung from her neck as simple as ever.

"You should spend more time on your own appearance, Mary, instead of trotting off to help someone else at a time like this. A little more effort on your part may tip the scales to your favor," said Mrs Bennet as she adjusted the trimming on Mary's hair and smoothed out her gown. Mary let out a sigh of despair. Her mother was never pleased with her appearance and she had no concern for the guests below. Her allegiance was to Miss de Bourgh's happy recuperation and not the acquisitioning of a husband, at least not through fashion and coquetry. She wanted a man of content, someone she could converse with and exchange points of view. Her eyes were set on Daniel and he was not so shallow. She would not give her appearance extra care when in reality it meant so little.

"Well, you do look fine in spite of yourself, Mary," said Mrs Bennet pleased with her final observation. "Will you make your entrance with me and Mr Bennet?"

"No Mama. I will be accompanying Miss de Bourgh and Daniel."

Taking a deep sigh, Mrs Bennet left the room. Mary stepped in front of the mirror to take a second glance. She took a long look at herself. Leaning into the mirror, she slowly removed her spectacles. 'No sense in taking chances,' she thought as she pinched her cheeks and pushed her hair behind her ears to expose the tiny baubles. When she was at last satisfied she slipped her glasses on again and left for Miss de Bourgh.

Anne was standing in front of a full length mirror when Mary arrived. She looked refine in her gown as it was of the highest quality satin. It was very well tailored and fashioned to camouflage the excessive frailty of her physique.

Daniel, wearing his best starched clergyman outfit, reviewed the ladies before him making the prediction of both becoming the most handsome ladies in the room tonight. Anne felt more impassioned than ever to partake of the festivities. She could not conceal her confidence as she was up to the task and enthusiastically faced what she considered to be the social event that would alter her life. Daniel and Mary admired her new attitude. They knew she was capable of it and felt that in some small way they helped form her new point of view.

*   *   *

The ballroom at Pemberley exhibited the grandeur and richness appropriate for the formality of the occasion. Only the glow of Georgiana's face and the shimmer of the ladies' sparkling jewels compared to the brilliance of the room. Fresh flowers displayed on the consoles enhanced the air with the aromatic fragrance of a botanical garden as the amiable atmosphere felicitated smiles and excitement from every guest. Mr and Mrs Darcy, Georgiana and Lord Watney formed the welcoming committee while the background music invited guests in. The entrance of Mr Carrington had, at last, placed Mr Darcy in a favorable position to secure a dance with Miss de Bourgh.

"Mr Carrington, shall I take the liberty in suggesting a partner for you at the commencement of the dance?" greeted Mr Darcy to fulfill his obligation.

"It is very kind of you, Mr Darcy. I am grateful for your concern but I have been fortunate enough to make some engagements already. The first two have been promised to Miss Bingley and the third to Mrs Hurst. Afterwards, I hope Mrs Darcy will avail herself to compliment me with a dance besides," he answered graciously.

"My concern was just for your entertainment. I am delighted you have already procured a few partners. Do go in and enjoy yourself," said Mr Darcy ending it in the face of defeat.

The Bennets were entering next while Mr Darcy took the opportunity to lean toward Lizzy to convey his news of failure. "He thought I was acquiring a dance for you, Elizabeth."

Mrs Darcy was amused. "Then I suppose I will be dancing with Mr Carrington tonight, Mr Darcy," she laughed.

"I have never had the propensity for the task at hand," he explained. "I couldn't carry the conversation past the initial offer. The mere mention of her name never even passed my lips."

"Do not be so hard on yourself. After all, it was Lady Catherine who put it on you. It is a precarious situation," she said. "In any case, you must secure a partner for Miss de Bourgh. Your cousin, Colonel Fitzwilliam is at present without a partner. He will happily dance with Miss de Bourgh and I am sure you are not reluctant to ask it of him," she conspired as she waved her parents in. Mr Bennet stopped for a little chat with his cherished daughter.

"My dear Lizzy, you look radiant tonight. Allow me to thank you on behalf of your mother, for reaching into the depths of her life's interest, at least since Jane was born, and realizing them with this bountiful ball. It is a generous gesture on your part," he said as Lizzy suppressed a chuckle.

"Oh, Mr Bennet," began Mrs Bennet ignoring his comments as they entered the ballroom, "take a deep breath." She inhaled with exaggeration bringing on a rush of adrenaline. "Invigorating isn't it?"

"Is it the blue blood that stimulates your senses or the scent of helpless bachelors trapped in an elaborate snare?" he asked. "My heart goes out to those unsuspecting souls."

"You are mistaken, Mr Bennet. They are not unsuspecting for they have come for the very same reason or why come to a ball at all?" she asked rhetorically. Turning to face the room with her hands spread out before her, Mrs Bennet embraced the moment saying, "Look Kitty! So much eligibility and wealth assembled in one room! You are certain to attract the noblest and richest of all."

The Bennet's entrance turned heads. Mrs Bennet's resonant voice caught their immediate attention while Kitty's poise distracted it. In no time, all eyes were on Kitty. Her attire and posture charmed her spectators as she formed an immediate following. Mrs Bennet was aglow with aspirations when she saw the impact her daughter made. She stepped behind Kitty strategically, taking Mr Bennet along with her to allow Kitty to sort through the gentlemen as they passed by.

Miss Bingley and Mrs Hurst, already present, realized the potential hazards of Kitty's appearance. They feared that Mr Carrington would naturally follow the example set by the others and cause Caroline to lose her advantage. Together they conspired to keep a watchful eye over Mr Carrington.

Dr Kindrel soon entered. Not easily intimidated by formal settings, he felt a little overwhelmed at the immensity of the room. Strengthening his conviction, he thought only of the promise the evening brought to being with his beloved Kitty. The sight of her made him lose his breath as the men surrounding her reveled in her magnificence. Without hesitation he descended toward her to take his place by her side until Mr Bingley stopped him fast in his tracks to introduce him to, "someone very much worth meeting."

"Mr Bennet," asked Mrs Bennet, "which one of these young men do you find attractive?"

"Do not ask which young man attracts me, Mrs Bennet!" snapped Mr Bennet in alarm. As usual Mrs Bennet did not care if she was overheard but Mr Bennet would not have it. The slightest misunderstanding could mar his integrity beyond repair. "I will not have you ask me questions of attractions for what attracts me is not being here at all! You may begin the process of elimination on your own. I trust my voice will not rise above your opinion at any rate."

"There must be someone whose reputation goes before them," continued Mrs Bennet unphased as she would enlist his cooperation just the same. "Someone immense and prominent, with the breeding of Mr Darcy and the personality of Mr Bingley," she said reviewing her requirements aloud.

"Madam, I have not the interest you do."

"Oh, you are full of humor tonight, Mr Bennet. You know my interest is only for Kitty and Mary and yours should be as well. Go ahead. Make rounds, inquire and return better informed. Find them husbands, Mr Bennet!"

"My dear, I will not assist in bringing the poor soul to the slaughter, nor will I remain with you as the crime takes place. The business of procuring a husband is your forte!" He turned to find the card room when he stopped in midstream. Reconsidering the high cost of his investment for this affair versus the even higher stakes in the card room, he chose the lesser of the two evils and stayed to observe his investment at work. Reluctantly, he returned to Mrs Bennet and asked, "Have you sighted your first victim?"

"Just remain at the ready, Mr Bennet. I will dispatch you when the time is right," she answered as her prediction of his cooperation was realized.

The room stirred with excitement when Lord Watney and Miss Darcy officially opened the dance floor. Mrs Bennet stood vigilant to observe who Kitty might choose. Increasing her expectations, she saw Kitty ignore those standing beside her as she began to scan the room. Dr Kindrel set himself free from his circle with a polite bow and boldly pardoned himself as he made it through the gentlemen surrounding Kitty. He reached out his hand to her, pulled her forth and proudly escorted Kitty to the dance floor. Col Fitzwilliam escorted Miss de Bourgh while Mr Carrington escorted Caroline. The Darcys, Bingleys, and Hursts soon followed leaving the rest of the guests to join in.

"Were you here all along?" asked Kitty. "I didn't see you."

"I was making my rounds," he jested as they continued in step. The two were all smiles.

"Dr Kindrel," Kitty said playfully, "you do not mention my attire. Don't you find it beautiful? My aunt Gardiner selected it for me during my stay in London."

"Could this be the much anticipated dress you had me escort you to Gracechurch Street for?" he said trying to get a better look at it while they danced.

"Yes. You do have a good memory but you do not mention that you like it!"

"You do not need to adorn yourself in this manner to have my compliment, Miss Catherine. I had the honor of seeing your gentleness and compassion in London and have since found you in possession of complete and natural beauty. However, having said that, I am sorry I did not mention your loveliness tonight."

"Mr Bennet," cried Mrs Bennet disconcertingly, "She is blundering the whole thing. All she ended up with is Dr Kindrel! Stop them before it's too late." Mr Bennet walked away from Mrs Bennet to settle in at the far side of the room. Frustrated, Mrs Bennet surveyed the room to investigate what Mary was doing. To her chagrin, Mary was seated with Miss de Bourgh and Daniel.

"Get up, Mary. You must go out on the floor with everyone else. You should not be left behind. How else will you be seen?"

"Yes, Mama," whispered Mary trying not to attract attention, "but I have not been asked."

"With all these eligible men? It is your fault Mary for being cooped up in this corner. You must stand up and make yourself known. Go and take a turn around the room," she insisted lifting her daughter from her seat. She took a few steps when Daniel called out to Mary.

"Miss Bennet, a ball of this stature does not allow for a clergyman to begin a dance with a lady of your status, otherwise I would gladly escort you to the floor," he reminded Mary.

"We should not stand on ceremony. I do not fear giving the wrong impression and would love to dance with you." Daniel bowed humbly and took Mary out to the dance floor.

Mrs Bennet was dumbfounded as she was taken by surprise at the sight of Mary and Daniel's advancement to the dance floor. Surmising that her daughters were set to destroy their chances for marriage among the elite, Mrs Bennet declared them the most unthinking of women and turned hastily to locate Mr Bennet.

"They do not think of themselves, Mr Bennet. What will our neighbors in Meryton say when we come home with a common clergyman and a doctor for all our troubles? Is there nothing you can do about it?" agonized Mrs Bennet.

"I will promptly return to Longbourn to gather a consensus if you wish," volunteered Mr Bennet.

"Do not nettle me. This is no time for jest, Mr Bennet. At least Mary will be seen now but my hopes for Kitty will be destroyed if she does not elevate the rank in her selection of partners. We must act with urgency, Mr Bennet, before our daughters are done in by their own deeds."

"She can only dance with one partner at a time, Mrs Bennet," he said reasoning with his wife while she scanned the room for an immediate substitute. "Allow her to do her own choosing. I am certain she will choose better next time as I trust she has nothing more in mind than your image and good reputation in Meryton."

Ignoring his sarcasm, she focused in on a gentleman with immense presence. He had an air of wealth and the subsequent allure of an attractive face. His shoulders were broad and his body well framed as he appeared strong and athletic, yet polished and debonair. "That young man just coming off the dance floor over there by Mr and Mrs Bingley looks very willing to make an attachment," she whispered with all the force her breath would supply fearing that someone else would discover her catch.

"Mrs Bennet, your eagerness to have me act on your intuitive skills never fail to amaze me. Dare I ask you, at a time like this, how you can so easily surmise that he has a willing look?" asked Mr Bennet calling her on her remarks.

"Just go make his acquaintance so we can introduce him to Kitty. Make haste, Mr Bennet and let no one prevent it! There may be time for her yet if it is done directly!" she instructed enthusiastically.

"I shall not be pushed. Let Kitty meet him on her own. She doesn't seem to need our help anyway," he retorted as he pointed out that Kitty was once again surrounded by her share of young men. "How should I arrange the introduction when I do not know if Kitty is available? No, Mrs Bennet, I will not be sent on a fool's errand."

"We cannot depend on her, Mr Bennet. She will be dancing with a servant next. Make haste! Her future is in your hands!" she said pushing him along. Mr Bennet walked across the room toward the direction of Mrs Bennet's chosen man. As he neared him, the gentleman became suddenly inaccessible. Young ladies from all corners descended upon him and he stood surrounded. Mr Bennet turned to look at Mrs Bennet. Giving a slight shrug of his shoulders, he refused to break through the ladies and hastily abandoned his mission. Seeing she would not get any further cooperation from Mr Bennet, Mrs Bennet went on to implement an alternate plan. She would have Lizzy arrange for Lord Watney to introduce the two.

The young man Mrs Bennet selected for Kitty was a prize selection. He was a Baronet named Sir Jonathon Nettington. He was both eligible and wealthy, and was an investor friend of Lord Watney who was to remain at Pemberley until the wedding. Sir Jon held himself in the highest of standards and selected his dance partners with discriminating care. Mrs Bennet was very proud when he accepted Lord Watney's invitation to meet Kitty. To her added delight, Sir Jon found Kitty to be not only beautiful, but the most impressive dancer at the ball, making her exceptionally worthy of his company. Observing Kitty's attentions from other men only added to his desire to dance with her. The fourth set was about to commence when he gave her his hand and escorted her to the floor. They danced the fourth and fifth consecutively as everyone commented on how lovely they looked together. Indeed, they formed a magnificent pair.

Mrs Bennet, pleased with Kitty's success, allowed herself a moment's rest and took a seat by Miss de Bourgh as she expected Mary would eventually return to her side. Anne sat the dance out having already overextended herself with Mr Darcy, Mr Bingley and Col Fitzwilliam. Her ankle was beginning to swell and she could no longer dance. Content with the evening's progress, Mrs Bennet conversed with Miss de Bourgh to pass the time.

"Miss de Bourgh, I have met your mother when she came to visit my Lizzy at Longbourn. I am sure, at the time, your mother had no idea the person she was visiting, my Lizzy, would soon become a relation of hers," volunteered Mrs Bennet. Mr Darcy was approaching to inspect Miss de Bourgh's ankle when he overheard Mrs Bennet say, "It is a small world, isn't it. And here we are meeting at the Darcy's. Mrs Elizabeth Darcy. That does have a lovely sound doesn't it? My daughter Mrs Jane

Bingley did not do so poorly either. Her Mr Bingley has such a fine disposition. He is not as stiff and distant as Mr Darcy. I have long desired that Mr Bingley's easiness should somehow rub off on him . . . ."

Mr Darcy froze in his stead with the familiar chill Mrs Bennet had so often cast upon him in Meryton and turned away with a distant look of condemnation on his face. Mr Bennet walked over to his wife and alerted her to keep her voice down as Miss de Bourgh sat speechless. She felt embarrassed and turned in her seat to pay particular attention to her ankle in an attempt to separate herself from the Bennets as inconspicuously as possible. She entertained the idea of moving her seat but was afraid it would cause a bigger scene if Mrs Bennet should call her back. Instead, she remained helpless as she searched to be rescued.

"Oh, Mr Bennet, what I say is no secret. It is known by all," said Mrs Bennet dismissing her husband. Turning to bestow her full attention on Miss de Bourgh once again, Mrs Bennet continued her conversation on a very different subject. "Miss de Bourgh, you are of marrying age. Surely your mother has thought of an alliance for you! I married off three daughters within two years and they have all married well," she boasted. "Are you familiar with a Mr Wickham? He is an ensign in the militia. He married my youngest, Lydia. They are with the regiment and are living up in the far north or they would have been here today. I miss my Lydia but marriage is a girl's first duty you know." She paused and said, "Mr Wickham's services must be indispensible." Seeing Mrs Bennet bent on making a spectacle of herself, Mr Bennet walked away to the library seeking permanent refuge for the remainder of the evening. Barely taking notice, Mrs Bennet drew her breath and went on, "There must be someone for you, Miss de Bourgh. Whatever is your mother waiting for!?!"

On the far side of the room, Lizzy pulled away from Charlotte. The sight of the uneasiness Mrs Bennet was causing Miss de Bourgh and of the entertainment she was affording that side of the room called for her attention. She felt the color rise to her cheeks as she went to check her mother's actions. Dr Kindrel was nearer to Mrs Bennet and noticed the commotion beginning to stir. Well aware of Mrs Bennet's annals, Dr Kindrel navigated his way to her. He felt he could be of help to the family as he was thoroughly charmed by the tales of Mrs Bennet's inclinations and knew he would delight in experiencing them first hand. He advanced on her before Lizzy could and with tact, and amusement, he gallantly pushed a footstool toward Miss de Bourgh and spoke out saying, "I am sorry to interrupt your conversation, Mrs Bennet and don't want to seem rude but I would like to advise Miss de Bourgh to elevate her leg if she wishes for a quicker recovery. I notice that she hobbled over to her seat and can see the swelling of her ankle." Turning to Miss de Bourgh he said, "I prescribe that you sit the rest of the dance out, Miss de Bourgh." He returned to Mrs Bennet, "It is a pity such a lovely young lady must sit out a dance, devoid of her own choosing. Have you a suggestion, Mrs Bennet, for her to enjoy the rest of the evening as best she can?"

"She should resign herself to hear the music and remain in good company. Mary and Daniel will do. Mary does not have the attention that Kitty has," replied Mrs Bennet, glad to be of service. She called for Mary to sit with Miss de Bourgh while Dr Kindrel glanced over to the dance floor where Kitty was dancing with the Baronet. He could detect the designs Sir Jon had set upon her. Discomfited by the sight of Kitty looking so happy with the winsome Sir Jon, he turned back to Mrs Bennet and continued his conversation.

"May I be so bold as to reveal that Miss Catherine has confided in me, through her great concern for you, that you have been having a problem with your nerves. It concerns me. How could it be that someone so full of youth and good health suffer so?" he said raising her from her seat to the dance floor.

"Oh Dr Kindrel, you do not know the half of it, although I do not complain and make anyone suffer with me! They first started twenty-five years ago . . . ."

Dr Kindrel looked forward to speaking with Mrs Bennet for some time and thought conversing with her now was as good a time as any. For him the allure of her conversations was not in what she said but in the way she said it. Her eccentricities, liberties and blunt manner gave him, a man who constantly dealt with sickness and death, the greatest pleasure, exceeded only by the memories they provoked of moments well spent with Kitty in London.

Between dances Dr Kindrel and Mrs Bennet had formed a viable friendship. They enjoyed each other's company as Mrs Bennet often provided him with exceptional amusement through her bizarre larks and commentaries of the guests surrounding them. Mr Bennet appreciated the distraction and came to like him very well indeed.

Lizzy stood back and watched Dr Kindrel's creative diversions. She appreciated his sincerity and gave him a grateful smile. Noticing her presence, he acknowledged her with a nod of his head.

Charlotte stood observing the guests with her husband. "Have you noticed, Mr Collins," she said snickering at the humorous distraction, "that everywhere Mr Carrington goes Miss Bingley follows? It seems to me he is a marked man."

"This evening captures the very essence of romance and provides the influence of attraction. If Miss Bingley is interested in Mr Carrington, it should be considered a blessing and not a means of aspersion and idle chatter." Charlotte tolerated the reprimand and, when Mr Collins was through, rose to tour the room.

Miss de Bourgh retired to her bedchamber during the banquet to give appropriate care to her swollen ankle, forfeiting any chance of meeting Mr Carrington as the rest of the guests enjoyed the remainder of the festivities that concluded the night. Mary danced with a variety of partners, yet managed to remain, for the most part, in the constant company of Daniel while Kitty danced the night completely away, mostly with the Baronet, making Mrs Bennet very pleased indeed.

*   *   *

That evening, Mr and Mrs Darcy made sure their guests settled in properly before they made their routine rounds throughout the house. Mr Darcy let their favorite dogs in and secured the doors while Lizzy accompanied him, hand in hand, to put out the final candles. When the chore was complete, the dogs followed them to their bedchamber where they obediently slept outside the door.

Sitting on the bed, waiting for Mrs Darcy to join him, Mr Darcy watched as Lizzy brushed her hair by the vanity. She listened as her husband reflected on the splendor of the night. "We received nothing but high praise for the success of the evening, Elizabeth. I give you all the credit. Where would I be without you?"

"It gave me the greatest pleasure. Georgiana deserves the best. She is as much a sister to me as my own. I will miss her when she is gone, but as Mama says, 'it is a woman's duty'."

"I am grateful she has followed our example and married for true love and affection. I could not let her go otherwise," said Mr Darcy.

"Nor could I," agreed Lizzy.

"And what about your sister Kitty? She has certainly come into her own!"

"Yes, she has finally acquired the fine manners and grace maturity brings. I am delighted to see it. She was so thoroughly influenced by Lydia's wild ways. Jane and I nearly lost all hope."

"Next to Georgiana, she became a main attraction," noted Mr Darcy as he reached out to Lizzy and motioned her to come to bed. "Now we move on to the anticipation of Georgiana's wedding."

"It will be lonely without her," Lizzy sighed in deep thought. She slid gently into bed as Mr Darcy assisted her with the covers.

"I'm not going anywhere," he said pulling her close to him.

Chapter 7

Quiet games of chess and cards were sufficient entertainment as the guests gradually recovered. The men planned for shooting birds early the next morning while the ladies, with the exception of Caroline and Mrs Hurst, planned on staying behind.

"The confinement of a house, when the day will be as warm and bright as tomorrow promises to be will not suit us at all," said Caroline. "I would like to follow the men as they hunt and shoot their foul. Wouldn't you Mrs Hurst?" Mrs Hurst promptly agreed as she desired for Caroline to remain near Mr Carrington as much as possible. Sir Jon expressed his disappointment in the other ladies' refusal to come along.

"I would like it if even more ladies would accompany us. It will increase the appeal of the event," he said invitingly. "I urge more of you to tag along."

"Kitty will go," volunteered Mrs Bennet to the complete amazement of the Bennet family, "She can shoot a few herself."

Seeing the look on their faces, Caroline took it upon herself to provoke them into the truth of it. "Miss Catherine, do tell me what your preference is. What sort of foul do you enjoy hunting for?"

"The larger the better," answered Mr Bennet. "About this tall." he taunted holding his hand out in the air above his forehead. "Not just any size would do for our Kitty, we should clear that up right now for too short would be an insult. What say you, Mrs Bennet? What should our Kitty hunt tomorrow?"

"Why, Kitty will shoot foul like everyone else, of course. You know that very well, Mr Bennet," she said unamused.

"Kitty, go hunting?" exclaimed Mary in confusion. "It sounds a bit bizarre if you ask me."

"No one is asking you Mary. You know very well Kitty loves hunting," insisted Mrs Bennet as she stared at Mary in agitation, "and we can do without your insolent remarks!"

"Of course, Mary, do remember Kitty loves hunting," said Mr Bennet being less than convincing. Mrs Bennet was grateful for his donation and was put at ease as he continued. "She has been thoroughly trained in the science. Your mother has taught her all she knows on the subject, though the shooting of foul would be new to her." Dr Kindrel laughed aloud as he grasped the full meaning of Mr Bennet's comments. Lizzy looked anxiously at Jane.

"Whatever are you saying, Papa? Mama does not hunt and neither does Kitty," insisted Mary. Jane and Lizzy wished Mary would not pursue the subject. It would only serve to aggravate Mrs Bennet into further discussion.

"Mary, if you have bothered to look up from your books every now and then, you would know that Kitty loves to hunt. I should know my own daughter, shouldn't I?" said Mrs Bennet sneering with dour emphasis.

"Mama!" responded Mary in confusion.

"Do not struggle for understanding, Mary. This is just a little beyond your scope," stated Mr Bennet. Lizzy and Jane blushed as Mrs Bennet sat seething in silence. They were afraid their mother would erupt in a way that would not be controlled. Mr Darcy saw the distress on Lizzy's face and placed a comforting hand on her shoulder.

"How she does expose us to comments," shared Lizzy in low spirits.

"Do not ever allow yourself to feel self conscious in your own home, Mrs Darcy. Their behavior does not reflect on you," he whispered. "If you look around you will notice that, with a small exception, you are surrounded by friends and family. Anyone disapproving will just have to tolerate it or leave. No one's opinions is of any significance but our own," he instructed with assurance.

"If she is as skilled as you say, Mr Bennet, I hope she does not kill all of the birds herself," continued Caroline at Kitty's expense.

"Not to worry," replied Mr Bennet, "she has never used a gun in her life!" Dr Kindrel could not suppress a hearty guffaw while his partner, Col Fitzwilliam struggled to suppress his.

"Let's not quibble over it. Whosoever should be induced to join us is welcome to come. Miss Catherine can come if she so desires," remarked Mr Darcy with finality.

"And she does!" assured Mrs Bennet.

Jane spoke out trying to save Kitty saying, "Perhaps Kitty, you can stay and help me? With Mr Bingley away with the men, I could use your help with the children."

Kitty quickly took the bait and insisted she would not go, preferring to aid Jane. Much to the chagrin of Mrs Bennet, the matter was settled for the night.

When morning came Kitty was prepared to leave with the hunters. Mrs Bennet had woken her early and insisted that she go. Sir Jon was very happy to see her and walked with her as they approached the fields. Mrs Bennet saw them off with a smile on her face and a gleam in her eye.

Within two hours, Kitty returned hurrying home. She could not endure the sight of the killed and injured birds. It sickened her and she declared the sport the most horrific of all. Entering the parlor quietly, so as to escape Mrs Bennet's detection, she found Lizzy sitting with the Collinses.

"Where is Mama?" she asked concealing herself behind the furnishings.

"She is with Jane and the children. Is everyone back so soon?"

"No, but I abhor the sport and had to return. I did not know their blood would spill so bright, Lizzy. I was becoming ill out there," she said disgusted.

"I do not blame you. What about Sir Jon? Where is he?" she inquired.

"Sir Jon was so preoccupied with looking out for birds, that he did not even notice I had departed. Dr Kindrel escorted me back," Kitty replied.

"How are the other ladies doing? Did they return as well?"

"No. Actually, they are enjoying themselves very much. Mrs Hurst stands by Miss Bingley, who sticks to Mr Carrington and praises his every shot. He is very good at the trigger but he never hits anything. I would wager he is as much a sportsman as I am! Besides, they will not leave his side at any cost. There must be an attraction or I do not know how he endures it." Looking around she said, "I am going up to my bedchamber. Please do not let Mama know I have returned ahead of the party without Sir Jon." Lizzy and Charlotte gave their word as Mr Collins observed them in silence. Kitty crept her way up the stairs fearful of being discovered by Mrs Bennet.

"It is lovely to find amour blossoming right before your very eyes, isn't it Mrs Collins." said Mr Collins charmed by the cycle of life. "You see, dear cousin, Mrs Collins had perceived the attraction Miss Bingley had for Mr Carrington the night of the ball. I, too, have seen how inseparable they are. Mark my word, there is a match in our midst. All the better if it would resolve itself in wedlock."

*　　*　　*

Groups were formed for touring through the parks of Pemberley. Miss de Bourgh, though invited, did not want to walk about and stayed behind with Mary and Daniel. They sat in the parlor reading quietly while Mr Collins wrote Lady Catherine a note saying:

To The Honorable Lady Catherine de Bourgh,

> You will be delighted to hear of the glamour your daughter displayed at Miss Darcy's ball. She was radiant and danced the night away. She opened with Col Fitzwilliam and danced solely with familiar faces thereafter. However, you must not

fear. She did not overexert herself as she left the ball before the buffet. The food was exquisite and was displayed with fine artistic finesse. It was equaled only by the elegance of the ballroom. The orchestras played such wonderful music that I could not resist a dance or two with my Mrs Collins. At present, Miss de Bourgh sits by my side as the other guests tour the grounds of Pemberley. She is in good spirits and sends her love and happiness. I remain your humble servant,

Rev William Collins

In the meantime, the walk around Pemberley was too vast for guests to enjoy in one day. For the most part, they remained in the well cultivated gardens where bright cheerful flowers blanketed the landscape with an attractive array of shapes, fragrances and hues. The variety of flowers were so expertly arranged that they appeared to have sprouted as naturally as nature would allow. It seemed as though anything would grow there at its best. The noon sun swept over them as the sound of running water from a nearby brook flaunted refreshing completeness.

Mr Carrington was consumed by Miss Bingley as expected. Sir Jon enticed Miss Catherine to break away from the main crowd, where she was in happy conversation with Dr Kindrel, to sit with him under a tree. After some moments of polite dialogue, Sir Jon took the liberty to express his feelings for Kitty.

"I must say, I did not think I would find much to interest me here but myself. Yet when you stood there looking incredibly striking at the ball, I knew I had to know you better." He slid slowly closer to Kitty and took her hand when Dr Kindrel made a sudden appearance.

"Excuse my abrupt interference, Miss Catherine, but refreshments are being served back at the estate. I recommend you take advantage of the offer, as the combination of the warm sun and the long stroll may have exhausted you," suggested Dr Kindrel extending his hand to her with a smile. Sir Jon immediately rose to his feet and placed her hand on his arm before it reached the doctor. Kitty accepted Sir Jon's arm and walked back conversing with both him and Dr Kindrel. She did not notice the offense she caused Dr Kindrel but Sir Jon placed a great significance in her action and gave Dr Kindrel a repudiated look, considering his appearance extremely intrusive.

Sir Jon strategically ushered Kitty to a table so occupied, it left no room for Dr Kindrel. The good doctor excused himself graciously and took a seat next to Mrs Bennet, Col Fitzwilliam and the Bingleys. There he partook of refreshments and joined the pleasant conversation his affable companions afforded. Both Mrs Bennet and Dr Kindrel bestowed occasional glances toward Kitty's table. Mrs Bennet wore a grin. Dr Kindrel did not.

Sir Jon had Kitty's complete attention as he engulfed her in dialogue that, as he put it, "would benefit her greatly in times to come." He invested a lot of time in instructing Kitty to beware of her associations as their image can profile who she was. "I shall overlook your ignorance of the obligation superior people have to maintain airs and ambiance at all times. Country life has kept you unacquainted with the ways of the upper class. Take my advice you must always be conscious of your relationships as they portray your position in life," he said with authority. "You must allow me to aid you as you claim your proper standing in high society, Miss Catherine, for I will manage you to your full potential."

Kitty listened in awe, as a student would listen to a teacher who had insight and knowledge beyond her means. She thought he was wonderfully altruistic, freely offering vital information for her own good. There was a world out there she had no knowledge of and she decided it may be worth remaining in his good company, as her mother desired, after all.

*   *   *

The next day, Mary, Daniel and Miss de Bourgh chose to remain indoors again as they found a book of interest and were not yet ready to give it up. Lizzy led the women to Lambton in the barouche to spend a portion of the day shopping and browsing through the stores. Mr Darcy and the men rode along the countryside to fill their morning and decided on archery matches for the afternoon. Mr Carrington was shooting arrows with Sir Jon when he remarked on how wonderfully tranquil the day had been.

"It is a fine peaceful day, isn't it Sir Jon?" noted Mr Carrington trying his hand at archery.

"It is a dull and uninteresting day. Must be the lack of women. I, for one, would always forfeit quietude for a lady. Ladies should always be around when men are exhibiting their athletic prowess. Games, in particular, provide women the uncommon advantage to sit and stare at our figure without want of prudence. Oh, how they have admired my strength and abilities. It is a natural attraction like bees to honey," said Sir Jon. "For our part, it stimulates the talents to perform at peak ability. I admit I thoroughly enjoy the display."

"I'm afraid I will do little to earn their admiration. It would hardly be worth the seat. I have never invested the time necessary to develop my talents well enough to consider them worthy of an exhibition. In fact, I prefer to remain indoors and maybe read a good book," confided Mr Carrington.

"Is that why your aim is so poor? Dear fellow, I was a very determined athlete since my youth. I live for competition and the smell of victory. I plan to always be the best and surround myself with the best," boasted Sir Jon with hubris.

"Again, I do not share in your ideology. I am quite comfortable with my situation in life. I can accept my position and the solitude of my manor with bliss and a complete sense of fulfillment. I would be there now if my father did not make an appeal that I go out and find a wife."

"I expect to experience more out of life than humble domesticity. I must travel and never settle in one place for too long. A beautiful wife by my side is the very thing I desire as well—one that will be the envious desire of all men. And one that will do as I say."

"The envy of all men may be too much for one man to handle," jested Mr Carrington.

"Not the way I calculate it. She will be a lady of exceptional social standing who has had a naïve country upbringing. Those can be better trusted and provide less trouble than one who has adopted the cunning and sophistication of city life. An undemanding wife is vulnerable in your hands and can be molded any way you desire," stated Sir Jon arrogantly. "I am considering Miss Catherine Bennet, but the thought of having her parents in the family requires further reflection."

"They are a little animated for proper company but harmless nonetheless. Besides, they carry the potential to provide for a little humor in the day, don't you agree?" said Mr Carrington in a supportive fashion.

"I shall never be laughed at. How Mr Darcy endures such aberration is beyond my comprehension. Quite frankly, if I am to be with Miss Catherine, she must be removed totally from them." Having that said, Sir Jon and Mr Carrington completed their match and were joined by the other men. "Ah, someone with true skill and ability," said Sir Jon. "What should we wager?"

*　　*　　*

The ladies returned late that afternoon. Observing the men fully absorbed in their sports, Lizzy arranged for the servants to provide refreshments outdoors, enabling the ladies to watch the men while she reviewed the dinner menu with the cook. Caroline and Mrs Hurst applauded Mr Carrington's every attempt while Mrs Bennet overtly admired the Baronet. She was very proud of his mastery in archery.

"Look Kitty, he strikes the target every time. He is a man of true perfection. I will brag to the highest degree about him to Lady Lucas and Mrs Philips back in Meryton. He will be a splendid addition to the family and make a fine husband for you!" she said excitedly.

"As far as I can tell, it is Col Fitzwilliam that hits the mark with every shot. Sir Jon hits the target but not the mark, Mama. I think Col Fitzwilliam is a much better marksman than Sir Jon," answered Kitty with honesty.

"That doesn't count Kitty! He works all day with weaponry. Of course he is better!" said Mrs Bennet belittling Col Fitzwilliam's accomplishments.

"Our men do not fight with bows and arrows, Mama!" exclaimed Kitty exhausted by her mother's prejudice.

Mrs Bennet brushed Kitty's comments away, defending her stand saying, "Swords, arrows, muskets or slingshots. Aiming is aiming and Col Fitzwilliam gets all the practice in the world! Where is your loyalty?"

*   *   *

Armed with their hands full of paints and easels, the large party clambered their way up to the rustic wooded hill side that captured the spectacle Pemberley so generously offered in the bright noon sun. Mary and the Mr Collinses stayed behind to befriend Miss de Bourgh who feared her ankle was not yet completely out of peril.

While they ascended, Lizzy pointed out the formidable sights of lavender fields that mimicked ponds of clear blue water as they swayed in the wind. As they continued to climb she directed their attention to the cows and sheep that grazed lazily on the heath reminding everyone that Pemberley was a successful working farm as well. She brought attention to the trees ascending sparsely on their left, gathering closer as they met up with the tightly knit forest. Everyone agreed its natural beauty was obligingly picturesque.

Georgiana and Lord Watney, equally talented in sketching, chose a theme close to their heart. They sketched each other, one at a time, sharing the same canvas. Georgiana was sketched by Lord Watney facing left while Lord Watney was sketched by Georgiana facing right cleverly giving the impression that they posed together sitting on the edge of a hill. The result of their first joint effort brought them every delight as they could not resist looking into each other's eyes with the tacit admiration lovers exhibit for one another.

Kitty was not so adept in the art and selected to use water colors which would not require a well trained hand. Using a variety of colors and spontaneous strokes, she managed to capture the landscape, reproducing the likeness through its semblance, with little precision, yet suggesting nothing else but the image itself. Dr Kindrel commented as to his fascination with her unique talents.

"You have done a magnificent job capturing the perspective, Miss Catherine," he complimented. "Your angles, shades and blending of colors do you justice. You have a way I have not seen before and it works well for you." His joy was true and he stood as enthusiastic of her accomplishment as she did herself. The compliments, overheard, brought the officious attention of Sir Jon to the forefront. After a brief analysis of her artistry, much less impressed with her skill, Sir Jon required that Kitty try her hand at improving it by adding another subject to the painting.

"Miss Catherine," he began looking perplexed by her work, "I hazard to say that your colors blend together so chaotically that it functions to bewilder the eye. It makes me disoriented with my own surroundings! Which is the sky? Where are the grounds? Why do they look so barren? Surely you can take the liberty to add a bush or two to make the scene complete! It is obvious, you have no fixed technique," he critiqued. "You can do yourself a bit more credit if you would sketch someone into the picture to draw the necessary distinctions. I will be your model and place myself within sight of your composition where you can add me in with little difficulty," he demanded.

"I thank you kindly, Sir Jon, but do not trouble yourself. I will require no such services," she said accepting the humiliation. "It is true, I am no expert and will thereby never attempt the human form," she said shying away from the suggestion. She would agree she had an eye for colors as she enjoyed utilizing them to form a worry free expression but she would not alter her painting with a figure as difficult as a living being.

"Nonsense, Miss Catherine, I am decided," he insisted with total disregard for her desires. "You must have faith in what I say. I have an eye for art and predict that the picture would be vastly improved with a subject in it." He went forth egotistically and struck a pose. Reluctantly, Kitty reached for her brushes and took up her paints.

"Miss Catherine, do not feel you must comply with his wishes if they are not your own. You should never allow yourself to be so easily persuaded," advised Dr Kindrel disturbed that Sir Jon forced himself onto her canvas. "You and I were content with what you had prior to his remarks and for my part, I believe the harmony will be lost once he is placed within. Why would you compromise yourself for his satisfaction? Why allow his opinion to be worthier than your own?"

"He is well cultured and I believe him when he says he has the expertise to make the suggestion," she said defending her decision to abide by his will. "I have a high regard for his opinion. I should respect it. After all, he is only trying to help me. I do not mind giving it a try if he doesn't mind posing," she said beginning to feel insecure with her decision. She did not know who to please. "Please allow me to concentrate so I can do my best."

Dr Kindrel saw the confusion in her eyes and, in attempt to decrease her anxiety, did not beleaguer the issue any further. In keeping with her best interest, he stepped back to allow Kitty the room she needed to paint unencumbered. Scouting around the immediate area, he found the affable Col Fitzwilliam wandering about enjoying the view. He stepped away to converse with him briefly.

Committed to her challenge, Kitty began to paint. She gave serious attention to every detail, constantly comparing her sketch to Sir Jon. Having his figure fully outlined, she went on to give her attention to his features. She was deep in concentration.

Quietly, so as not to disturb her work, Dr Kindrel returned and observed her as she drew. He saw the intensity in her eye and the deficiency of her hand. Encouraging her, he remarked on her strengths and revealed nothing about her weaknesses. 'Not everyone can get proportions correct their first time out,' he thought. Indeed, he did consider Sir Jon as having a uniquely large head.

"I daresay, I would not have painted him any differently. You have captured his true image as it is much like the character," he said to Kitty as she continued with increased fervor. "Come Col Fitzwilliam! Do tell. Isn't Sir Jon as dapper as he has been made out by Miss Catherine? Doesn't she have an exacting eye for her subject? A more measured stroke could never be achieved."

Col Fitzwilliam scarcely glanced at the picture before he took a deep bow to conceal his snicker, feigning the presence of greatness. "Most freely I confess that by what you say, the likeness is true. Your talent abounds," he said smiling to repress laughter. "But if you will excuse me, I would like to view the other's paintings as well to show no preference." Kitty was very pleased and with that the Colonel moved on.

"There!" she said after a short time. "I am finished." Dr Kindrel gave her a reassuring smile and a nod of the head signifying his complete approval. Sir Jon, seeing Dr Kindrel so struck, hurried toward the canvas and, to his disappointment, found his figure abused.

"I don't see the resemblance at all. Your talent cannot be approached with a serious eye," he said grievously. "In fact, I have resolved this very moment that you must take lessons. A master will benefit you immensely. Only then will you excel!"

"Kitty, you certainly are passionate in all you do," said Lizzy as the Darcy's stopped to study Kitty's picture with curiosity.

"I just wanted to try my best, that's all. In either case, I am done with this painting and was about to pack up as you approached," said Kitty.

"Good. We are beginning to lose the sun," announced Mr Darcy. "I am suggesting to everyone that we collect our items and begin our descent."

"Mrs Darcy, why haven't you mentioned those woods standing tall over there," inquired Sir Jon pointing to a portion of woods he had noticed earlier. "They beg to be explored."

"Actually, there is a delightful river hidden well within those trees. Mr Darcy fished there with my uncle Gardiner once or twice when he and my aunt came for a visit," answered Mrs Darcy while Mr Darcy motioned for them to get started. "We can walk within better range of it on the way down if we are careful. The ground there is not very reliable."

Walking parallel to it, getting a closer look at those woods, Mr Darcy pointed out a path that led to the running river. Unanimously, the guests expressed their desire to experience their own hand at fishing.

Satisfying their requests, Lizzy arranged for a fishing picnic to be enjoyed by them all tomorrow. Upon her return to Pemberley, she instructed the servants to meet them at the river's bank with a light and satisfying lunch to be consumed in the late afternoon.

*   *   *

That evening, when everyone settled in for the night, the housekeeper knocked on the Collins' door. "I am very sorry to disturb you at this late hour sir," she explained, "but you are to be summoned down to the foyer to personally receive a dispatch from Lady Catherine via special messenger. The dispatcher claimed he was well paid to deliver it into the hands of Mr Collins himself."

In a sudden burst of energy, Mr Collins threw on a robe and hurried to the foyer. "It must be critical! We must not keep him waiting!" he said in alarm. He thanked the messenger and went directly to a well lit nook to read the letter in haste. It read:

Mr Collins

Receiving your letter was of the most upsetting nature. I am so highly incensed by the whole affair that I have sent you this urgent dispatch. You were not aware, but Miss de Bourgh was to be in the constant company of Mr Carrington during the ball. Her future happiness depended on it. This was my reason for traveling so far to Greenfield Castle. I had assigned the task of the introduction to my nephew, Mr Darcy, who has proven himself extremely incapable of serving me with the fulfillment of a simple request. Since I now realize that I cannot rely upon his assistance, as he has become disagreeably unreliable ever since his marriage to your cousin Miss Elizabeth Bennet, I must now insist that you, Mr Collins, make the proper introductions and induce them to keep company so as to become familiar with one another. I must remain in Greenfield Castle to comfort Mr Carrington's father as planned for my sudden removal will cause him alarm. You may inform Mr Carrington that I am with his father and he is as well as he can be. I am adamant about your new appointment, Mr Collins. You are all I can rely on. Do not fail me!

Lady Catherine de Bourgh

Mr Collins received this news with immense distress. He recalled Charlotte's observation that Mr Carrington was being actively pursued by Caroline. He was stupefied into total frenzy when he recalled how he defended, even encouraged, their alliance. Devastated, in a daze, he staggered his way up the stairs to confide his business to his wife.

"I have dreadful news, Mrs Collins," declared Mr Collins wiping the perspiration from his brow. Charlotte became anxious as he was barely coherent.

"Whatever could be causing you such distress, dearest?" she asked with deep concern. Failing to get the words out, he handed her the letter. She read it through quickly at first and then again concentrating on every word feeling the weight of the letter. She considered it for a moment, then put it down to console her husband.

"Introduce them and induce them to keep company!" he recited from memory. "What an undertaking, Mrs Collins! How ever can I perform my duty when these past few days he has been in the faithful company of Miss Bingley? It is not my place to separate the two. What will I do? Her Ladyship is relying on me!"

"Do not be so despondent, dearest. Her Ladyship writes that she is with Lord Carrington and brings good news of his health. Use that information to initiate your introduction. He should like to know who the offspring of the woman caring for his father is, especially when Miss de Bourgh is in his present company," said Charlotte bolstering him up. "She shows promise of joining the group very soon. Do not despair. I am sure it will be much easier than you think!"

"That is good, Mrs Collins. It is reasonable. I will do as you say but I must inform him of her existence with urgency. Every minute counts! Where are they to go tomorrow? What are they to do?"

"They are planning an angler's picnic, dearest. I promised to join them. Lizzy said Miss de Bourgh should go as well since, as of this morning, her ankle was fully recovered. You should come along too."

"Very well, then. I shall. This has to be handled with all delicacy," stated Mr Collins as he disrobed and went to bed. "Nothing can go wrong!"

While Mrs Collins slept soundly, Mr Collins spent a sleepless night. He rehearsed a variety of introductions, made plans and prayed that nothing would go wrong. The hours passed quickly as he turned restlessly in his bed. It was not until he concluded that his objective was indeed attainable and his plans infallible that he dared to finally close his eyes, still running through his lines. Eventually, the audible rehearsals transformed themselves into dormant mutterings as he fell asleep in the wee hours of the breaking dawn convincing himself that the deed had to be done and it would commence immediately at breakfast.

* * *

That morning, everyone sat for an early rousing breakfast. They were in the proper spirit of things as the day promised to clear up despite the foggy skies. Friendly conjectures were provoked as the men prompted to gamble for the title of The Greatest Angler which was to be awarded with indisputable braggart's rights. Mr Collins sat sedately with little appetite, awaiting the arrival of Miss de Bourgh, not daring to speak a word for fear of losing his train of thought. Halfway through the meal, he became concerned that Miss de Bourgh failed to appear. With breakfast completed, he approached Mrs Darcy to make his inquiries.

"Dear cousin, please tell me why Miss de Bourgh has not joined us at breakfast?"

"She will breakfast later at a more reasonable hour with Mary and Daniel. Mrs Jenkinson thought it unwise for Miss de Bourgh to take on a crude walk in the woods so early in the morning when she would not be at her best. To be sure, Mr Darcy and I would have very much enjoyed her presence but we must respect her desires and trust in her nurse," Lizzy answered hopelessly.

Mr Collins was completely beside himself. Not only would Mr Carrington and Miss de Bourgh avoid the chance to meet, but Caroline would increase her hold on Mr Carrington by accompanying him for the whole experience as has been her custom. Mr Collins could not be pacified, though he did not let on to anyone but Charlotte.

The company assembled itself outdoors and the outing began. Mr Collins had to reconsider his strategy and thought it wiser to send Mrs Collins on ahead while he fell back to gain a better perspective of the situation.

"It is a travesty that Miss de Bourgh did not agree to come to this outing. I would have introduced them and they would have been bonding as we speak! Moreover, I could have stayed behind for some much needed rest as I tossed and turned all night long," he said feeling sluggish from the enormous drain of energy. "But, oh, who can think of resting at a time like this? I have been contemplating the turn of events ever since breakfast, Mrs Collins. I must not let anymore time pass without addressing the matter and I do not think you should be with me when I tell him," he said planning carefully. "You should go on ahead and join the others for I feel I would have the advantage by speaking to him alone. It might prove to be very sensitive indeed."

"If that is the case, I can understand how it could be uncomfortable for everyone concerned and therefore, agree I should not be present," she said readily conforming to his wishes. She left his side and caught up with Lizzy and Jane. The mood was jovial and everyone was ready for the challenge of angling. With Mr Carrington close by, Caroline and Mrs Hurst spoke intimately to their brother, Mr Bingley, recalling the splendid memories of childhood fishing trips. Mingling amongst themselves, deeply absorbed in conversation, Mr Collins saw the opportunity to draw Mr Carrington's attention. Quietly racing up behind him, trying not to distract the sisters, Mr Collins made his bold attempt. He stepped directly in Mr Carrington's path and kept him separate and apart from the others.

"It is my deepest pleasure, Mr Carrington, to relay the good news that your father Lord Carrington is benefitting from the hands of the very capable and caring Lady Catherine de Bourgh. Through her correspondence, she has licensed me to inform you of your father's good health," affirmed Mr Collins bowing humbly as he spoke, choosing to be direct.

"That is good news. I thank you for your message. It has been gratefully received and you should pass that on to your patroness. My father hasn't always the ability to take to the quill and news from home is always a comfort. I shall write him in good time."

Considering the conversation over, Mr Carrington circumvented Mr Collins and ran ahead to catch up to the other members of the party. Fatigued with the chase, Mr Collins struggled to keep up.

"I am very glad to be of humble service. Did you know, Sir that her daughter, Miss Anne de Bourgh is in our little assembly here at Pemberley?"

"No, I did not! I thought we have all met each other by now! How could it be that she is amongst us without my knowing?"

"You have not yet met her, Sir, I assure you. She is not of our little party here because of her fragile, delicate nature. But she is in Pemberley. The other Bennets and my brother, Daniel remain behind to enjoy her most worthwhile companionship this morning as they have done almost everyday here."

"I shall be pleased to meet her when we return. Thank you again for your services," he said and strode off leaving Mr Collins to himself.

Caroline noticed Mr Carrington lagging behind. She slowed Mrs Hurst down to allow him to catch up, alarming Mr Collins to no end. He did not appreciate the rivalry for Miss de Bourgh. He shadowed them relentlessly as they proceeded to the edge of the woods that led to the river.

Mrs Hurst was first to feel the burden of his uneasy presence. In time, Mr Collins became an irritating annoyance to Caroline as well. They tried to separate him from their little group but discovered that Mr Collins was tenacious and intent on following. The women, offering Mr Carrington a better view of the flora in the area, maneuvered him in and out of narrow unmarked paths they remembered from their exploration in earlier years. Determined to lose Mr Collins, they carefully navigated themselves through the most difficult paths the woods afforded. Aided by thickets and branches, they encumbered the already exhausted reverend.

The fog in the woods had not yet lifted. It was patchy, heavy and dense making it difficult to see ahead but Mr Collins dared not risk losing sight of his prey. He would not look down to secure his footing no matter how unpredictable the ground below. Regrettably, he tripped over and over again on jagged rocks, fallen branches and unearthed roots. Many times the hapless Mr Collins bumped his elbow on the rubble and suffered immense sharp pains. In addition, he found his coat snagged on sharp limbs that pulled him into the bushes and ripped their way through to the skin. He even plunged his feet directly into an otherwise insignificant stream that was most inconveniently concealed. Having fallen solidly on the ground, finding it difficult to rise yet once more, Mr Collins sat for a moment to assess the physical damage. After careful examination, he rose to survey the woods around him finding himself completely alone. The ladies, intent on losing him, had succeeded. Mr Collins was lost and could not find his way. Mrs Hurst and Caroline, now a safe distance from him, triumphed as Mr Carrington remained completely unaware of the entire affair.

The three did not meet up with the rest of the group until they reached the river where everyone had already arrived. Blankets were laid upon the ground under canopies constructed to provide shade. Fishing tackle had been distributed and Mr Darcy was already pointing out the better sections of water which provided the most sport. The servants were still busy setting up a table for the refreshments as Caroline and Mrs Hurst scouted around for Mr Collins one last time. Finding him nowhere in sight, they considered the entire event a job well done. For them, the rest of their day should proceed without further intrusion allowing Caroline the personal contentment of joining Mr Carrington out in the fishing spot of his choice.

"Do you fish often?" inquired Caroline trying to keep an interest in his present endeavor.

"Not at all. Angling is no passion of mine," replied Mr Carrington with sincerity. "I have never been proficient at it, but, I daresay, that does not stop me!" he said poking fun at himself.

"I have fished as a child and used to enjoy it, but now I find that I have quite outgrown it myself," she replied.

"I believe I have a good form but I never catch a thing."

"Well, you do strike a pose," teased Caroline.

Mr Carrington gave a nod and a smile and brought the conversation to an end so as to concentrate on the fish. After a few quiet moments, perceiving that conversing on fish would not do, Caroline sought another subject.

"What I still enjoy is sailing out in a canoe. There is nothing finer than floating on the water to cool oneself from the heat on a hot summer's day," she said to discover if he shared her joy of canoeing. Getting no reaction from him again led her to rethink the day as becoming an increasingly unexciting, drawn out, disagreeable ordeal. 'He is too absorbed in his fishing,' she thought. After a moment she asked, "Please, then, tell me what you do enjoy doing most."

"I like to live in the moment and attempt and enjoy everything that comes my way for life is too short. However, for the foreseeable future, I prefer to sit at home with my father to dream the days away," reflected Mr Carrington looking very pleased with his plans.

"Are you planning to put all your time into dreaming when you have every means of actually fulfilling your fantasies," she inquired.

"Well, there is always an intriguing book of mystery and suspense to break the peaceful sedation of a trance whenever necessary."

"You can not be so taken by a mere book! It cannot be enough!" declared Caroline perceiving a conflict in personalities. She much more preferred to be out embracing the world. She considered books useful only when traveling long distances in a coach. Even then, she paid little attention to the subject and theme. Still, she considered her displeasure in this knowledge and would make further inquiries before she cast her final judgment on him as it did not, as of now, look like a very promising fate.

"I read constantly to Lord Carrington for he has little ability to do so for himself now that his eyes fail him. I do what I can to comfort him, you know." He thought she could relate to the attention he paid his father in his time of need.

"Why, yes, of course!" she said giving it a second thought. "But I am curious. Who remains with him while you are not at home, for a father could not expect his son to entirely restrict his own enjoyments for his sake!"

"He does not need to hamper himself with guilt in the matter. I am not known to leave his side for any long period of time whatsoever for many years now. Furthermore, I would not care to. Similar to how you would not leave your sister, Mrs Bingley, in her time of need. In that, I would presume we are of one mind," he said in earnest.

"Yes, I see," she responded. "But haven't you been in London for a significant stay prior to your coming to Pemberley? Does that not indicate that you leave him to himself for longer periods of time than you lead me to believe?" Caroline needed to be clear on how he led his life. She had no intention of staying at home with a shriveled up blind man and his lackluster son.

"I see why you struggle with it so. You fear my traveling will not do. I have traveled extensively this past year, but only for the distinct purpose of altering a way of life that, as I shall not conceal from you, Miss Bingley, a life which any man, alone in a vast estate, would eventually wish to change. I feel I can be frank with you, for we are both searching to fulfill our lives," he said bluntly. "I am determined. Where my carriage left Greenfield Castle with one, it shall return with two."

Caroline could hardly believe her ears. 'How much more forthright could he be? Why else would he take the liberty to express such confidence in me!?! It is unmistakable! Mr Carrington has every intention to propose! To think moments ago it was beyond detection and I almost turned from him,' she thought, grateful she held herself back. 'Temporarily forfeiting a life of merriment for the attainment of title and fortune is very much worth the investment in time, for his father cannot live forever! Then, I shall dispose him of his ways and acquire in him a new understanding. He, himself, shall soon wonder to what benefit it would be to gain a title and not flaunt it! In any case, even if there is no commonality in habit, I can execute a grand tour on my own. After all, Mrs Hurst survives her marriage and Mr Carrington is not half the sloth Mr Hurst is.' She now focused dreamily on her impending increase in rank and stature, basking in sweet silent thought, allowing Mr Carrington to concentrate on the fishing, as idle conversation was no longer a necessity.

*　　*　　*

Up river, Sir Jon kept company with Kitty. Normally Kitty enjoyed fishing but under the dictatorship of Mrs Bennet, she was dressed too fine for it today. Sir Jon, in the spirit of competition, guided her to where he judged was one of the best fishing spots on the river. The only problem was that it was across the rushing water at the opposite end of the bank.

"Follow me, Miss Catherine. If there is one thing I know, its angling. I can determine the ideal location on my own," he said referring to Mr Darcy's suggested fishing spots, "and I see one way over there on the other side of the bank."

"Sir Jon, I don't see how I can make it over there without wetting my good shoes. I would prefer not to go," she said disinclined. She looked unfavorably at the water rapidly charging over an obscure line of protruding boulders. "Those stones look too slippery to cross safely. Let's stay on this side of the bank. Surely Mr Darcy's judgment can be relied upon!"

"Nonsense. There is a wager to win and I must claim it. Take off your shoes and I will assist you across." Kitty felt oppressed by his insistence but did as he said to appease him. At that time of the morning the water was especially cold and she shivered as she crossed it.

"Now," he said as he led her onto the bank, "it will take some time before the fish realize the disturbance has subsided. We must stay very quiet or they will swim away for good."

"I'll just sit over here," said Kitty as she sat to dry her feet before she could warm herself over with her shawl.

"Shh," demanded Sir Jon going to the bank's edge. "Extreme silence is vital!"

Sir Jon became deeply consumed with his fishing. Not once did he turn to Kitty for conversation or to acknowledge her presence in any way. She simply sat quietly, as he ordered, and found it could not make a difference to him if she was there or not. Realizing the hours she would have to spend in a state of suppression, she found herself becoming increasingly downtrodden, cold and uncomfortable.

True to his expectations, Sir Jon soon caught a fish. Cries of jubilation eventually came from the groups across the way as the others caught a few as well. There was laughter, mocking conjectures and gaiety among the competitors on the other side. A good time could be heard from them as the morning soon passed into noon.

A servant collected everyone together at the orders of Mr Darcy. The time had come to terminate the fishing and commence with the measuring and weighing of their catch. It was the moment Sir Jon awaited. His haul was very successful indeed! In fact, he was faced with the dilemma of having to choose between the heavier and the longer of his fish.

"I must select which fish to carry across the water, Miss Catherine. I have thrown back the smaller ones but kept these two in particular which would win this wager for me. Could it be at all possible that you would be accommodating and allow me to carry these two across? My arms will be full but you can cross the stream without my assistance, can you not?" he asked already picking up the fish he intended to carry over. "There must be an easier crossing for you. If you walk up a little further you shall find it. I believe I can see it from here! It is not very far off for you have time to spare but I may miss the evaluations if I do not make haste and return in the manner in which we have come."

"You may make your way on your own if you wish," Kitty said freely. She was anxious to get back and did not care if she returned with him or without. Assessing her situation, she thought, 'These rocks will make me unsteady and the flowing waters are especially cold. It should be easier for me over there as he suggested.' She turned to him and said, "Do not worry about me. I shall follow at my own speed."

"You are a good sport, Miss Catherine," he declared as he secured his prized catch and brought them safely across. Kitty stayed back to watch him go, preparing herself mentally for the crossing. She was beginning to feel a bit disheartened. A part of her was waiting for him to turn back for her but the chances were slim as he did not even glance back.

Looking up and down the river, in search of a better path, she walked up a little way. Anxious to get across, she hastened to brave the bitter water. She struggled as she held up the hem of her dress to keep it from getting wet while holding on to her stockings and shoes. She was laboring steadily to get across before she lost her footing. Stumbling, she began to plunge into the harsh water. As she felt herself falling, she noticed a fish fly by her, hitting the water with a splash prior to herself when, at the same instant, a strong familiar arm wrapped itself securely around her from behind.

"Miss Catherine, how is it you are caught up in these rushing waters?" asked the doctor deeply concerned. "What could have recommended you to go swimming at a time like this," he said easing her hardship with humor, attempting to hold her steady at the same time. Kitty spoke to him as candidly as she always had and summarized the incident with reliable accuracy. When the facts were completely disclosed, Dr Kindrel could not be contained.

"He was wrong to put you in such a predicament! His manners are remarkably selfish to say the least! You of all people do not deserve such treatment." He stopped himself before he said too much. Lifting her up in one fell swoop he escorted her safely to the opposite bank. There, he retrieved two blankets and to the neglect of his own sodden feet, tenderly wrapped one around her shoulders and tucked the other over and around her legs. He rubbed her cold, clammy feet vigorously to increase their circulation and promote their warmth. In the meantime, Sir Jon, preoccupied with the flaunting of his catch, never once noticed the applications Dr Kindrel bestowed on her.

"I sure am fortunate to have come by you in the river when I did!" exclaimed Dr Kindrel massaging the balls of her feet and the tip of her toes. She thought how lovely this attention would be if it wasn't genuinely essential for her good health as he did have a way with his hands.

"I think you mean I was fortunate you came along when you did," corrected Kitty as she secured the blanket around her shivering body. "I was led to believe that we were quite secluded on the opposite side of the river. Sir Jon said it was his own discovery!"

"It was one of the sites Mr Darcy suggested yesterday," he said dismissing her ideas that they were secluded in some forgotten location. "Either way, I do mean that I am the fortunate one. I insist! I don't wish to have another Bennet for a patient ever again. They keep me entirely consumed with long drawn out illnesses. You, of all people, must know I would not leave your side until you have improved and thereby goes all of my fortune!" mocked Dr Kindrel. "It would have been most inconsiderate of you."

"You jest, Dr Kindrel but I do wish to thank you for surrendering your catch to rescue me. I cannot swim you know. I fear I might have drowned," she said in all seriousness. The gravity of her words wiped the smile completely off his face. It had not occurred to him that she could not swim. Seeing him quit the massage, she tucked her feet under the blanket, grateful for his care. Dr Kindrel was piqued.

"All the more reason Sir Jon should not have abandoned you. He put your very life in jeopardy," he said in a huff adjusting the blanket on Kitty's shoulders. Brazenly, he wrapped his arms around her while angrily staring over her head in the direction of Sir Jon. "I tell you, I am not impressed by a man who professes to be good while his character is so blatantly bad. Even a vial of medicine wears its skull and cross bones for all to see when it can go both ways. The man stands in stark contrast with himself! All his fortune and property could not sway me to desire his company."

"You should not be so hard on him. He is not altogether objectionable. He has a very generous side," she said feeling Sir Jon was not complete adversity. In his defense she added, "He is not what you think." Dr Kindrel was amazed. Sir Jon did not deserve her charitable representation and he would not allow that low individual to earn her precious favor. He must persuade her.

"Whatever happened to the Catherine I knew in London who disavowed any connection to callous, unprincipled, egocentric persons such as he?" he asked critically.

"This is different, Dr Kindrel. Sir Jon has selflessly offered to instruct me on the niceties of the upper class and expose me to new acquaintances that shall enrich my life. That is all goodness for me as my father has kept me so confined since Lydia's elopement that I am not up to par with these modern times. Sir Jon is cultured, in the midst of things, always traveling and broadening himself. I would say, even more favorably, that he is discerning and generous to spend his invaluable time on me wouldn't you?" She saw the disbelief on his face and continued her argument before he could say more. "And if you do not believe it would benefit me, I shall share with you in confidence that Sir Jon was selected by Mama. Surely, you cannot deny that her concern for me and my future is true. As it is, she worries constantly for Mary, who shows no interest in marrying at all," she said further explaining herself. "Mama has to be sure her daughters will be ample providers for Mary's future as well! You are not aware that Longbourn is entailed to Mr Collins upon Papa's death and there alone is where our present security lies. I must marry and if he should ask me, I believe he will be a better provider than most. He is a good man. I assure you," she said trying to convince her caring confidant. She looked into his eyes to assure him she knew what she was doing as he gazed at her anxiously.

Suddenly noticing that his clothing was saturated with river water, she spread out her blanket to drape over his legs as well.

The sound of her voice pierced his very soul as he knew he could not compete. He was not a poor man by himself, as he was earning a good and proper living, but he had no stable roof over his head nor could he establish one for a family in the near future. If he had anything to offer Kitty, he would do so this very minute. 'Marry me,' he thought, 'and I will love and protect you for the rest of my life. Anything you want will be at your disposal for I have secretly admired you all these months.' However, they were just words he wanted to say for how fair would it be to ask her to take this chance on him. To do so now would be an injustice to her. 'If I ask her to wait for me and do not achieve an adequate fortune, where would she be then? The wife of an itinerate worker. I would have no security to offer her and that is what she seeks. She has been straightforward about that. Miss Catherine would resent me and so would her family. Her whole life is in front of her with Sir Jon. I cannot think about myself at a time like this. It is her direction in life and I must release her,' he concluded with a heavy heart.

Dr Kindrel never responded to Kitty's comments. He sat in melancholy contemplation and concluded that, for now, he would enjoy her company and observe her beauty so as to imprint it in his mind for future recollection. Together, they spent their limited time observing the wilderness of the woods and the gallery of God's lovely creations, among which Dr Kindrel considered Kitty the most appealing.

Sir Jon continued in the preoccupation of his boasting. His was the biggest fish of the lot and he stood in the glory of the moment. He was unabashed of his illustrious catch and displayed it for all to see. After a period of careful measurement, and re-measurement for those who would disagree, Sir Jonathan Nettington was officially declared the winner.

The disappointed found it hard to concede but Mr Carrington and Caroline observed silently acknowledging the facts without prejudice.

"I'm afraid your ante is totally lost," noted Caroline with little surprise since they had not caught but a single tiny fish.

"That is entirely tolerable. It was a gentleman's wager and I participated solely for the support of the game," consoled Mr Carrington.

*   *   *

Luncheon was served as the servants put the fish into cold water containers and placed them on a cart for its return to Pemberley and dinner preparations. It was deliciously uplifting and restored everyone into a complacent state of mind.

Dr Kindrel had Kitty stay on the blanket while he served her a cup of hot tea. Sipping it slowly, she felt herself recover. Being there with Dr Kindrel, felt natural and comforting. She treasured his friendship and thought, 'he is the most pleasant man I have ever known.'

Thoroughly warmed by his unrelenting care, and the heat of the noonday sun, Kitty declared herself fit for company. Dr Kindrel suggested that she partake of the lunch being served to maintain her strength as he offered to retrieve some for her.

"I thank you for your generous offer, but they will be searching for us soon. I think we should join them now, don't you?" she suggested getting up to leave.

"Perhaps, but there is no need to hurry for you should not be seen in such disarray," he said referring to her bare feet and damp hem.

"You are right. There will be too many questions I would not care to answer. We shall wait a little longer."

The rest of the party ate to their satisfaction and rested well in order to prepare for the journey back. Dr Kindrel and Kitty made their appearance in time for the last bit of luncheon. Suddenly noting her arrival, Sir Jon called her to his side.

"You have missed all the fun, Miss Catherine. I have been telling everyone of the large number of fish we caught, but do not worry, I did not reveal our secret location. It remains in our confidence," he said, neglecting to ask how she crossed the river. He took her elbow and eagerly escorted her to the barrel of fish already stowed on the cart. "Come look at how my fish diminished the competition," he commanded as he had her peer into the barrel. Kitty gave a nonchalant nod of approval and turned to join the others who were collecting themselves for the return trip. She did not give great significance to his personal gain and rejected hearing anymore of it.

Mr Collins finally made his way through the woodland to the river. He emerged dragging his feet as his shoes were bogged down with the weight of water and mud drawn from every stream, brook and puddle inadvertently discovered between one location and the next. His face and hands were wholly lacerated from the branches that slapped him as he championed the perplexing unmarked path. He was devitalized, fagged and fully overcome by the experience. It was unfortunate that the scraps of food were already discarded and the dishes completely packed away as everyone was assembled to leave the very instant he arrived.

"My dear Mrs Collins," said Mr Collins in a haggard state, staggering toward his wife. He grasped for an arm to lean on. "It will do you no harm to know that Pemberley woods is a great and fearful wilderness! There is not a smooth or rounded stone in the whole forest. Everything is sharp, piercing and cutting." He stood on his own for a moment to exhibit his wounds and frayed garments.

"Whatever happened to you Mr Collins? I assumed you turned back!" exclaimed his bewildered wife.

"I took a detour and lost my way," he explained leaning on her once again, trying to recover himself.

"We are just about to leave and the refreshments have all been consumed, dearest. This is a pity. What are we to do?" remarked Mrs Collins looking to Lizzy for help.

"You are in no condition to walk, Mr Collins," Lizzy observed. "You must ride with the servants to recuperate while the rest of us hike back." Mr Collins, in no mood to put up a fight, promptly sat in the back of the cart. Mrs Collins waved to her husband with sympathy as he was carted away.

"Take heed to my warning, Mrs Collins and do not wander off the path!" he warned with his last bit of strength. Caroline and Mrs Hurst could not repress their hysterics in the background.

Once out of sight, Mr Collins slumped carelessly over the cargo being transported back to the house. He was determined to close his eyes for a much deserved respite. However, despite his attempt to sleep, he did not travel long before he was overcome by an irritating whooshing sound. It disturbed his tranquility and he could not rest.

Upon its investigation, Mr Collins discovered he was leaning against a container of floating fish. Surrendering to his relentless misfortune, he collapsed in defeat, listening to the splash of fish filled water all the way back to Pemberley.

Chapter 8

Mr Collins came down with an unmerciful case of poison ivy and desperately coveted a return to Hunsford Parsonage. Unable to join in proper company, Mr Collins sent for his brother. He informed Daniel of his most recent obligation to Lady Catherine and allowed him to read her letter, keeping in mind that the task would now be transferred to his own custody.

"I am in despair, brother," cried Mr Collins. He had a notable reluctance in passing on the charge. Scratching himself through his compresses he continued to speak. "This persistent itching and offensive rosy blistering appearance has me so far removed from my sensibilities that I cannot complete Lady Catherine's delicate request. I regret I have no choice but to rely on you to fulfill the mission. I fear Lady Catherine will not approve of a substitute for she does not wish to make sport of her daughter but I am beside myself. I warn you, it shall not be easy. Do you feel you can handle it?"

"I do not dislike it, brother, and find nothing objectionable about it. You will discover no want of spirit in me!" he said responding agreeably. Daniel perceived it as an act of forgiveness from his brother for his recent trespasses with Miss de Bourgh. "I am sensible to your predicament and assure you it bears no further discussion for I will pursue it with enormous speed," he said as he turned to leave. "Rest well and care for yourself with peace of mind. You may consider it all under control, but now, I must make haste! There is no time to spare."

"Make haste cautiously," warned Mr Collins with renewed trepidations. "There is no room for error!" He felt Daniel complied almost too expeditiously for comfort. "Delicacy and compassion!" he cried to Daniel just before he disappeared down the corridor.

"I would remind you brother," said Daniel as he stopped in his tracks and turned to Mr Collins one last time, "that I have the greatest compassion for our Miss de Bourgh. Did we not, Miss Bennet and I, prepare her for the dance and sit with her faithfully during her healing?"

"Oooh," moaned Mr Collins as he shut the door. "As if matters were not sufficiently complicated . . ." He removed the soaks from his cheek and sat on the edge of the bed. Taking one deep breath he clasped his hands together and bowed his head in prayer.

*   *   *

Daniel took on the mission with eagerness promising himself to make short work of it. The first thing he did was to apply to Dr Kindrel for an examination of Miss de Bourgh's health.

As suspected, Dr Kindrel assessed nothing wrong with her and strongly advised Miss de Bourgh to get out of the house to enjoy the revitalization of fresh clean air. "Your ankle is entirely healed Miss de Bourgh. Nothing would improve your health, and complexion I might add, faster than a little sun and exercise. It confounds me that you remain so sheltered on such fine days as these. What else could keep you so confined?" he asked in bewilderment.

"Mrs Jenkinson recommended my continual avoidance of the walks to prevent further damaging my weak ankles and I did not want to become a spectacle hobbling about," explained Miss de Bourgh.

"No one would consider you a spectacle if you did have to hobble, which you don't. It is inconceivable that you have been kept indoors all this time," he said. "The others are involved in outdoor activities today. You should make every effort to join them, without your nurse, for I expect to see you there!" he prescribed. "Nothing should keep you indoors now," he ordered as he gave Mrs Jenkinson a stern look of reproach.

Simultaneously, Daniel confided in Mary and employed her assistance once again. Unable to refuse him anything, they planned to increase Miss de Bourgh's involvement with the assembly below. Encouraged by Dr Kindrel, Miss de Bourgh was ready to make her appearance.

Once outdoors, they discovered teams of two being formed for the friendly competitions in archery. Jane and Kitty decided to go in out of the noon sun with the children. Mary implored Miss de Bourgh to join her in a match, taking Kitty and Jane's place.

Needless to say, this particular team was of no threat to the others. They were immediately disqualified and sat out with Daniel to watch the competition proceed without them. Mr Carrington and Caroline were defeated next, for Caroline, though proficient in the sport, did not want to outdo Mr Carrington. Recognizing a new face, noting it must be Miss de Bourgh of newly found fame, Mr Carrington escorted Caroline back to their table. Mary made the introductions and offered them a seat so they may enjoy their refreshments together.

"I am especially pleased to make your acquaintance, Miss de Bourgh. I have been informed that your mother, Lady Catherine, is with my father as we speak. Her companionship is very much appreciated," said Mr Carrington with every bit of sincerity.

"I will send your compliments to Mother when I see her at North Courtlandt. My mother is a selfless woman and is genuinely concerned with what goes on about her," commented Miss de Bourgh. "You can rest easy that he is well if she said so."

Exchanging mutual looks of triumph, Mary and Daniel were extremely pleased with the effortless flow of their conversation. Daniel decided to further their communications by edging them onto an advanced stage.

"I do not wish to interrupt your discourse, but new teams are forming and I am sure you do not want to miss out. I suggest you team up with Miss de Bourgh so you may continue your conversation. I am positive Miss Bingley would not mind," urged Daniel. Caroline was about to protest when Mr Carrington rapidly approved of the idea.

"Why certainly! Miss Bingley would not mind," he assumed as he bowed his head to Caroline. To her chagrin, Miss de Bourgh and Mr Carrington removed themselves from the table. Caroline rose to find her sister.

Daniel could not be satisfied with the results of his effort for long as Mary soon directed his attention toward Mrs Hurst. Before you knew it, she was promptly at work, rearranging the matches, pairing herself with Mr Carrington, eliminating Miss de Bourgh from the game. To their dismay and to Caroline's delight, Miss de Bourgh returned to the table.

"Miss de Bourgh," interviewed Daniel in amazement, "why did you return so quickly? The matches have not even begun?"

"Sir Jon has increased the stakes by making a wager," she answered. "Mrs Hurst was kind enough to suggest I sit it out to increase Mr Carrington's odds for winning."

"Behold, the formation of a most unholy trinity," Daniel told Mary as he looked at Caroline, Mrs Hurst and Mr Carrington. "They shall have their way temporarily," he continued, "as I perceive the mission has become a tad bit more difficult than it was but a moment ago."

After giving it considerable thought Daniel concluded that it would be best to acquire Miss de Bourgh's undaunted cooperation which could only be accomplished by exposing his newly appropriated role of matchmaker. "I must be straight forward with you, Miss de Bourgh and reveal my awareness of your mother's specific wish to have you earn the hand of Mr Carrington. The mission had been assigned to my brother, Mr Collins but his unfortunate circumstances prevent him from being here and accomplishing it himself, so I have been called upon to replace him. If you heed my advice, we should be able to get this thing done with relative ease." Miss de Bourgh admitted this communication to be true and sat in earnest to hear what he would advocate. "I am of a mind to say to you that your timidity will not do! Modest principles cannot dictate at a time like this. You must increase his inclination to familiarize himself with you through your enticements. Once he gets to know you, Miss de Bourgh, he would by all means give in to your charms. Only there is no time to waste. We will be departing within a few days, each of us going our own way," said Daniel.

"You must make a remark about him that makes him have to provide you with an answer. This way you will stimulate his mind and maintain his attention. You keep it going until he develops a stronger interest in you or you discover commonality and he finds he cannot leave your side!" said Mary.

"It is too much for me, I cannot do it," insisted Miss de Bourgh in apprehension, waving her hands in front of her to make them stop. "I do not know how to go about it. How am I to begin? What shall I say?" Mary and Daniel were encouraged with her response. She did not reject it for substance. She rejected it for content and it would be simple to coach her on dialogue.

"Watch us. We shall act it out," volunteered Daniel.

"That was a fine game you played Mr Carrington. Do you play often?" began Mary.

"Why, yes I do. I enjoy the sport immensely. Do you?"

"Actually, I am a far better dancer."

"Well, then, we should dance tonight if dancing is to be had."

"Yes, of course. You are so kind."

"You are so lovely."

"I think I love you."

"I love you too."

"Shall we marry?"

"How could we do otherwise? I shall write Mother and let her know—and that is that! Wedding bells and all the rest," said Mary convincingly.

"Could it be so easy?" asked Miss de Bourgh not yet convinced. "I have often heard Mother say that it was by such means, and then some, that Mr Darcy was won. I should like very much to make an attempt but I am afraid I cannot make my words come out as easily as they have for you."

"You just need to practice. There is much to say for repetition," explained Daniel. Finding Miss de Bourgh willing, they proceeded to coach her as the others continued with their sport.

The competition proved very entertaining and compelled both spectators and competitors for a very long time. Teams were finally divided further into one on one meets. Mr Bingley, Col Fitzwilliam and Dr Kindrel were very much in the humor of the sport. They gave bows and cheers or jeers when appropriate. Sir Jon would not submit to comedy as he continued to play with all seriousness.

Mr Carrington completed his game as he was the first to be defeated. Mary and Daniel's eyes were on Miss de Bourgh inducing her to commence with her well rehearsed lines. As Mr Carrington came near, Miss de Bourgh glanced down shyly and delivered a nervous trembling smile. He sat down by her side as he had before. Mr Carrington readily returned the smile and Miss de Bourgh was encouraged. "That was a fine game you played Mr Carrington. Do you play often?" she began nervously.

"I would not have been disposed of so soon if I did. However, it was kind of you to think so," he replied with a chuckle. "I would be excellent at it if the objective was to miss the target." Disarmed by his unexpected reply and laughter, she ceased any further attempts and turned all her attentions to the game. In the blink of an eye, Caroline and Mrs Hurst were soon eliminated and joined the table. Excluding Miss de Bourgh from the conversation, they offered Mr Carrington useful tips on taking aim. Mrs Hurst urged Caroline to give him proper instructions on the field so he could practice before the next round.

"Mr Carrington, you and I are not very skilled with the bow but I notice there is something in Miss Bingley's style that may benefit us both. If we can entice her to give up her little secret we may present a more formidable challenge for the next go round. Do show us, Caroline," she pleaded playfully. "Come Mr Carrington. Let us sharpen our skills to rejoin the competition. Miss de Bourgh will understand, won't you?"

"Absolutely," she responded without a moment's hesitation. "You must go Mr Carrington and learn your lesson well!"

He rose to accept the offer excusing himself from his present company giving Miss de Bourgh an exclusive smile and a gallant kiss on the hand. Caroline and Mrs Hurst were offended by his actions and saw to it that Mr Carrington could not find his way to Miss de Bourgh's table again for the remainder of the day. As evening fast approached, Daniel suggested they go in to prepare themselves for dinner.

"I dare say, that was an admirable beginning, Miss de Bourgh. I saw how he returned your smile and even kissed your hand!" encouraged Daniel. He continued instructing Miss de Bourgh saying that she should smile as much as possible and continue exhibiting an inviting persona since Mr Carrington responded to it rather well. "After dinner, you should sit on a sofa and instruct Mrs Jenkinson to have a seat apart and away from you, allowing room for someone else to sit with you," he said. Giving it a second thought he boldly suggested, "Mrs Jenkinson should be relieved of her duties altogether since you are no longer ill. Remember, Dr Kindrel said all you needed was fresh air and exercise and you do not need her for that."

"That is true," admitted Miss de Bourgh giving him more credence.

*   *   *

Daniel stopped to visit Mr Collins in his bed chamber before dinner. He reported that Mr Carrington shot arrows with the enchanting Miss de Bourgh, assuring his brother of their compatibility. "He gave her an inviting smile and a most proper kiss on the hand before they parted. She was, of course, receptive." Mr Collins thought this was the best account ever and said he would write Lady Catherine that the matter was at hand. When Daniel left for dinner Mr Collins wrote:

To The Right Honorable Lady Catherine de Bourgh,

I have the happiest of circumstances to relate to you. You shall first and foremost desire to know that introductions were made between Mr Carrington and your daughter, Miss de Bourgh. It was received with much pleasure by both. They spent the day sitting outdoors together, in proper company, taking refreshments and involving themselves in joint activities. I cannot account for further confrontations, for I have inadvertently come into contact with poison ivy and must remain in my chamber for the rest of the stay. However, I am pleased to announce, as it is advertised, that she and he will form a match in good time. I pray your forgiveness for not writing more, but I find myself quite uncomfortable these days, encased in soothing wraps. I look forward to returning to Hunsford Parsonage tomorrow as I am in no condition to attend Miss Darcy's wedding. I remain yours

Rev William Collins

That following morning, Mr Collins removed himself and Mrs Collins from Pemberley. Mrs Collins was reluctant to go but agreed her husband would be more comfortable at Hunsford Parsonage. Daniel promised to write and keep Mr Collins informed on Miss de Bourgh's amorous prosperity. Lizzy was sad to see her good friend leave so soon, even missing the wedding, but took refuge in the knowledge that the visits had resumed and extracted promises from Mrs Collins to return to Pemberley some time next spring.

The ride home was most irritating for Mr Collins as he itched and scratched unrestrainedly all the way. Mrs Collins received no relief from his complaints until they finally reached their home where she escaped into her own private salon.

*   *   *

Caroline, giving due recognition to Miss de Bourgh's newly found charms, set a plan underway to eliminate her threat. Caroline and Mrs Hurst, having long been acquainted with the de Bourgh family, had the advantage over Miss de Bourgh. They knew very well that she did not possess the slightest interest or ability in physical exertions and used the intelligence to their benefit. Beginning early at the breakfast table, the ladies set their ruse in motion.

"Mrs Darcy, Mrs Hurst and I were quite put out when we heard that the men will go riding through Pemberley while you confine the ladies to walk. We, too, can appreciate the exercise a good hard ride would provide," stated Caroline. "Wouldn't we, Mrs Hurst?"

"Yes, though we have taken great pleasure in our short treks, we would appreciate the larger expanse and the brisk ride!" added Mrs Hurst.

"I confess, I am no horsewoman and did not make such recommendations from my own lack of desire to partake of it. However, now that it is known, we shall, with Mr Darcy's approval, provide the stimulation."

"Without question," agreed Mr Darcy. "We shall go after breakfast."

The men readily adopted the idea. Dr Kindrel turned to Miss de Bourgh and suggested she accompany them.

"I would enjoy a ride through Pemberley if I were able to, but as it is I, too, am no rider," she said with regret. Daniel and Mary protested. It was contrary to their hopes and expectations for Miss de Bourgh and Mr Carrington.

"Lizzy," began Mary, "is it acceptable that we should be without the company of the entire party for the whole afternoon? Would it not be better to set up a game of croquet that we can all enjoy as a group?"

"Bravo, Miss Bennet! Croquet would be just the thing for this fine day," supported Daniel.

"Alas, Caroline," said Mrs Hurst with her most pitiful sounding voice, "we should never get to cantor or break into a gallop throughout Pemberley as we used to in the good old days. We must only treasure it as a memory never to be repeated."

"I see no reason why we could not satisfy everyone with their own preferred activities," said Mr Darcy putting an end to Mary and Daniel's objections.

"I would enjoy a game of croquet with those who stay," volunteered Lizzy happily working in harmony with her husband. "There should be enough of us left behind to form an impressive game. Jane would continue to be close to the children and Mama would not remain alone!"

"That is a wonderful solution. A splitting of the baby, isn't it Mr Collins?" asked Mrs Hurst curtly establishing her success over his insubordinate interference.

"I have not heard Solomon's wisdom used quite that way," afforded Daniel feeling the full effect of his defeat, looking downcast at Mary.

Over the next few days, Caroline adhered to Mr Carrington relentlessly preventing Miss de Bourgh from ever attaining his good company exclusive of herself. Despite Daniel and Mary's faithful attempts, the rivalry was always won by the Bingley sisters as Miss de Bourgh's allies were outmatched by the wit and cunning of these two seasoned veterans.

The days flew by quickly as the wedding was on the morrow and the party guests would soon vacate Pemberley. The women made one final essential visit to Lambton for some last minute shopping. Caroline and Mrs Hurst left reluctantly as only they alone could approve of and pick up their specially ordered items. Mrs Hurst left Mr Hurst in charge of guarding Mr Carrington for Caroline, a job he fulfilled with the same vigor he approached every task and as soon as the carriage was out of sight, he retired directly to the parlor. There, he sat on a secluded easy chair mulling over his assignment until the very thought of the distasteful chore faded away into the dark abyss of his vacuous mind.

Without the women around, Sir Jon suggested that the men drill their fencing skills, himself being in need of the review. They all agreed, except for Dr Kindrel. Having no fencing skills behind him, he preferred simply to observe. Mr Carrington fenced with Mr Bingley who was kind enough to make compensations for his lack of skill while Sir Jon sparred the ever capable Lord Watney. Mr Darcy and Col Fitzwilliam were still preparing for the duel when they stopped to converse with Dr Kindrel in a corner of the room.

Mr Bingley, an able swordsman, graciously allowed Mr Carrington to prevail. He wanted Mr Dacy's guest to remain excited and experience the glory of winning. After Sir Jon won the match between himself and Lord Watney, they were asked to exchange partners. Mr Bingley challenged His Lordship next, leaving Sir Jon to cross swords with Mr

Carrington. Quickly surmising the talents of who he was to fence, Sir Jon became agitated by what he viewed as a blatant insult to his reputation as a formidable opponent. He had no desire to cater to the inept as he took his practice seriously and wanted to employ the full extent of his skills. Determined to dispose of him quickly, Sir Jon reluctantly accepted Mr Carrington's challenge.

After a quick "On guard" Sir Jon advanced with one reprisal after another. He did not hold back. He pressed Mr Carrington to try harder and become swifter but Mr Carrington could only respond with elementary parries. "Come on, man. Give it a little more. Give it all you bloody have!" he taunted as he thrust his sword forward for a flank cut.

Sir Jon fenced Mr Carrington as an equal, with full force attacks, honing in on all his skills. Mr Carrington made his best attempts at vindicating himself against Sir Jon but was terribly outmatched. His sense of timing was off and all he could offer was a strong, distant stand. A feint attack by Sir Jon forced Mr Carrington to parry without a riposte enabling Sir Jon to attack relentlessly. Mr Carrington could not easily recover. "Make this worth it!" cried Sir Jon.

Suddenly, what should have been a mere exercise was now a serious feat of self defense for Mr Carrington. Sir Jon redoubled his attacks and finally drew blood. Mr Darcy and Dr Kindrel were astounded. A slash on the arm could have only been deliberate since a foil's target is limited to the protected torso and nothing more. Everyone wondered how Sir Jon could have gotten so carried away. Yet, before anyone else could react, Mr Darcy took up the sword and without protective garments, came between Mr Carrington and Sir Jon. He executed one swift, uninterrupted action to the hilt of Sir Jon's foil and took the blade. The force landed Sir Jon on the floor where Mr Darcy pinned him with his point.

"You must learn to pick your fights carefully, Sir Jon," enlightened Mr Darcy with an austere voice of reason. "Victory over the defenseless is no victory at all." Throwing his sword down in protest of Sir Jon's actions, he turned to Dr Kindrel and asked, "Is Mr Carrington alright?"

"It is only superficial but highly uncalled for," related Dr Kindrel as he assessed the wound. Sir Jon rose slowly from the floor and apologized with all gallantry to Mr Carrington and Mr Darcy. Without a sign of true repent, he explained he only wished to encourage Mr Carrington to fight harder. "I will not fence anyone again who is not up to the challenge," he vowed and proceeded to take up the sword against Col Fitzwilliam. Mr Carrington accepted his apology and excused himself to cleanse his wound and change his shirt.

Miss de Bourgh, who had no investment in Lambton, had remained behind in her chamber. Leaving her room to return a book to the library, she came across Mr Carrington. Observing him holding his arm with blood stains on his sleeve gave her cause for alarm. Immediately, she took a fervent interest in his injury and insisted on an explanation.

"You are bleeding, Mr Carrington! What happened?" she inquired with true concern placing her hand over his to cover the wound.

"Do not worry yourself, Miss de Bourgh. I shall mend readily. It is only superficial. You see, I am merely going to my room to change my shirt. It will stop bleeding post haste," he said surprised at seeing her. "Please, do not think of me as imposing, but why have you, once again, alienated yourself from the rest? I have searched for you among our friends but you are never there?"

"I am afraid I am not the athletic type. I have lived a quiet life, mostly under the strict guardianship of my mother who needlessly feared for my health and had never allowed me to become actively involved in any sport," admitted Miss de Bourgh.

"Sports are very much overrated in my opinion," confessed Mr Carrington in agreement. "But, have you been ill as a child, Miss de Bourgh?"

"I have been led to believe so but Dr Kindrel suggests there is no ailment in me that should call for the intensive care and attention I have been getting. He feels all I need is fresh air and exercise. I have spent so much of my time here in Pemberley analyzing my past and have concluded that after the death of my beloved father, Mother became fearfully concerned with preserving my health and well being as I was all she had."

"Understandable! We should talk more. If you will allow me to change my shirt, Miss de Bourgh, I would like to escort you about the grounds to continue our conversation as I am quite through with my swords play." Miss de Bourgh accepted smiling shyly.

"I will return my book to the library and meet you below," she proposed. Mr Carrington was agreeable.

In a short time, they met in the vestibule. Mr Carrington escorted Miss De Bourgh to the flower gardens that led to the avenue of trees and finally to the inconspicuous benches. There, they sat in each other's company, quietly passing the time, discovering their many similarities which were plentiful indeed. They enjoyed staying at home, had long family histories that entwined with one another from generation to generation and neither of them was any good at sports.

Mr Carrington appreciated Miss de Bourgh's sweetness and gentle compassion. She expressed true concern for his father and thought it only natural that Mr Carrington would move back home to care for him stating she would do the same for her own mother.

"I could not ever imagine enjoying myself if my mother, who had given her every thought and concern to my well being, should need me," she said in serious conversation. "A parent gives their youthful energies to their children selflessly until they are spent. We should feel honored to have the opportunity to share our energies with them while we can!"

"But, by your own account she has kept you from enjoying your life thus far! How is it you would not find it in your heart to go out and make up for lost time?" inquired Mr Carrington testing her sincerity.

"Please, do not confuse true affection for neglect. As I once told you, my mother does her best for everyone who crosses her path. She is charity itself. In my case, she has troubled herself immensely to ensure my well being. She protected me since my youth with such zeal that she did not see the harm. But I am grown now and understand it very clearly. A portion of her very being was taken from her with the loss of my father, never to be returned. I would not want her harmed that way again through any performance of mine. I should always want her to feel secure and in good spirits as you do with your own father," explained Miss de Bourgh.

"And so there are no grudges or hard feelings on your mother's over protectiveness?" persisted Mr Carrington, admiring her evermore as she spoke.

"None whatsoever. The thought does not even occur to me. She has done it all out of love. The past cannot be altered. It is only the present and future that can be amended, but never in the name of retaliation," she said nobly.

"You have captured the very core of my sentiments toward my own family. Our parents have done a good job with us and so we gladly return the services," agreed Mr Carrington.

Through her tacit gestures, he detected her shyness and realized how difficult it was for her to speak freely to him. He made it easy for her with his own patient manner, never rushing her opinion or speech, sitting quietly during moments of silence and promptly agreeing with her when the conversation was very much to his liking. Her innocence and his tranquil nature allowed them to spend a wonderful afternoon of personal exploration, discovery and enchantment. Time passed so quickly they were sorry to see the sun setting so soon.

"I am sorry we have not the time to sit out here all day in this loveliest of gardens. If it were my home, I would have the servants come out and set a table and candles for us but as it stands, I should think it the proper time to dress for dinner," suggested Mr Carrington dutifully rising to give her his arm. Miss de Bourgh rose and held onto him tenderly.

The two of them felt they were in the presence of the most compatible companion ever to be met. Their satisfaction with one another left them desiring more than just friendship. A few more chance encounters would certainly work to bond their relationship and secure their fate.

Their newly formed union became obvious as they slowly strode across the lawn to return to Pemberley. The harmony of their ambling gait and the contentment expressed in their eyes could not be misread, especially by the two observing them from the carriages returning from Lambton.

Caroline was horrified when Mrs Hurst directed her attention to them. Mr Carrington never assumed a leisurely glide nor smiled in quite that fashion when she was in his company. 'It could not be that the drab wan Miss de Bourgh has so completely won the interest of Mr Carrington in such a brief space of time!?! He could not abandon me for her in just one afternoon! It is not possible! At least it must not be so,' determined Caroline.

Apparently, Mrs Hurst's thoughts were functioning in accordance with Caroline's as she relayed a shrewd look of confidence to her sister. "It seems I must advise your Mr Carrington on the proper behavior toward Miss de Bourgh. As I see it, it is entirely inappropriate," she said patting Caroline's hand. "Leave it to me, Caroline. It shall be under control by dinner time tonight."

*　　*　　*

Dinner conversation was filled with talk of the wedding. "Miss Darcy, do reveal your plans to us. Where will you take your wedding tour?" Mrs Hurst inquired.

"Lord Watney and I are obliged to go first to North Courtlandt for one week to address some minor matters before we leave for any extended period of time," answered Miss Darcy. "Once they are sanctioned, we shall be free to go to Lyme just before the onset of the busy fall season. We shall remain until early October when we will return to North Courtlandt as we wish to be settled back before Michaelmas after which, in the spring, we will begin an official wedding tour to Switzerland, Germany, Austria and other neighboring countries."

Spending the autumn season on the beaches of Lyme was the envy of all. Nothing could be more contemporary. The moderately sized, elite resorts offer a limited number of lodgings difficult to procure when the season was in full force. A great many visitors, most of which were gentility, flocked to Lyme in the fall to benefit from the medicinal brisk chilling sea water of the coast. Distinguished bathers traveled far and wide to reserve the bathing machines that stood ready for them in the little bay that curved around the Cobbs.

Other attractions surrounding the district of Lyme were the quaint neighboring towns, like that of Pinny with its charming tranquil countryside of herbage and various orchards that came to life in the free blowing wind of Charmouth, another hamlet, boasting its own unique combination of high grounds and fragmented cliffs that allowed a spectacular view for sightseeing or painting. UpLyme, a nearby village, likewise complimented these locations offering a fully wooded area of its own distinction, standing strong, for anyone to frequent.

"It may be very probable to see you there. I have had plans of going to the shore for the season and having been well informed that my father's humors remain steady intend on going after all. It will round off this year for me before I return home in mid fall. I am going early to have my choice of accommodations as well for I hear it does fill up rather quickly as the change of season progresses," said Mr Carrington.

"I can't believe it. What a happy arrangement it will be! Here, Caroline was mentioning the loss of Mr Carrington's company, when we are all going to the same destination," said Mrs Hurst cheerfully. This was a revelation to Mr Hurst and Caroline. Lyme was never discussed as their next destination but Caroline thought it a delightful revision.

"It will be a pleasurable season," cried Caroline as she came to life with the news.

"Through Divine design, I'm sure," rebuked Daniel mockingly aloud to Mary.

"Fateful coincidence!" she answered sharing in the irony of the Bingley ladies statements. The ladies were not fooling them.

Miss de Bourgh was surprised at Mr Carrington's sudden mention of traveling so far away directly after the wedding without ever mentioning it before. In fact, his conversation led her to believe he would remain to further their friendship. "Perhaps we can get to know one another better when everyone has vacated Pemberley. We can remain a day or two, just you and I," he told her on their stroll through the garden. 'Perhaps the attraction has faded away,' she thought reconsidering his announcement, listening with deep interest to his future plans.

Mrs Bennet had no interest at all in their discourse. She was sufficiently intrigued by the quiet discussion she overheard between Sir Jon and Kitty, thrilled by the constant mention of the magical words "marriage and engagement'. She listened as Sir Jon asked Kitty, "how favorable would it be for a mere country girl to be thrust into fast society as one of the benefits of marriage?" Desiring to share her discovery with Mr Bennet, she kicked him haphazardly under the table and motioned with her head for him to eavesdrop on their daughter. Mr Bennet gave her a swift scornful glance as he adjusted his seat to the outer limit of her range so as to continue eating in peace. Disappointed with his disinterested response, Mrs Bennet resorted to sharing the heart of their conversation to her more immediate circle consisting of Dr Kindrel, Mary and Daniel instead. "Sir Jon should soon request permission to visit at Longbourn as he has naturally developed an acute interest in Kitty. Of course, he will be given permission!" she said peering triumphantly at Mr Bennet. "I knew we would make a conquest here at Pemberley. A baronetage for my Kitty! Won't my friends be envious!" she whispered to the equally concerned Dr Kindrel.

*   *   *

After dinner, the men came to the sitting room to join the women. Mr Darcy revealed a surprise he had in store for his wife and all of his guests were to share in it. "I thought a last night out in the warm evening air would bring about a nice change for our guests, Mrs Darcy. Do you agree that we should head out for a few late night cocktails?"

"That sounds wonderful. Mr Darcy and I have enjoyed many nights out in Pemberely's moonlight," shared Lizzy appreciating her husband's spontaneity. She could sense this evening would hold certain delights for her. "Shall I have the servants light the torches?" she asked.

"No, my love, everything is prearranged," he said as he took her arm and led the party out the rear doors. Stepping onto the patio, the guests were greeted with a fluted glasses of champagne. The incandescent glow from the beautifully arranged candles surrounded in rings of freshly cut flowers gave an especially fragrant and romantic air as Mr Darcy instructed a violinist to play softly in the background. There were many "oohs" and "ahhs" as the guests expressed their delight. It proved to be a nice surprise for them as well as for Lizzy. Mr Darcy's thoughtfulness and attention to detail made her very proud to have him for a husband. "It is perfect!" she said looking amorously into his eyes. That was all the compensation he required.

"Look, Elizabeth. The stars shine brightly for us tonight," said Mr Darcy holding her close, grateful for nature's generous cooperation.

"Mrs Darcy! If you were not so already, Mr Darcy has just made you the envy of every woman here tonight," said Jane overjoyed for her sister. "Everything is so tastefully done and can only be admired with awe."

"Good show, Mr Darcy!" agreed Mr Bingely patting Mr Darcy on the back. "We must do a thing or two like this at Netherfield some time, if not but to recall this momentous occasion."

Jane was pleased Mr Bingley was so affected after they shared such hard times in London. She was glad to see he had put the past behind him and looked forward to being home again in Netherfield. Mr and Mrs Bennet were as captured by the ambiance as was everyone else.

"You have never planned such an evening for me, Mr Bennet," commented Mrs Bennet.

"There is legitimacy for the situation here, my dear. These young people believe themselves to be enamored with one another!" he responded.

"That will not provoke me, Mr Bennet. I do recall a time, not so distant, when your fancy for me induced you to surprise me with an indiscretion and a trinket as well. You need not own up to it but I know your weakness has not yet been exhausted, not even after all these years. Has it Mr Bennet?"

"Do not ask me for confirmation, Mrs Bennet. I won't reveal myself to you," he answered playfully. "And if this is what is to be had from such an evening, I, for one, should be excluded. It is an imposition to a man of my nature."

Mrs Bennet knew very well her husband would never have thought up such an evening and was impressed with this aspect of Mr Darcy that she had never known to exist. "Mr Bennet, could such a man as Mr Darcy have thought this up himself?" she asked.

"It is Lizzy that inspires him. She deserves this and much more," said Mr Bennet.

"If only Mr and Mrs Collins were still here to see what Mr Darcy does for Lizzy. They would realize, once and for all, that we have no remorse in Charlotte marrying that odious Mr Collins and inheriting our house. Then, when we are dead, she would never enjoy her life at Longbourn half as much as she should! Well, never mind. I shall relate it with minute detail to her mother, Lady Lucas. I shall tell her what Charlotte has missed, as I will not let this lovely gesture go unrecounted."

Dr Kindrel was particularly appreciative of the enchanting distraction. It opened the opportunity for him to steal another intimate moment with Kitty. He caught her attention and smoothly maneuvered their position to where they could finally have a private word. "Miss Catherine, I will be leaving tomorrow immediately after the wedding ceremony. The morning will be filled with so much activity that we will, most likely, not get a chance to have a proper discourse and say good bye," he said.

"Say goodbye?" questioned Kitty suddenly discovering she may not ever see him again. "I did not realize! The time has gone by so fast! Are you to return to London or will you continue your travels to an even more adventurous path?" she asked playfully.

"I will not be returning to London any time in the near future, Miss Catherine. I had only a miniscule amount of furnishings there and have already notified my landlady to store them for me. She is a good sort and I can trust that she will put all in good order," he said calmly. "Colonel Fitzwilliam has graciously arranged to employ my medical services for the militia. I will have the honor of reviewing and updating physician's practices from regiment to regiment. It is a wonderful opportunity for me as my travels promise to gain me great recognition. I look forward to the experience with eagerness. Yet, I admit, I leave Pemberley with immense apprehension," he said coming to terms with his melancholy. His appearance grew grave as he collected his thoughts. His manner was hesitant disclosing confusion and uncertainty. He gazed at her for a moment and then looked away wondering how to proceed when Kitty spoke instead.

"What could be disturbing you? You are such a happy person, in good spirits at all times," asked Kitty. "Please, feel free to share your thoughts with me. I cannot bear to see you in such a state."

Through these words he saw the mutual concern they shared for one another. It emboldened him and drawing a deep breath he proceeded by saying, "If I may have your permission to begin our conversation by focusing on you, Miss Catherine . . . ."

"You should not tolerate any burdens on my behalf. There is nothing about me that should grieve you in any way! We have always spoken freely. Speak out and have it said," she proposed with true compassion.

"For one thing, I wonder if you will rethink your understanding with Sir Jon," he said with hesitation for this inappropriate intervention.

"Rethink what understanding! Sir Jon is a personable caring man. He is a gentleman. I am sure I don't know what you are speaking of," she answered surprised that Sir Jon was brought into their quiet discussion. Dr Kindrel turned away disappointed in her answer. Confused Kitty confronted him again and urged him to continue.

"Through your mother, Mrs Bennet, I have been informed of your probable marriage to Sir Jon. It grieves me deeply," he said. "I wish to . . . I am compelled to advise you to alter your regard for the Baronet," he said deciding to be straight with it. "I am afraid I must take on the very unpleasant task of discouraging you in your choice of husbands. Your observation of him is so contrary to what I see. He is not at all in your league. You do not belong with him, Miss Catherine, and you are not meant for the kind of life he will provide you. You are not of his sort."

"Why am I not meant for that kind of life?" she asked in offense.

"What I am saying is that you do not belong with that breed of people. Did we not establish that their genus is the most shallow of the entire human race and that their strict civility only masks the contempt they have for natural affection and the common man. Their species will not accept you, Miss Catherine, for once you are revealed to be legitimately gentle, you will be swallowed up. They will be vindictive and it will turn him around. He will resent you and side with his peers. You have seen how he places the utmost importance in how he is perceived by others. Even a mere fish carried more significance than you did!"

"That was such a triviality!" she said protecting Sir Jon's reputation.

"Triviality!?! Do not alter your self respect for anyone Miss Catherine," he replied hurt that she was giving in to Sir Jon. "Can't you see how your very existence is disregarded by him and can you not foresee how, if you never accustom yourself to their likeness, his people will slight you as well. Furthermore, if you cannot keep appearances he will think you unworthy and abandon you to yourself. I have seen this in family after family," he said earnestly. "You will be all compromise to remain with him. You are choosing poorly and will pay for it dearly. All happiness and vivacity will be lost in you as he will intercept and deprive you of your very thoughts until you lose all mastery of yourself!"

"Again you cast aspersions against Sir Jon," she said feeling her temperature rise.

"Please, think Miss Catherine. Follow your own instincts when it comes to who you are to marry. You have allowed your mother, who I respect and adore very much, to tie you to that Baronet and that will not do. Believe me, he is all wrong for you," he explained.

"Now I am convinced that you have overstepped your place and it is a disservice to me. I do not honor your opinion. My instincts tell me to listen to my mother. Unlike you, she thinks of me and my security. You, of all people, know that. But you have only pretended to be my friend. See how you take liberty to demean me in believing me incapable of making up my own mind. I have been very much mistaken by your affable facade, Dr Kindrel," she responded strongly. "I have confided my family's dubious financial security with you but that should not mean that I am destined to be forever without fortune, just because you are. I thought you would only want the best for me. I must marry someday! Why shouldn't I marry into a better life? How dare you determine I am not meant for improvement in rank and situation! And as for my dissolution, my sisters have all married well under my mother's guidance! Look about you and see how Mr Darcy honors Lizzy," she snapped back.

"It is my understanding that each of them married for love as you should too. This man is cold and pompous. He admires you for the way you attract attention, because you are beautiful and dress in high style but it is not appearances that make a marriage. You are a medallion to him. Someone he can display while he exhibits himself. You shall have no life of your own, spending your days listening to him speak of himself as you do now. To him, every sport is a personal conquest and I believe he considers obtaining you much the same. You see, it is not that you fall short of that sort of life but it is he who is not worthy of you and your most precious companionship. I daresay, he does not love you nor do you love him. He is all foppery with a cavalier nature that will become increasingly reckless as the years go by. You could only be injured at his expense," he said realizing that his words were not penetrating. He could see her eyes turn cold at his continuance.

"Sir Jon admires me apart from how I dress and I take him the way he is, as he takes me the way I am," interrupted Kitty. "He is a man of refined gentility."

"He is not taking you the way you are. You are free and alive. He is already stifling you, taking your soul from you day by day. I am only thinking about you and I fear you will regret your decision if you marry him."

"I will not have any regrets. And I do not see how you dare involve yourself in this way. Your talents lie solely in healing the body," she said trembling with the force of the truth of what he was saying though not amenable to concede. "Do not extend yourself where you are not trained."

"Then examine yourself! You do not have the appearance of a lady in love. You are constantly distressed and uneasy. A lady who has found her completeness does not frown as you do. You should emit light and happiness with smiles and easiness as does Miss Darcy! You will waste your life being miserable while trying to keep up appearances of happiness."

"It is your desperation for destroying my prospects that make me appear so although I cannot believe that any marriage would be the tragic experience you describe for me."

Dr Kindrel paused to reconsider. He did not want her to lose focus of his message. Believing he had said enough, he conceded, saying, "If you believe yourself in love and trust he can bring you true happiness I will yield and leave you to your decision."

"I will not listen to anymore of this anyway since it is clear you are resigned to challenge and refute me no matter what I say," she said indignantly.

"Trust your heart, Kitty. It is not too late," he urged tenderly with aggravated devotion. Turning to walk away he added, "Think hard. Someone who loves you just the way you are will come to you in good time, if only you would wait. Take that as my advice if you will. Wait for love so that when I return you may be happily married." Dr Kindrel struggled to keep himself from proposing to her now. He knew it would discredit his justified accusations of Sir Jon and he wanted them intact for Kitty to consider. For now he would say no more.

Confused, Kitty turned herself from him forcing a final conclusion to the stinging confrontation. Dejected, Dr Kindrel politely excused himself from the company and entered the house. Kitty walked in the opposite direction trying to come to terms with the bitter encounter but she did not afford two steps before she was called upon to join the others.

As she stood there, disconnected, she was grateful for the shadowy darkness that shielded her face. No one noticed her faze as they were too absorbed in their own happy thoughts and conversations. Surrounded by their glee, Kitty found herself discouraged and feeling more alone than ever before.

Chapter 9

The exchange of vows early the next morning provided the opportunity for every couple in the room to reflect on their own nuptials. It was a very emotional time for Mr Darcy as he thought about his parents, Lady Catherine, Elizabeth and of course, Georgiana. Mr Darcy looked upon his only sister with pride. He had watched over her so lovingly, for so long, that he could not see her go so easily. He hoped that Georgiana would be as happy and fulfilled as he was with his precious Elizabeth.

Kitty was sitting next to Sir Jon as she heard the exchange of vows orated by Pemberley's pastor. She fancied herself reciting the same pledge and closed her eyes to legitimize her fantasy with the seal of an imaginary kiss. Her dream was so vivid that she felt the kiss, so soft and gentle, become much more passionate than she had ever thought it could be. It was hypnotic and filled her emotionally, warming her blood as no other dream had ever done before. As she slowly opened her eyes she could not release the image of herself kissing her beloved Dr Kindrel. 'Ah me! Dr Kindrel! I don't know why I was dreaming of him so affectionately. Could it be? I would have never overlooked him for all this time if I perceived that I had such feelings and yet I now know that I truly love him,'she thought as her mind would not let go of her trance. 'It felt so natural and true.' She drew a clearer understanding of her feelings as she reconsidered their last encounter. 'Why had I thought so ill of him? What aberrant pressures compelled me to take such an attitude? He was harsh on Sir Jon, with so many objections. However, confronting me was not as egregious as I made it out to be. My trumped up pride required me to see want of propriety in him and not see his sincerity. Indeed, I have always been fond of him. In fact, I have loved him and have never been equally impressed by Sir Jon. It was just the flattery of his advancements and Mama's most desired approval and pride in me that fostered my own happiness. If I had the slightest suspicion that I was disregarding my true feelings I would have seen the justice of Dr Kindrel's charges against Sir Jon. I am excessively sorry to have been so curt with him. I was wrong. He said I should wait. It is heedful advice. I must meet with him again, this morning, before he departs and tell him it was not such an indelicate intervention as I made it out to be. I must tell him I wish to see him again and again. And he is here, in the same room only a few rows behind.' She turned to look back and locate him but was distracted by Sir Jon's imposing eyes. She satisfied him with a brief smile and thought about him for a second, 'Sir Jon. He is menial and can't compare to Dr Kindrel. Why should I customize my proper feelings by altering them to please him? I have never revised my ways to accommodate Dr Kindrel and I would never feel so affected by a kiss from Sir Jon as I would be from my most excellent doctor! How could I have made such a horrible mistake? It is all so clear to me now. I cannot let Dr Kindrel go without at least revealing my own feelings and if the affection is returned, I shall put an end to this charade with Sir Jon and wait for Dr Kindrel's return. I must tell him before he goes or how would he know!' she thought as she wrung her fingers with anxious anticipation.

Immediately following the ceremony, Kitty hastened to Dr Kindrel. The church was very crowded and everyone rushed out in unison to see the bride and groom take their first journey together as man and wife. Lord and Lady Watney made their way through the well wishers and climbed into the brand new, posh barouche presented to them by the Darcys. Waving goodbye the coachman drove them to the Watney's home, North Courtlandt. In all the commotion Kitty lost sight of Dr

Kindrel. "Miss Catherine! Do not hurry so. A man would think you have never seen a wedding party before!" called Sir Jon holding her back by the arm. Kitty refused to be held back and continued to move aggressively out the door. He followed her as she ran out of the church with deliberate speed.

Col Fitzwilliam and Dr Kindrel were exchanging their own goodbyes outside the church doors. They were surrounded by Pemberley's guests who bid them a safe journey. Sir Jon continued to pursue Kitty as she ran up to the pair. She peeled her way through the crowd fully intent on drawing Dr Kindrel's attention but was taken aback, speechless as she stood before him gazing wide eyed at what she beheld. There he stood, as noble and as debonair as any gentleman garbed in regimentals. Naturally, Col Fitzwilliam required that Dr Kindrel wear the attire while working with the regiments. Kitty was awe struck. She thought him the most handsome man in uniform she had ever encountered and it immobilized her.

Detecting her presence, he turned to take her hand, not to kiss good bye on the cheek as he had done to Mrs Bennet, but to pull her toward him to have a final intimate word. He was searching for her as eagerly as she was searching for him. He had something to say and the expression displayed on his face matched the look in her eyes. The attraction was palpable as the desire to be with one another was their only objective. They eliminated the world around them, drawing successfully closer by what seemed like an eternity, finally taking hold of each other's hand when the abrupt appearance of Sir Jon interfered. Sir Jon resumed his position at her side, taking her by the arm and intentionally hoarding her as his, once and for all. Dr Kindrel drew back momentarily, to assess Kitty's reaction, but she just stood there, silently paralyzed, much as before allowing Sir Jon to have his way. Assuming their indestructible allegiance, Dr Kindrel released her hand and said good bye with a stiff chivalrous bow. Kitty was overwhelmed and could not speak as Sir Jon placed her arm in his. She remained stunned as she and Sir Jon watched Dr Kindrel and Col Fitzwilliam mount to finally ride off.

After brunch, the parties dispersed to make last minute arrangements for their departures. Soon after, many of the guests vacated Pemberley. The Darcys, Kitty and Mrs Bennet were at the door to bid Sir Jon farewell. He turned one last time to Kitty and said, "I regret that I did not break my previous engagements when we first met. At this late date I could not possibly alter my plans. However, I will tolerate my departure more gracefully if you would allow me to correspond with you at Longbourn," he suggested.

"That would do just fine, Sir Jon," said Mrs Bennet who was lingering to hear these glad tidings. "Kitty will check the post three times daily!" she added. With that Sir Jon bowed, thanked the Darcys for their hospitality and made his exit.

Mary was to stay a fortnight to help Lizzy return the house to its usual state. To her delight, Daniel had a day or two before he was to escort Miss de Bourgh and her nurse to North Courtlandt.

The Bingleys departed immediately for Netherfield in their coach while Kitty and the Bennets took young Charles and Elizabeth with them and followed in theirs. Kitty was grateful the children were with them. They provided amusement and entertainment for Mr and Mrs Bennet, leaving her to her own thoughts. She could not dismiss the picture of the attractive uniformed Dr Kindrel. He was handsome and good-looking all along but she could not see it. She was too busy regarding him as a friend and confidante. How could she have been so simple not to have viewed him in any other way? He was compatible, easy to talk to and caring. 'How dare he fool me that way!' she thought in anger. 'He shouldn't have cloaked himself under the veil of friendship. I would have welcomed his advances as far back as London if I was thinking clearly and thought of him as a mere man and not a doctor. Foolish me,' she concluded helplessly.

The carriages traveled one behind the other, all the way to Netherfield where the Bennets fondly deposited the children and continued on the next few miles to Longbourn. Kitty sat quietly, continuously weighing the past events at Pemberley. Despite all that occurred, she kept recalling what transpired within the last few hours there. It was difficult for her to grasp that she had found and lost love in one spontaneous moment. She could hear her mother mentioning Sir Jon repeatedly to Mr Bennet but was not moved by the mention of his name.

"You can be very proud of Kitty, Mr Bennet, for Pemberley was not as uneventful as you might have anticipated. I was not surprised one bit by her attracting a man of his high rank and dignity. You were right prohibiting her from Meryton for she certainly would have been spoken for by anyone of the officers. And now, a Baronetcy! Lady Catherine Nettington! It is an aristocratic name and our Kitty will wear it well. Who would have thought we would have this in store for our humble family!" shrilled Mrs Bennet in a boast.

"He has not mentioned anything to me about it yet, Mrs Bennet," commented Mr Bennet.

"I have seen it with my own eyes, Mr Bennet. They are discovered. He has tossed his design toward our Kitty and will soon make his applications to you. I have done right by our Kitty, wouldn't you agree?" she happily pointed out.

"I can hardly wait to see what you have in store for our Mary!" replied Mr Bennet lightheartedly.

"That Mary! Don't speak of her to me. She did nothing to better her position. She will have to live off of her sisters for the rest of her life when we are withdrawn from this earth. That is most inconsiderate of her. Fortunately, Kitty shall have ample assemblies, as will Jane and Lizzy, to introduce Mary. Won't you Kitty?" Hesitating only a moment, without receiving an answer, she continued, "See Mr Bennet, Kitty is thinking about her Sir Jon. I am all anticipation for receiving him at Longbourn as he will eventually need to make a visit to see you. I will have the Philipses and my good friends the Lucases there for introductions. It will not hurt to show him off. Sir William Lucas is so proud to have been knighted but he will be nothing to a Baronet who has background and lineage behind him. Besides, his daughter Charlotte married a common clergyman! What connections could she bring for her younger sister, Maria. Maybe Kitty can invite her to an assembly or two once Sir Jon knows more of the family. You would, wouldn't you Kitty?" she asked.

"Poor, desolate Maria," sighed Mr Bennet sarcastically.

*   *   *

That very night, Mr and Mrs Darcy made their usual rounds to secure the house. He was very pleased with what he was able to provide for Georgiana. He told Lizzy how he thought his parents would have been proud of their children and their choices of marriage partners.

"They would have adored you and the way you worked to make this day all it could be for Georgiana," explained Mr Darcy. Lizzy knew it meant a lot to him and was grateful for the admiration he had for her performance. Together they basked in the moment as they walked slowly arm in arm. "I do wish my aunt would have graced us with her presence. As my mother's sister she should have witnessed Georgiana's wedding. She should have danced at her ball. Instead, she placed me in charge of the ill fated matchmaking between Mr Carrington and Miss de Bourgh," related Mr Darcy as he held the door open for the dogs. "I fear all hopes of reconciling with Lady Catherine are lost forever as she is not easily inclined to forgive.

"She cannot have realized how difficult it is for you to act reliably where matters of the heart are concerned. It was most arduous for you to approach me and you loved me! It could be no easier to match a stranger with a repressed young lady such as Miss de Bourgh, lovely as she is," consoled Lizzy. "She cannot be put forward when she, herself was not ready and Miss Bingley cannot be forced back when she was acting in proper context. True, you were not help or hindrance but both situations were beyond your reach. Ease your mind, Fitzwilliam, Lady Catherine will forgive you at some point."

"I did not try hard enough. I had hoped it would work itself out in the end as I was caught off guard with Mr Carrington and Miss Bingley. Nevertheless, I was not about to estrange potential suitors again. No, I have learned well enough not to interfere with relationships," confessed Mr Darcy as they climbed the stairs.

"Indeed, your judgment was right in this case. Let romance take its own course. You must trust that all will be right in the end and we, for our part, shall remain open to Lady Catherine despite herself."

*   *   *

Miss de Bourgh was preparing to leave Pemberley when she received a dispatch from her mother. It read:

Dearest Anne,

I am writing to inform you that I shall not arrive at North Courtlandt within the next few days as planned. Lord Carrington has grown accustomed to my company and insists that I remain at his estate longer. Clearly, I cannot deny him. It would be inexcusable to desert a cherished old friend when he would be destitute without me. I plan to stay an extra few weeks. Do inform Georgiana. If she is not at North Courtlandt when I arrive, I shall have to see her another time. Congratulate Lord Watney on my behalf and give Lady Georgiana my best wishes and hopes for all happiness. Your mother

Lady Catherine

Miss de Bourgh shared the news with Daniel. She thought they should take advantage of the extra time and invite their good friend, Mary, to see North Courtlandt's Parsonage. Daniel agreed he would be eager for Mary to see the parsonage and invited her to join them. Receiving Lizzy's assurance that the housekeeper would be equally capable in returning the house to itself, Mary accepted. Miss de Bourgh, Daniel, Mary and Mrs Jenkinson proceeded to North Courtlandt but not before Daniel wrote a letter to his brother Mr Collins.

Mr Collins was anxiously awaiting the final confirmation of Miss de Bourgh's and Mr Carrington's successful alliance. He was delighted to receive the letter Daniel sent him. Sitting happily in the garden he made himself comfortable as he read:

Dear Brother William,

I am about to embark on my final journey to North Courtlandt. I cannot explain the excitement and anticipation I am experiencing with the mere thought of encountering my first commission. You can trust I will dedicate my full body and soul to the parsonage's successful turnover and make the Watneys proud to have selected me as their cleric's successor. But I must be quick with my correspondence for Miss de Bourgh and Miss Bennet are to share in my jubilation. They are seeing to their boxes as I write.

My main function in writing you is to inform you that Mr Carrington has left Pemberely with Miss Bingley and the Hursts for Lyme without yet making his promise to Miss de Bourgh. In fact, nothing in the way of commitment was ever established. I hazard to admit, we leave Pemberley with Miss de Bourgh as unattached as when I was first assigned my fortuitous office. I write with deep regret to give you such adverse news brother, however, it is truth and cannot be manipulated from where I stand. It must be given up. Miss de Bourgh appears resigned to the fact as she wears a face of content. Yet, I confess, I can detect the loss in her eyes as they are the windows to her soul. I remain your brother &c

Rev Daniel Collins

This news was far from what Mr Collins expected to hear. The shock of it made him quiver. He held every expectation that this communication would announce the agreeable union Lady Catherine envisioned. Instead, this most unhappy state of affairs has become his own undoing.

Mr Collins could not blame his brother as he visualized himself swiftly escorted out of Hunsford Parsonage with neither a good reference nor a fond farewell. He would never forgive himself for carelessly plunging into Pemberley's poison ivy. 'What adverse set of consequences that dreadful day has brought. It has cost me my entire livelihood. It was Armageddon itself. Now Mrs Collins and I must restrict our economies to our fullest ability for I do not know where we shall reside once Lady Catherine returns to find me so miserably failed.'

Chapter 10

North Courtlandt was a grand estate with grounds equal in expanse to Pemberley. Its approach was direct and afforded a picturesque view of the grounds, in all its magnificence, extending one full quarter mile from the gate. It was evident that an extensive area of forestry had to be cleared before the immense mansion and its surrounding parks could be situated. The natural landscape yielded to a stone courtyard, softened by potted trees strategically placed to provide a proper amount of color and shade. Every bush and shrub was deliberately bred and manicured to cast a formal display as nature, if left to itself, lacked the structure and incentive to form its own impressive design as it did for Pemberley.

North Courtlandt Manor was well constructed and beautifully architectured to assert nothing but wealth and family history. The pale exterior, with creeping ivy, stood resplendent with white on white clutches of flowers and creamy pink roses that stood out beautifully amidst their respective shades of green. Indoors, the rooms were large and needed a woman's touch to soften the rigid gothic interior.

There was a novelty in being the first greeted at North Courtlandt by Lady Georgiana. Proper titles were used and good humor was distributed by everyone. Georgiana was delighted Mary was able to join her little group and promised numerous balls and various forms of entertainments after the honeymoon period. Wasting no time Daniel was shown his new home.

Courtlandt Parsonage was located one mile beyond the gate, off the road leading toward the village. It was a large house, big enough for a ready made family, adequately furnished. The chapel was humbled by its simple exterior but praiseworthy within due to the softly emitted rainbow effect of its stained glass windows.

Observing his parsonage for the first time proved to be an emotional experience for Daniel. It was his dream come true. He vowed, once again, to do his very best and become the most competent, discerning parson anyone could ever be. Plans to play games and promenade about the grounds of North Courtlandt with Mary and Miss de Bourgh throughout the duration of their stay were graciously declined. He was anxious to begin his duties and accepted to be in their company for evening events only. Instead of games and walks, he would use the mornings to acquaint himself with his flock as he wanted to get started as soon as possible. The ladies fully understood and honored his wishes. Lady Georgiana excused herself to return to the house providing Miss de Bourgh and Mary a chance to explore North Courtlandt until late in the afternoon. While on their explorations, Mary thought about Daniel and his parish.

"Miss de Bourgh, don't you have the slightest curiosity to see the villagers that will compose Daniel's new flock? It is a curiosity to me. I should like very much to accompany him in his circuit to acquaint myself with them, wouldn't you?"

"That is an excellent idea. It should benefit Daniel to have friends with him and would allow Lady Georgiana more time for herself to fulfill her obligations before her departure," added Miss de Bourgh as they set off to find Daniel.

"It is extremely generous of you to help me like this," he replied happily. "A new parish is a huge responsibility and who else would I take more comfort in than you two. If it is acceptable to my benefactress, we shall get an early start in the morning," condoned Daniel with a gleeful spirit.

Georgiana took no exceptions to their occupying themselves any way they desired. They were to consider their initial visit at North Courtlandt as unceremonious and as casual as they deemed. Reserving their joint entertainments to dinners and evenings would be very satisfactory to her as she utilized the time to instruct and acquaint herself with the housekeeper and the servants.

*   *   *

Early the next morning, Daniel began establishing himself throughout the village. Miss de Bourgh and Mary were delighted to accompany him. The townsfolk were friendly and encouraging to Daniel as the majority were faithful churchgoers.

His rounds proved to be of even greater value as he was able to identify the infirmed and indigent citizens who required more frequent house calls and extra assistance. At their evening gatherings, Daniel and the ladies reported these circumstances to Lady Georgiana, enabling her to pay these tenants a special visit with food and remedies while Daniel brought them spiritual comfort. During that time, Mary and Miss de Bourgh lent themselves to the young ones making sure they were cleaned, fed and read to.

Mary petitioned Lady Georgiana to donate books to the parsonage so they can be readily available to take on the road to read to the children, or to be distributed among them if they possessed none of their own.

Many times, on her visits, Mary recounted bible stories she had known since childhood. The children loved the stories and the very youngest absorbed them as if they had never heard them before. After a few days of storytelling Mary came to realize that they were genuinely unfamiliar with the stories of the Bible.

Informing Daniel that the children were particularly ignorant of the scriptures encouraged him to divulge what he had learned about the previous pastor. The Reverend Robert Morris was a man of celibacy and had no wife to aid him with the parish's children. He left that charge to the parents, who were preoccupied with their daily chores and could not satisfactorily educate their children on religious matters, accepting their weekly sermons as their only means of study. This neglect left plenty of work ahead in guiding the children with their spiritual needs.

Daniel immediately decided to establish a session for the children that would be attended by them directly after the weekly sermon. Mary helped in setting it up by gathering and organizing children's books, slates and other materials that may be helpful. Daniel wrote sermons that related in some way with the stories the children would be learning so the adults could aid them with their instruction more easily. The two worked diligently to prepare for the next sermon.

While Mary remained involved with Daniel's classes, Miss de Bourgh and Georgiana inspected the house and immediate grounds to list the necessary alterations. So much had to be done that it was determined the house would need a major overhaul when Georgiana returned from the honeymoon. She planned to seek out particular items on her future travels throughout Europe to make the house her own. She was happy to have this task before her and considered it a pleasure to revamp the house with a modern look, as she had seen Lizzy have the pleasure of doing in Pemberley, slight as the alterations were. His Lordship welcomed giving North Courtlandt Manor a fresh, new personality and gave Georgiana a free hand.

Sunday arrived and Daniel delivered a dynamic sermon reinforcing the need children have to acquire scriptural knowledge at an early age. The flock was inspired and embraced Daniel with open arms. Immediately following, the children remained to be educated on David and the giant Goliath. Mary sat through this class to provide her support and quickly developed a sense of satisfaction as she was able to provide a helping hand. She took on the task with enthusiasm and felt she could easily perform this function for the rest of her life. Outdoors, Georgiana and Miss de Bourgh chatted with the tenants. Everyone bestowed high praise for the new pastor and thanked Lady Georgiana for the unique find.

The following week the Watneys embarked on their travels to Lyme. Mary had to leave as she was to be escorted back to Pemberley, where a manservant from Netherfield was to collect her and deposit her to Longbourn. Mary, Daniel and Miss de Bourgh promised to maintain their friendship through faithful correspondence until they could meet again.

Miss de Bourgh remained at North Courtlandt with Mrs. Jenkinson for the remaining week. She and Daniel arranged to walk throughout the village for daily exercise. They, of course, enjoyed each other's company but felt the loss of Mary as she had become a very important addition to their lives.

Miss de Bourgh visited the parsonage one last time to help Daniel prepare for his next meeting. "Where would you like these books, Daniel? They are not well organized just lying on the table from when the children scanned through them last," asked Miss de Bourgh.

"Frankly, I didn't pay close enough attention to how Miss Bennet managed things because she was so efficient. I should have observed her more closely when she was here," admitted Daniel. "For now, just leave them on the table as they are. I am beginning to understand how the previous pastor could not be encumbered with the children's needs. If it wasn't for Miss Bennet, I may not even have noticed their neglect nor devoted much time to them."

"It is a hardship to be without her, isn't it Daniel," observed Miss de Bourgh. He could only admit it to be true as the villagers missed her contributions claiming the children were especially disheartened that she was not there. However, after a while, it was of no consequence. As he feared, he did not have the time to make his visits, write his sermons and care for the residence adequately enough to maintain the addition of the children's education. He bid for volunteers to aid his cause but no one filled the position with the excellence of Mary.

*   *   *

In these months away from Rosings, Anne had enough fresh air and exercise to improve her look dramatically. She increased her appetite, felt stronger and developed a passion for freedom and independence.

Lady Catherine arrived as scheduled. She was optimistic and jubilant to see her daughter again and commented that she looked remarkably well. Anne described her days at Pemberely and at North Courtlandt with brevity explaining that she was much more active than ever before.

She informed Lady Catherine that Georgiana had proceeded to Lyme leaving word that she was sorry to have missed her and that she was very pleased with Daniel.

"Of course she is pleased with Daniel. I have an eye for these things. But do tell me, Anne, how did you like Mr Carrington?" asked Lady Catherine, anxious for the good news.

"Mr Carrington is a very fine gentleman. We had a good time together," said Miss de Bourgh with spirits elevated by the mention of his name. Her pleasure with him showed on her face.

"That pleases me. I knew you would develop an interest in each other. I don't know why I didn't think of him before. He shall soon be visiting us at Rosings, won't he?" inquired Lady Catherine.

"He is gone for the fall season, Mother. He went to Lyme," explained Miss de Bourgh.

"Why would he go to Lyme when you are here? Why would he want to leave you? It must have been terribly unavoidable. Very well then, when has he arranged to see you again?" she asked. Detecting a sudden change in Miss de Bourgh's demeanor, her suspicions began to rise. "Do not hesitate in telling me Anne, I wish to know," she demanded sensing something amiss.

"Mr Carrington received good news of his father's health and thought he should round off his travels with a view of Lyme. He said it was part of a previous itinerary he had designed for himself. Afterwards, sometime in late September, he is to return to Dover. How have you left Lord Carrington, Mother? In good health, I presume?" She shared all she knew of the matter and hoped her mother would put it to rest with a diversion.

"Lord Carrington's health is very good, but I need to understand, Anne. Did he or did he not promise to see you again!?!" insisted Lady Catherine.

"No Mother," admitted Miss de Bourgh suddenly feeling insecure and withdrawn. Her eyes cast down to her feet.

"Then we must hurry back to Rosings and pack for a stay in Lyme. There is no time to waste, or I should like to stop and visit our Mr

Collins, but I will put that off for now. I will leave a note here for Georgiana while you get a servant to pack your boxes immediately." As Miss de Bourgh ran to do her mother's bidding Lady Catherine sat down and wrote:

Dear Lady Georgiana,

I am sorry to have missed seeing you off on your wedding tour. I regret not being here sooner but I was needed elsewhere. When you return, you must call on me at Rosings. I shall advise you on how to redecorate North Courtlandt Manor with as little expense as possible. No doubt Lord Watney can conceivably get the better grains of mahogany and satin wood from one of his islands but I shall recommend the better cabinet makers in the district. Remember the lessons I have taught you. Do not discard anything, but have them stored in a lodge or somewhere little occupied. In any case, I can see there is much to be done to modernize your arrangement in furniture and décor. I shall assist in any number of ways. Best wishes to you and your husband. Your aunt

Lady Catherine

*   *   *

Upon her departure, Miss de Bourgh confirmed her promise to correspond with Daniel. He ran along side their barouche to the gate and waved them off. When they were beyond his sight, he turned to face the immense estate from the view of the gate feeling quite secluded. It was a lonely walk toward his large house and once inside, he listened to the overbearing silence that was now his only companion. He sat at his desk to write his brother a letter. It read:

Dearest Brother William

So much has happened since I wrote you last. Lady Catherine arrived at North Courtlandt to be disappointed in not seeing Lady Georgiana. The Watneys could not wait for her late arrival and set off for their season in Lyme. This event was followed by a second disappointment as Lady Catherine learned from Miss de Bourgh that Mr Carrington is in Lyme with absolutely no intention of returning to be with Miss de Bourgh. I do not know if she is aware of the tenacious Miss Bingley and their occupation of Lyme as well. As far as I have been informed, Lady Catherine and Miss de Bourgh are returning to Rosings post haste. It was said she is not pleased with you. Remember, in times like these, we can put all matters in prayer to assure the best outcome for all. Your brother,

Rev Daniel Collins

To consume his solitude, Daniel walked into town to post the letter himself. He saw a few friendly faces but they were busy with occupations of their own. He returned to the parsonage slowly, finding himself reluctant to get back. Having arrived, he walked through the parish aisle and stepped up to the pulpit to look upon the empty benches. He remembered the past weeks fondly recalling how Lord and Lady Watney sat with Miss de Bourgh in their pew. He was glad to see they were attentive listeners. Then he recollected how Mary sat with the parishioners making herself one of them despite the fact that she was invited to sit with the Watneys. She had the children about her and a glow that he did not fully realize until now. He reminisced about the time they played potential lovers in Pemberley for Miss de Bourgh and he was grateful he complimented Mary the way he did. 'Heavenly days! Miss Bennet is especially fine with her nature so altruistic and pure. She has an indelible sweet and gentle soul. In fact, she is as alluring as she is intelligent,' he thought to himself. 'She is inspirational and helpful, always embracing the call for assistance whether requested for aloud or silently implied. Her incomparable contributions would be an asset to me and North Courtlandt Parsonage. Truth be told, I find I am very fond of her and my affections are growing steadily, even in her absence.' His spirits became animated when he thought of her, and from this day forward, he did so with increased frequency.

*   *   *

At Rosings, Lady Catherine and Miss de Bourgh readied themselves swiftly for Lyme. Anne stopped her mother's scramble for servants long enough to make one special request as she had learned from Daniel and Mary that you had to venture the effort in order to achieve. In this case, she was decided. From this day forward, she would hold her own. She did not think her mother would approve but bravely presented her plea just the same.

"Mother, I feel that I am in good health and do not need a nurse anymore. I would like to leave Mrs Jenkinson behind. After all, you have remarked yourself that I am no longer off color," she said confronting her mother with confidence and respect.

"You do look remarkably well, Anne. If that is what you wish, it is alright with me. I don't have time to argue with you in either case," claimed Lady Catherine thoroughly preoccupied with the task at hand. "I shall send Mrs Jenkinson to Dover to care for Lord Carrington. It will be a good gesture on our part and he could benefit from her unwavering care."

Overjoyed, Anne was instantly reborn. She was empowered by her success and gained new courage. No more overshadowing escorts, no more overburdening guidance. She felt relieved.

Mrs Jenkinson was apprehensive and forlorn but promises were made to reunite them, in the future, to care for Miss de Bourgh's own children at Greenfield Castle.

Making good time on the road, the de Bourghs found themselves promptly in Lyme. Their accommodations were not up to par, as the season had a devoted early following and was well underway. They had to manage in the small apartment they were fortunate to secure.

The streets were heavily congested and it was difficult to locate anyone specifically among the dense crowd. Lady Catherine directed her footman to search the lodges and inns for the name of Mr Carrington, but the footman consistently returned without success. In addition to those attempts, Lady Catherine and Miss de Bourgh took every opportunity to make their presence known throughout the rest of the week but it was all to no avail for Mr Carrington was no where to be found.

Miss de Bourgh corresponded faithfully, keeping Mary and Daniel well informed of her situation. She wrote them that she and Lady Catherine were in search of Mr Carrington and were having a difficult time locating him. In her eyes, the way things stood, her prospects seemed very poor indeed.

*   *   *

At Longbourn, Mary wrote:

Dear Miss de Bourgh

I have heard from Daniel and was very glad to hear his parishioners sent me their regards as I too, wish I could have spent more time there with them. Indeed, I was very happy to have had the opportunity to help establish Daniel in his new employment, small as my contribution may have been. I felt very productive and look forward to any future invitation North Courtlandt shall bestow.

In any case, I am anxious to relay some important news to you about your Mr Carrington. Your efforts shall not reap you any positive results for you are searching in the wrong place. My brother, Mr Bingley, has recently received word of their whereabouts as Mr Carrington continues in the company of Miss Bingley and Mrs Hurst. It seems they began their excursion in Lyme but are in Charmouth for a week or two to explore the cliffs and sands until which time they shall return to Lyme. I wish I could be of further assistance by giving you the name of the lodge but that is not known to us. Do not lose hope. There is no mention of anything deeper than friendship as far as Mr Carrington is concerned for Miss Bingley has not made any announcements. I shall keep you informed if I receive any further news.

As for finally dismissing Mrs Jenkinson I say it was a brilliant move. She should have been strolling in someone else's parks long ago. Daniel shall be ecstatic with the news. I remain your trusted friend,

Miss Mary Bennet

Of late, Mrs Bennet had been watching Mary and Kitty write and receive an increasing amount of correspondence. Mary, in particular, scrambled to meet the post three times daily to rummage through the dispatches in search for a note or two.

"There is so much writing and receiving here, and yet I, with three daughters gone, never receive any letters," she complained as she saw her daughters engulfed in their mail. "With all that reading and scribbling, it is no wonder I never see you girls about the house anymore." She was thinking mostly of Kitty who, from the very onset of her return to Longbourn, behaved in a distant manner.

Quite the reverse, upon their return, Mrs Bennet promptly arranged for small socials with friends and neighbors creating a means by which to boast of her days in London and Pemberely. She would speak of her emerald necklace and, most of all, about her success in finding a potential son in law in the aristocratic Sir Jon. Mrs Bennet wanted Kitty to join her in some of her engagements to thereby allow her guests to envy her evermore as she would speak of her good fortune. She urged Kitty to break out of her trance just long enough to help spread the word, declaring that two wagging tongues were quicker than one, but Kitty profoundly declined. There was no possible way she would sit and listen to talk of Sir Jon when Dr Kindrel weighed so heavily on her mind.

"Where are you going Kitty? I had hoped you would linger about the house today. Mrs Long, Lady Lucas and your aunt Philips shall arrive soon! I have arranged for them to pay me a social call. It is the first of its kind since my return. We shall have a splendid time talking over all the news of Meryton dating back to when I first left. You must stay and join us," insisted Mrs Bennet.

"Mama, I have never joined you before and have no interest in news of Meryton since I am never allowed in town these days anyway," answered Kitty disapprovingly.

"It is not to receive gossip that I invite you to sit in but to deliver it. I have it all planned," she said with merriment sitting Kitty next to her as she would a trusted confidant. "First, I shall boast of Jane's endearing, darling twins. They are by far the grandest pair of children Hertfordshire has ever seen if I do say so myself. Then, when Mrs Long has completely resigned to the fact that she cannot compete with her lone grandson, I shall address Lizzy's insufferable task of governing the expansive, flawless estate of Pemberley and go into vast detail of all its glory and Mr Darcy's ardent love for her. I shall mention Mr Bennet's necklace, let them view it, of course, and then," she said grabbing Kitty's hands with excitement, "to throw them into a head spin, I shall end with my account of the impeccably, refined Sir Jon!" she squealed with exaltation. "That is where you come in. You can talk about how handsome he is and how every woman at the ball sought out his attentions, but he desired only you as his chosen partner. I shall sit back nonchalantly to observe Mrs Long and count the shades of green as they appear on her face. It will be more than she could endure! Oh, it promises to provide so much entertainment and amusement! Mrs Philips and I are sure to laud over it for many months to come!"

"Mama, I will not speak so of Sir Jon," declined Kitty standing to leave the room as hastily as possible.

"Don't be so timid Kitty. We are only speaking the truth, and when he proposes, I will handle all the bragging by myself," assured Mrs Bennet.

"What makes you believe he will propose? And if he does, what makes you think I shall accept? You should not depend that I would," refuted Kitty.

"Why shall I not depend on it for even one moment?" berated Mrs Bennet. "He is a rich, able handsome aristocrat and he has exhibited a definite interest in you and you will not refuse him for people would think you unstable. But do not be so somber Kitty. I don't know why you doubt yourself. He shall write soon and set your mind at ease. Have more confidence in yourself. I saw how constant he was to you. He remained at your side the whole stay!" she said comforting her daughter. "Your coquetries were very successful. You have made me so proud," she said with brilliance giving Kitty a kiss on the forehead. "But that is enough of that, for I must remember to remind Mrs Philips to prevent Lady Lucas from buffering the impact of my chronicles. She is so kind and empathetic that she would not allow me to antagonize Mrs Long for any significant length of time. Well, go on with yourself, Kitty, you need not stay after all. She might divert you and change the direction of everything, for she is very clever like that!" dismissed Mrs Bennet. "Hill!" she called leaving Kitty in the parlor. "Hill, you must not rush with the meats when the guests arrive . . . ." can be heard as she faded into the kitchen. Kitty just sighed, feeling totally inundated by the whole affair.

*   *   *

After a few days of moping around the park to avoid Mrs Bennet, Kitty found her only solace was in keeping entirely to herself. She strolled about the small grounds and sat at the swing where she and Lydia spent most of their time together a few years past. The gust of the wind had therapeutic effects on her as she swung back and forth recalling when lovesick soldiers used to push them to and fro. Absorbed in her memories, she suddenly realized that she had totally overlooked a great ally in her cause. She could not believe her oversight! 'How could I not have thought of her before! My sister Lydia Wickham! Wife of a military man! Resident of a military encampment!' She jumped off the swing with revived spirits and without losing a moment, wrote to her sister in Newcastle. Her letter read:

Dear Lydia

We have recently returned from Lady Georgiana's wedding. It was lovely and all went well. But do forgive me for not giving you the fullest detail about it now. It is not my purpose in writing you. I have met a man who, I confess, I have fallen deeply in love with. His name is Dr Alexander Kindrel and he is presently touring with the militia to instruct the physicians on his unique techniques in medicine. I did not know how much I loved him until now that we are parted and are most likely never to see each other again. During the wedding, I wished so much that I was reciting my vows to him but became speechless at the opportunity to tell him when I saw him standing there for the first time in beautiful regimentals. I couldn't move at the sight of him. Lydia, I shall come to visit you if he should come by your camps for, although I am sure Papa would not like it, I would surely attain his consent when he knows why I depart. Please write with any news you hear of him. My heart is aching. Your sister,

Kitty

The days seemed to pass slowly for Kitty. Mrs Bennet could not understand the urgency Kitty displayed as she waited for the dispatcher but decided to dismiss it by attributing her daughter's impatience as a sign for a long awaited word from Sir Jon. Finally, Kitty received a response from Lydia.

160

Dear Kitty,

Isn't love grand? It is the best feeling in the world. I am so glad to hear you have finally found someone. I was beginning to lose all hope for you. If you could have visited us last summer, as I have repeatedly extended the invitation, you would have already been in love and probably married by now. The single men are so friendly and stand proud in their red coats. If I have not been happily married these past three years, I could have very well become taken in by any of the handsome faces I see daily. However, my duty is to my Ensign Wickham and to my marriage, which in itself, is wonderful. I can recommend the institution very highly. It gives us women liberties you know not yet. My Wickham continues to be very successful in the militia and has hopes of becoming a Lieutenant soon but finds he cannot make the promotion stationed here. It seems his friends are not what he thought they were and, as the army has it, you need connections to make your advancements feasible. We are continuing on to another encampment as soon as we are able. My Wickham has already put in a request. By the way, it will give me lots of pleasure to search for your Dr Kindrel in my new situation as he is not here. You can count on me to make a thorough investigation and write as soon as I can if I learn anything.

Do not worry yourself about describing Lady Georgiana's ball. My Wickham and I have not thought about it. I am sure it must have been as drab and droll as the Darcys themselves. Poor Lizzy. Give Mama my best and tell Papa we look forward to hearing from him as well.

Mrs Lydia Wickham

Kitty's hopes fell as she would have to wait longer still. It was agonizingly painful for her as she discovered she did not possess a very patient nature when it came to personal matters of the heart and coping with Mrs Bennet's excessive babbling to the neighbors about Sir Jon made it too much to endure. 'She already hosted three teas for the bragging. And if I don't find Dr Kindrel soon, I am going to have to marry Sir Jon or how can I ever refuse him now?'

*   *   *

In Lyme, Miss de Bourgh shared her letter from Mary with Lady Catherine, never expecting her mother to react in such an irate manner. Lady Catherine could not believe her daughter was not only communicating with one of the Bennet girls but referring to her as a true friend.

"Do you not realize that the Bennets are the lowest of our class? What could be their objective, if not to elevate themselves and gain footage into our level of society as they have done with the older two girls? I shall not sit idly and allow them to use my own daughter when I so adamantly oppose it. They have cunning and have taken advantage of you as they have done to our Mr Darcy," she said outraged. "You must stop all correspondence with this Miss Bennet at once! You are forbidden to write to her again!" she demanded. "The liberties those girls take are inconceivable!"

"But Mother, Mary is a sincere friend to me. Has she not informed us that Mr Carrington is in Charmouth? Has she not told us that Miss Bingley is with him? This is important to know and we would never have found out otherwise," explained Anne.

"We would have done well on our own in finding Mr Carrington. And what is this business about Miss Bingley? Why should his being with her be of consequence to us? He is already promised to you. Lord Carrington has made it his specific wish and it shall be carried out. You have formerly met him and made the connection, there is nothing more to the matter than that. It is that simple."

"Mother, Miss Bingley has been attempting to impress Mr Carrington since Pemberley. She has given me a difficult time by merely standing near him. If she is in Charmouth with him, they may very well return engaged as she is sure to work with expediency to impound him."

"This will not happen again!" declared Lady Catherine with eyes bulging. "I shall not become victim to the blatant disregard this modern generation displays for contracts, good manners and protocol. Miss Bingley shall not take possession of Mr Carrington. Your slighting will not be repeated. I will see to that! According to this letter they are to return to Lyme within the week. They can be arriving any day now. We shall wait until then to set matters straight," she confirmed indignantly.

Regretfully, Miss de Bourgh ceased corresponding with Mary as Lady Catherine ordered. Days passed with the de Bourghs in Lyme and still no sign of Mr Carrington.

Lady Catherine continued to send her footman to make the inquiries at every inn and lodging in Lyme. Every clerk and innkeeper was to notify her at once, should Mr Carrington take residency in their establishment. For their part, she and Miss de Bourgh remained conspicuously in the public eye, making Lady Catherine especially uncomfortable. She did not appreciate the late August sun's intense rays beating down on her unscrupulously. They walked to the Cobbs where it was cooler, pausing only when they needed rest. Fervently, they sought out signs of Mr Carrington but it was always to no avail until one day, as Lady Catherine and Miss de Bourgh took their daily constitutional on the highly populated main street, they encountered Miss Bingley and Mrs Hurst deeply involved in conversation. Lady Catherine stood directly in their path demanding their attention.

"Lady Catherine! Miss de Bourgh! What a pleasant surprise seeing you here at Lyme! I had no idea you were to join us in our little bay," exclaimed Caroline in surprise.

"That is quite understandable for it was not planned," admitted Lady Catherine. "As you can deduce, the sun is not very good for delicate complexions such as ours and we are not here for the plunge. Anne and I have come here purely on business."

"Actually, the sun is doing wonders for Miss de Bourgh. She looks quite beautiful with her sunkissed glow. Where are you staying?" asked Mrs Hurst trying to remain composed.

"Our accomodations are at the Red Sea Gull. They are not what they should be since the season began before we arrived. We had no reservations but it will do for the time being. The season is beginning sooner than usual, I dare say, though I do not see the benefit of it," Lady Catherine said coolly. "Tell me Miss Bingley, we have been searching for Mr Carrington. I am aware you travel in his company. You must inform me as to his lodgings as I must arrange a meeting with him concerning an urgent message from his father."

"Mr Carrington is indeed traveling in the company of Mr Hurst and myself but he has not arrived in Lyme from Charmouth as of yet. We expect him to join us shortly. Please trust us to deliver your message to meet with him the moment he arrives," replied Mrs Hurst nudging Caroline into agreement.

"That will do very well. You may deliver that message as you wish. However, I shall send him an additional notice when I get back to my rooms. This way you may continue on with your own errands without further concern for my affairs. I fear they would be forgotten since you seemed to be in such a rush," suggested Lady Catherine. "Now, where is he to stay here in Lyme?"

Informed of his apartments in the distinguished Sandy Nook, they said their goodbyes and went their separate ways. Satisfied that communications with Mr Carrington would soon be at hand, Lady Catherine, not seeing the need to walk any further than necessary, instructed Miss de Bourgh to return with her to their rooms. "You see, Anne, we did not need the aide of outsiders like that Miss Bennet. Working through your own people shall always bring about positive results. We are bred with a deeply rooted sense of respect, decency and honesty that lacks in the lower classes."

As for the sisters, when they were far enough away from the de Bourghs, Caroline turned cravenly toward Mrs Hurst. "I was dumbfounded when you told Lady Catherine Mr Carrington was not here in Lyme! I would never have been able to fabricate such deception!"

"Lady Catherine's business with Mr Carrington's father could only mean that she has set her eyes on Mr Carrington to marry her daughter and here you are, so close to converting Mr Carrington from a mere acquaintance to a devouted fiancé! You have been seen everywhere with him and those in our society expect him to make a declaration soon. We cannot let Lady Catherine interfere with the security of your future. As distasteful as it is to deceive a long time acquaintance as Lady Catherine, we must continue with our deception. We will allow their reunion only after you have announced your engagement. In the name of self preservation we cannot otherwise risk the encounter."

"Oh, agreed! It must be done. I see no other way. How are we to proceed?" asked Caroline.

"We must have Mr Carrington removed from Lyme immediately!" said Mrs Hurst.

"Shall we tell him you left something back at Charmouth and have urgent need of it? He is courteous enough to retrieve it," suggested Caroline.

"No, he might see through the deception when there is nothing to recover. Let us say we are to meet Lady Georgiana in Pinny. We can say she is expecting us tomorrow and we did not realize it until now. He will not wish to disappoint them. Now, we must return to our lodging posthaste to intercept Lady Catherine's note."

"But we are late for our luncheon appointment with Mr Carrington. I will go on ahead and say you cannot make it," conspired Caroline.

"Keep him out as late as you can. I am sure Lady Catherine will not spend one moment without dispatching her note to Mr Carrington. I shall stay at the lodge all day if necessary until it arrives. He will not be the wiser," said Mrs Hurst turning back to the rooms.

True to their expectations, a letter was left for Mr Carrington later that afternoon. Mrs Hurst skillfully recovered it saying Mr Carrington knew of the message and asked her to retrieve it for him. Lady Catherine, never doubting their cooperation, did not realize a great ruse was underway. Two whole days passed by before she finally made a visit to the lodging herself. Once there, she was notified of the party's unexpected departure.

"How dare they escape Lyme without notifying me," she fumed when the clerk informed her of their departure. "Their conduct is inexcusable as they have willfully undermined my authority. Such insubordination is unacceptable!"

"They are returning within the week, Madame. Perhaps you can see them then," explained the humble clerk. "They asked me to keep the rooms available for them and have paid me well to do so!"

"I see. Very well.When they return, you are to notify me without their knowledge. I shall take care of those crafty felines myself," she said as she placed some coins in the clerk's hand.

Chapter 11

M rs Bennet was occupied directing Hill with the housekeeping while Kitty languished about the house waiting for the post to arrive. When the carrier came to the door, Kitty secured the mail before the servants. She shuffled through the letters hurriedly until she found what she was looking for—a letter from Lydia.

She ran up to her room and impatiently ripped it open. Lydia wrote:

Dear Kitty,

I am sorry to have taken so long to write you again. My dearest Ensign Wickham will do his best to locate your Dr Kindrel as he has renewed hopes of finding an endorser in him at Warminster. I have spoken to some of the wives at our farewell party who said friends of theirs have heard of your Dr Kindrel. He has a growing reputation amongst the troops and dances with all the ladies of worth. I am told he is a favorite amongst them. Alas, I had every intention of finding out more about your doctor, but as things go, I found myself interested in discovering what assemblies, public recreations and entertainment our new encampment would bring. Before I realized it the evening events were at a close. I am sorry to say I shall not be seeing them again before our removal as I

am so busy with our packing! I have enclosed a tally for Papa.
Tell him not to forget us.

Mrs Lydia Wickham

Reading this most coveted letter caused Kitty more anquish than
ever before. 'It is all so defeating to hear he is a favorite amongst the
ladies. It's not fair! It's not possible!'

She lay on her bed and wondered, 'Can I depend on Lydia or Ensign
Wickham to track him down? If they do, what could they tell him when
I alone have to tell him I was wrong to have argued with him our last
night together? I alone have to tell him that I love him. But how will he
be convinced after the way I treated him. I never gave him a sign or the
inclination that I felt this way about him. How could I when I did not
detect it myself, although I loved him all along and still do while he is
dancing every night, certain to fall into one of those women's snares.
Why is he wasting his time dancing? Why isn't he thinking of me when
I cannot do otherwise but think only of him? To be certain, they are
all vying for him! How could they resist? They are only human!' she
thought with heavy heart and wrenching tears. 'Men are so unassuming
where women are concerned. He must be told he can belong to no other
but me!' The hollow in her chest and the green in her eyes deepened
as she continued to sob. 'Even now, some horrible detestable freckle
face woman is certain to trap my innocent, naïve doctor and seize upon
him. And she won't be as difficult as I was,'she groaned. 'He is lost to
me forever. Ah me! What have I done? How could I have let him go?'
She cried incessantly into her pillow until she fell into a melancholy
slumber.

After a short respite of quiet reflection, Kitty believed her doctor
lost to her forever. 'With all his social distractions, a man so attractive,
charming and agreeable, he shall certainly be ambushed in the blink of
an eye. Even if I were there, in his most cherished presence, my chances
would remain remote. There is no other option for me as Lydia does
not provide consoling news and Mama would never prefer a doctor to

a Baronet. She is already persuaded. In so much as Mama could never have stopped me from uniting with Dr Kindrel, the reality that all hope of winning him remains in vain. Clearly, there is nothing else to do now. It is settled. I must marry Sir Jon.

*   *   *

That evening, in Lyme, the Hursts were the first to return from Pinny as they came ahead of Miss Bingley and Mr Carrington. Mrs Hurst asked the clerk for any letters that were addressed to her party. The clerk handed her a note in her name.

"Is there anything for anyone else of my party? For Mr Carrington perhaps?" she inquired.

"Yes Madame, but with all due respect, I am under strict orders to deliver it to Mr Carrington himself," responded the clerk.

"I am certain the sender did not mean that I could not take possession of it. You can be sure I shall make certain he receives it," she urged.

"I am very sorry but it is of the utmost importance that he receives it personally," he said nervously shaking his head. Mrs Hurst became increasingly agitated.

"Our coach is returning to Pinny to retrieve him for us. If it is that crucial, I must read it to inform him of its contents since he shall be late in his arrival and precious time may be lost. If it will provide you with more comfort, you may retake possession of it and redeliver it to Mr Carrington himself when he returns but I fear he would not appreciate it if it was something so urgent that I could have informed him about in good time."

Convinced by her argument, the clerk thought it best to allow her to read the letter for its content and replace it in its cubby to wait for Mr Carrington's arrival. From his perspective, it would do no harm but hopefully, be of service. Mrs Hurst read the letter and returned it to the clerk with some monetary compensation. In the end, the clerk thought himself happy to have performed the courtesy.

The note said:

Mr Carrington

I have a personal message to deliver to you from Lord Carrington. It concerns your immediate future and a specific wish of his. It is most urgent that I see you since your father and I oblige you to perform a certain duty where my family is concerned. I am waiting for your response at the Red Sea Gull. Please come alone. The message is for your ears only.

Lady Catherine de Bourgh

Mrs Hurst went up the stairs preoccupied with formulating a plan to intercept the note from Mr Carrington. She removed her hat and looked out the window in deep concentration before she even remembered her own letter. Finally, sitting on the bed she opened it to read:

Mrs Hurst and Miss Bingley

I am departing for Rosings but have no intention of leaving without seeing you one last time. Please accept my invitation for refreshments in my rooms at the Red Sea Gull. I am eager to see you both.

Lady Catherine de Bourgh

No sooner did she finish the letter when Caroline entered the room. "We are summoned to Lady Catherine. She will not leave Lyme until we visit her," said Mrs Hurst as she waved the letter under her chin.

"What should we do? Do you think she figured out what we did?" asked Caroline apprehensively.

"She would not have us over for refreshments if she did. She has also summoned Mr Carrington to call on her at the inn at his own time separate from us. It concerns 'his future and family business' and we know what that means," she said definitively. Mrs Hurst continued as Caroline was eager to hear what their next move would be. "Since she will not leave without first seeing us, we should not avoid her. If she brings up Mr Carrington we will have no alternative but to confront her on it once and for all. She will lose out and stop pursuing him since we, indisputably, have him in full possession. I believe we can see her for refreshments without Mr Carrington's knowledge. Fortunately, he is slow to put one and one together, after all, in all this time he has not yet asked you for your hand. What does he wait for?" she said very annoyed with him.

"We have an understanding," explained Caroline. "Sometimes words don't need to be spoken. Nevertheless, I feel he will propose in good time. Why else would he remain in my company? You are right, Lady Catherine must not interfere. Not after all this hard work."

"Well, if we can carry this out properly, you shall be free to wait as long as you need to," assured Mrs Hurst.

"Then let us go visit Lady Catherine tomorrow while Mr Carrington rests from his journey. Then we can enjoy our stay for the rest of the season newly liberated," stated Caroline with high expectations.

*　　*　　*

Lady Catherine was informed by her footman that Mrs Hurst and Caroline had indeed returned and soon after received a note saying:

Dearest Lady Catherine

Miss Bingley and I are honored you have waited for our return before departing for Rosings. Truly, you shouldn't have. However, we would be most pleased to accept your invitation. It gives us the opportunity to share some happy information with you, as you will be the first to know about Miss Bingley and Mr Carrington. We shall call upon you tomorrow. Please send confirmation.

Mrs Hurst and Miss Bingley

The confirmation was sent and Caroline and Mrs Hurst arrived at Lady Catherine's lodging in due time. "Come in," invited Lady Catherine. "I have been looking forward to seeing you. Please be seated. I shall be with you in a moment."

Lady Catherine discharged Miss de Bourgh telling Caroline and Mrs Hurst that she had her refreshments and a long constitutional would benefit her at this time as she had grown accustomed to the exertion. Miss de Bourgh left eagerly, knowing full well what was in store for the sisters.

The day was particularly hot as she strolled down the main street that led to the Cobbs. Her stride was taken in a slow leisurely manner allowing her every opportunity to enjoy the breeze blowing in from the waters that cooled the air ever so slightly. She ambled all the way to where the water seemed to come right up to the walk. As the waves crashed she closed her eyes to escape in thought and listen to the rambunctious screeches of the seagulls while drawing in the salt air with long deep breaths.

"Miss de Bourgh!" called someone from behind. "Miss de Bourgh! Hello there," said Mr Carrington as he stood watching her. "I hope I am not interfering with your soaking in of the fresh air but I am delightfully surprised to see you. I did not know you were in town until today. I hope you don't think it forward of me to approach you here at the Cobbs, in this way."

"On the contrary, Mr Carrington, I am very pleased to see you," welcomed Miss de Bourgh. She was taken by surprise and flustered about as she spoke.

"I see the sun has left its affect on you with a smart kiss of blush on your cheek. It does become you," he complimented enjoying her presence once again.

"Thank you," she blushed. Not used to receiving compliments, she felt more comfort in changing the subject quickly. "We have come here at the request of your father. My mother is inclined to speak to you on his behalf as soon as she could."

"Yes, I just received the message from Lady Catherine," admitted Mr Carrington, "and I was about to call on her in your lodgings to leave my card when I spotted you. I hope my father is well. Either way, I will be seeing him soon as I have every intention of returning to Greenfield Castle earlier than planned. Would you like to proceed with me back toward your lodging?"

"Actually, Mother is hosting a small party at this moment which is why I am out. She would prefer to entertain alone without interruption."

"Well then, if you would do me the honor, I would be in receipt of the greatest of pleasures if you would enjoy some refreshments with me. I should like to know what you have been doing since our last encounter at Pemberely. If we make haste, we may make it in time for a delicious snack at a nearby bakery," he said offering her his arm.

"Thank you. I would enjoy that very much," admitted Miss de Bourgh as she accepted his arm allowing him to lead the way.

The two spent a glorious afternoon together. They enjoyed each other's company so well they did not want to separate. Mr Carrington was reluctant to return her home as he did not know when they could meet like this again. He gave her his card to present to Lady Catherine saying, "She must inform me as to when it will be convenient to visit as it will be my pleasure to meet with her at anytime." Then he added, "Miss de Bourgh, I wish I would have met you sooner." Miss de Bourgh thought it an odd closing statement and not knowing what to make of it, responded with her winning bashful smile.

It was well into the evening when Miss de Bourgh returned home to find Lady Catherine vexed and disparaged. "Mrs Hurst and Miss Bingley are a pair of the most ill mannered brazen impertinent women I have ever known! They appall me! Those kind of people who do not honor convention have no place in our world, Anne. They are a threat to our very way of life. But fear not! Their reptutation shall go before them as I will ruin their name in proper society. After all, it will cause the decline of our culture if I do not do my duty in exposing them."

"Should I refrain to ask what happened?" offered Miss de Bourgh still feeling the delightful after effects of an entire afternoon with Mr Carrington.

"My dear, dear Anne, it has been revealed. Mr Carrington has shown significant interest in the unscrupulous Miss Bingley and she in him. In total disregard for any code of behavior they hope to announce their engagement very soon now as she will not give him up," she said disappointedly. "Well, no one can say that I don't learn from past experiences. When Mr Carrington visits I will only tell him his father has asked me to remind him that he awaits his prompt arrival, anxious for first hand news of meeting us. I will not inform him of the contract because he will disregard it as Mr Darcy had done before him and I will not put us in the destitute position of being humiliated all over again."

"Mother, I have spent these few hours with Mr Carrington. We came upon each other by chance at the Cobbs. He took me to eat and we talked for all this time. Be assured that I have found him as receptive of me as I am of him. Please do not yield yet. I cannot believe he doesn't care, as I have seen his fondness for me upon his face and I, too, have already developed an affection for him. Here, he has given me his card to present to you as you have requested a visit from him so do not alter your initial intent, Mother. I would like to give it my best effort before we concede," she said boldly. Lady Catherine was speechless. She did not expect to hear Anne make such a case when she was, herself, already predisposed to acquiesce.

"Anne," stated Lady Catherine with tender sincerity, "I would never have placed you in this situation if I thought it would end up this way. It saddens me beyond words. There is no greater stress than a mother, whose intentions, though well meant, continue to fall short. The world is rapidly changing and the younger generation no longer possess any sense of honor or consequence. No sensibilities toward decency. I shutter at the Bingley's unscrupulous conscience and fear that whatever you do will not rise to the challenge. We can no longer stand on principles as lover's bonds have recently become impenetrable. We must submit to the energies issued by two people determined to marry. They cannot be broken up. I assure you, this would not have happened in my time! However, if you feel you must make an attempt before we return to Rosings, I will not refuse you. If you will be reconciled that you have not relinquished him without one last attempt, so be it. It is the least I can do, although it will not ease my sorrow. But beware of Miss Bingley. Do not expect any cooperation from her as she will counteract any advancement and not let him out of her sight now that I have revealed our motives."

"I must have time to think, Mother," she said as she went to her room. She sat to reflect for a while before she came to another decision. Honoring her restriction against writing to Miss Bennet, Miss de Bourgh took hold of a quill and paper and wrote to Daniel. Her letter read:

Dear Daniel

I am still in Lyme and have reason to believe Mr Carrington and I would live in wedded bliss if Miss Bingley could be eliminated from our little circle. Mother has already attained Lord Carrington's approval to the marriage but Miss Bingley's constant interference has almost made us lose all hope. Please tell me what you think I should do. You and Miss Bennet have always been there for me in the past and I trust in your friendship to be here for me now. Do not hesitate to share this letter with Miss Bennet, for I cannot communicate with her at this time. I shall do nothing until I hear from you but please write back with haste. Mother has lost her patience. Your Friend

Miss Anne de Bourgh

*   *   *

Daniel wasted no time forwarding the letter to Mary with a request for her urgent input. He agreed that Miss Bingley had to be hindered in order to give Miss de Bourgh the opportunity she needed to see for herself if Mr Carrington and she could form an attachment.

Remembering the astute Miss Bingley caused Mary to become deeply concerned for Miss de Bourgh. It was a distress call that demanded the assistance of unfailing expertise. To do this right, she required the aid of someone with years of experience and profound abilities. Someone infallible, in whom there was a special talent, someone like her mother!

"Mama, please read this letter and give your advice. Miss de Bourgh, Daniel and I are in dire need of your excellent counsel and superior tactics in redirecting a man's heart into the path of a most deserving young lady. I can think of no one as adept as you in these matters. Please, read on and tell me if you think we can aid her with some of your insight."

Mrs Bennet examined the letter eagerly. "At last! A letter for me!" she said joyfully. She was delighted to be of service and read it through quickly. She asked Mary to fill in the details of their days in Pemberley when the Bingley sisters thwarted their every chance to get together.

After hearing enough Mrs Bennet turned to Mary with the oddest expression on her face. "I am so proud of you, Mary," she blurted with glee. "I never thought you had any concern for these affairs, yet, here, right before my very eyes, you have blossomed into the very young lady I had hoped you would be."

"It is not for me, Mama, but for a dear friend," clarified Mary before her mother would get carried away.

"I can see that! It is just that I was convinced you had turned a cold heart to the business as I believed the subject of marriage abandoned by you," explained Mrs Bennet.

"Lately, I have found it terribly intriguing, only I am not as skilled as you are. So, what do you think Mama, is there hope here?"

"Mary, you are the novice, which is precisely what you get for snubbing your nose at it for all these years. But I forgive you since a little cooperation from you should increase your prospects tremendously. Now, let us make a visit to Netherfield. Observe your Mama and learn," said Mrs Bennet with unbridled giddiness. "You may have need of such skills for yourself one day."

Mrs Bennet and Mary arrived in Netherfield unannounced finding Mr and Mrs Bingley together in the parlor keeping out of the noon sun. Mrs Bennet wasted no time setting her plan in motion.

"Where are my lovely grandchildren, Jane? I have thought of them and desired to see them immediately."

"They are coming, Mama. They have just finished their lunch and are being cleaned up by the nurses," explained Jane.

"The little darlings! Do tell me, Mr Bingley, when do you plan to christen them as it is a sincere concern of mine? I understand you have delayed because of your sojourn to Pemberley and because of your desire to baptize them in Netherfield, but time is wasting! It must be done as soon as possible as they are many months old now," said Mrs Bennet with consternation.

"We are waiting for the return of the Hursts and Miss Bingley. We cannot have this done without them. As you know, Mr and Mrs Hurst will be the godparents to Master Charles while Mr and Mrs Darcy will be the godparents to young Elizabeth. You see, we have been mindful of it. The Darcys can come to Netherfield at a moments notice but we do not want to interrupt the others' holiday," answered Jane for her husband.

"But you must realize the children are at stake here. Surely you do not honor a holiday as having priority to baptism!" continued Mrs Bennet. "The way illnesses spread so rapidly, it is shocking to me that you would take such a chance with your firstborn. Don't you agree Mr Bingley?" she pressed knowing full well he would be easily persuaded.

"You are right, Mrs Bennet. There is no need to wait longer. We should arrange for the baptism as soon as possible. We have often discussed it with our pastor, as he has made similar claims."

"Yes, we must call the family together from Lyme and Pemberley. It is of utmost importance to have this performed with haste," said Jane equally alarmed as she remembered her propensity for illness. "Our poor defenseless babies. We shall not delay any longer. I will send christening notices to the Darcys, the Hursts and Miss Bingley with the afternoon post. We shall restrict the affair to the family. It will be quicker that way," Jane declared.

"You are thoughtful parents," commented Mrs Bennet glancing slyly at Mary. The children entered the room carried in by their nurses. Mrs Bennet ran to them full of mirth. Her grandchildren were her pride and joy after all, they were to inherit Netherfield and all of Mr Bingley's fortune.

*　　*　　*

Mary sent a response directly to Miss de Bourgh not realizing that Lady Catherine demanded an end to their correspondence. Miss de Bourgh received the information she was searching for. The letter Mary sent her read:

Dear Miss de Bourgh

Daniel has shared your letter with me as you have allowed. You were right to depend on us. I have taken up your dilemma with Mama. She is an expert in these matters and has solved the problem of Mrs Hurst and Miss Bingley with ease. By the time you receive this letter, the Bingley sisters will be hastily called away to Netherfield. Do not be alarmed for it is with the happiest of occasions that they have been collected. Mama has arranged for the baptism of Charles and Elizabeth. The Hursts are to be the godparents and Miss Bingley cannot shun the invite. They will be confined to Netherfield for at least one week. Mama says if Mr Carrington is interested, you would know by then. Of course she wishes she were there to direct you but trusts your mother will know what to do if you ask her for help. We wish you the best of luck. Your friend,&c

Miss Mary Bennet

Miss de Bourgh sent a footman to investigate the whereabouts of the Hursts and Miss Bingley. As expected, they were suddenly called away, leaving Mr Carrington behind as he was leaving to return to Greenfield Castle. She then asked her mother to request an audience with Mr Carrington that very evening. The footman was dispatched with an invitation to dine and returned saying, "Mr Carrington gratefully accepts."

"Anne, how is it you have devised such a cunning plot? I am amazed at your abilities," remarked Lady Catherine.

"I put my trust in the devoted friendship of Daniel and Miss Bennet," she began. "I did not write to Miss Bennet as you have requested but Daniel acquired her help when I wrote to him about my dilema."

"You cannot possibly be serious! How could you involve others in your affairs, Anne? It was not prudent," said Lady Catherine still mindful of the success of her application. "There will be a price to pay."

"They befriended me when I was most insecure and withdrawn by my shyness at Pemberley. We spent all our time there together and have become very close. I knew I could trust them with this matter as they are as concerned for my happiness as much as you are. Miss Bennet went so far as to enlist the aid of her mother who graciously indulged us by requiring the Bingley's to have the children's baptismal sooner rather than later. Mrs Bennet was very pleased to do this for me requiring nothing in return," explained Anne.

"No, Anne, they do require something. They want to earn your confidence and assert their influence on you, taking what they can until they are through," her mother protested.

"Not true Mother, Mrs Bennet instructs me to rely on you for help."

"This is a revelation," admitted Lady Catherine stunned by the news. "I must admit the whole affair has given me much to consider as the matter has not left you unchanged. I must give this some more thought before I comment further. For now, we must entertain Mr Carrington and see once and for all where he stands on the subject of marriage and Miss Bingley."

"There is one more thing Mother. Please do not bring the marriage contract up to Mr Carrington. I insist that, if I am to marry him, he must care for me as much as I do for him. I shall not marry just for the companionship of a man and thanks to you I do not need to marry for financial security or social standing. I have seen the life two people can share when they are in love, at Pemberley with the Watneys, the Bingleys and the Darcys. I cannot desire less than that for myself."

"You have become an independent young lady, Anne, and I admire that. I will honor your request. It is, after all, your life and I have not done too well by you thus far where that is concerned," she said surrendering.

"Whatever are you saying, Mother. You have always done your best. I have nothing but the utmost love and respect for you. Everything will fall into place. You will see." With that, Anne kissed her mother on the cheek and ran to her room to dress for dinner.

*　　*　　*

Mr Carrington met the de Bourghs at Lady Catherine's inn promptly as scheduled. He was glad to be in the esteemed company of his charming Miss de Bourgh once again. Lady Catherine, already seated in a secluded corner of the dining area, welcomed him cordially. The evening commenced with the innocuous topic of Lord Carrington.

"I am extremely grateful you have sat by my father's side while I was away. I was very comforted with the knowledge of it. I am anxious to see him again and prepare to leave Lyme sooner than I thought."

"I should think you would stay the season through," remarked Miss de Bourgh.

"The landscape is remarkable and relaxing but I find there is nothing quite as satisfying for me as the chalky cliffs of Dover with its beautiful seaside," he described fondly as if he was already back home. "I have traveled extensively and, upon my word, I have discovered that I am not as equally overcome by anything I have seen yet. Lyme's coast was my last sojourn and I am full ready to go home now."

"The sights may not be of interest to you but you must admit the society has been satisfying, has it not?" asked Lady Catherine desiring to get on with it.

"I have made new acquaintances everywhere I've traveled and I hope I have left everyone with a satisfactory perception of me, but I confess, my thoughts always revert to my humble home, and the watchful care of my father. I have not been compelled by anyone or anything to do otherwise than return to Dover," he admitted.

"It is said you are constantly in the company of the Hursts and Miss Bingley. May I be so bold as to inquire, if there is not an attachment between you and Miss Bingley that would compel you to delay your return?" asked Lady Catherine.

"I have been in their company since Pemberley, it is true, but I have remained with them only because they continue to invite me to follow and I deemed it rude to decline since Mr Hurst implored me to accompany them, for he needed an additional male escort to make a convenient foursome of the group. And I can see why for I must say that where I thought we were journeying to Lyme for a prolonged stay, we have done nothing but commute from place to place and I am considerably tired out. They are social creatures and the energies of that lifestyle are not to my liking. These past few weeks alone I have been carted from Lyme to Charmouth to Lyme to Pinny and back to Lyme again. That is not my idea of fun nor can I continue in that fashion for the rest of my life as, I gather, is the custom of that family. To be blunt, there is no validity in the claim of an attachment and if it is said, I would like it to come to an abrupt halt. Why, Miss Bingley herself would surely take offense at being part of a rumor bearing no foundation. It should only work against her ever finding someone of her own. That would be an injustice to her as she speaks constantly of getting married!"

"Well, I was inclined to believe it because Lord Carrington had confided in me that you were out and about to make a proper search for a wife, as your Lord fears he would lose his eyesight altogether before he can enjoy his grandchildren. That was my simple message to you, that he remains adamant about your marrying."

"I confess, the women I have met may have been intriguing and even beautiful but they were not to my particular liking. To be frank, I desire one who is settled. A gentle home body. After all, I am most content upon the grounds of my estate and find it inconvenient, even distasteful, to travel about like nomads. Alas, although I have made a serious search, I have not found anyone like that along my crusade."

"She sounds like my Anne," said Lady Catherine jumping at the opportunity to promote her daughter. "She has been confined to her home as a child and to this day is content to remain among her natural surroundings, without having the need to find entertainment elsewhere."

Anne blushed at the mention of her name connected so fittingly with Mr Carrington. She agreed that what her mother stated was accurate but did not think she should be so blunt. Mr Carrington peered at her revealing an unmistakable look of admiration.

"I have learned that about Miss de Bourgh. She is exactly what I am looking for," he admitted, "but finding her already promised to marry has left me with no one as attractive and complete as she."

Miss de Bourgh was astonished. Confused, she did not know how to react. He continued to relay how charming he found her only to be disappointed at the news of her commitment to someone else. Miss de Bourgh was about to speak out for herself when Lady Catherine launched her own remarks.

"Miss de Bourgh is not engaged! Where did you get that impression?" she blared.

"Mrs Hurst and Miss Bingley have told me so," revealed Mr Carrington in bewilderment. "We were waiting to be seated for one of our last dinners at Pemberely when Mrs Hurst offered me her kind advice in turning my attentions elsewhere to prevent an embarrassing rejection. I distinctly remember because I found Miss de Bourgh considerably interesting after one of our long walks in Pemberely and inquired about her to Mrs Hurst. Fortunately Mrs Hurst volunteered the foreboding news." Anne and Lady Catherine were dumbfounded. Miss de Bourgh remained speechless as Lady Catherine found her tongue.

"Scheming, tawdry, spiteful girls! This is insufferable! Has every sort of integrity collapsed right before my very eyes? Oh, how well they wear their deceit but I shall repay their vicious acts of deception and falsehoods with God's pure honest truths. You must allow me to speak," she said catching her breath. "I must reveal to you what has been, of late, very distressing to me. I will be straightforward with it, for you are not attached and there is no reason for sugar coating. You, Mr Carrington, have been in association with two contemptable vixens, and their Mr Hurst is just the same. You have been deflected because of lies that have made you a victim of circumstance as they have led you through a path separate from the truth," she said ranting. "However, their day of reckoning is here. I too thought I knew them well, through Mr Darcy, but now they have shown themselves to be far worse. They are cannibals for they eat their own! Assassins, assassins!" she said uncontrollably agitated. "Well, I shall not go into great detail at this moment of their lurid behavior but they will get theirs. Their consequences will prove most disastrous since I shall see to that! I will make so much noise that all of Europe will speak of it and once our public's eyes are open they will be turned out by high society. I propose you to hold them in deep resentment keeping as far away from them as you can breaking all ties immediately once and for all," warned Lady Catherine with terrific vehemence.

"That is shocking news and I should not be spared any details as I would appreciate the more candid approach of hearing the truths as you know it," declared Mr Carrington anxious to hear everything since he has so thoroughly disclosed his affection for Anne. The discourse continued with the full intelligence of the Hursts' and Miss Bingley's willful misconceptions. It was significantly insightful as they devoted a good portion of their time unraveling the sisters' deceptions. Only as the evening progressed, did they eventually settle on the lighter happier topic of the sharing of good books, dancing and music. Directly after dinner, Mr Carrington requested that Miss de Bourgh escort him for a stroll in the late night air. Anne happily accepted while Lady Catherine was elated to see them out the door.

Mr Carrington requested Miss de Bourgh's faithful companionship for the next few days until, having enough of Lyme, they unanimously agreed to a prompt removal. No consideration was given to the return of the Hursts and Miss Bingley as Lady Catherine announced, "Their return will sour the environment."

Mr Carrington received a persuasive invitation from Lady Catherine to visit at Rosings so their acquaintance may be further extended. Grateful for her offer, he accepted cheerfully, sending his own carriage ahead to Rosings while he joined the de Bourghs in theirs. Lady Catherine was witness to the manner in which Anne and Mr Carrington related. His interest in Anne proved true and her quiet nature was camouflaged by her sincere interest for every word he uttered. When she did speak, it was with freedom and confidence.

'Anne would never have been as content with Mr Darcy,' concluded Lady Catherine overjoyed with the turn of events.

*　　*　　*

As the clomping of the horses drew them closer to Rosings, a servant at Hunsford Parsonage ran to call for Mr Collins as he had instructed them to do upon first sighting Lady Catherine's barouche.

"Excuse me, Mr Collins, sir," said Rebecca with a curtsy. "Lady Catherine's barouche is rapidly approaching."

"Upon my word! Quickly! Make haste and locate Mrs Collins! I want her to be here when they arrive. Lady Catherine will surely desire to stop and speak with me. Go quickly Rebecca!" he said rushing her away.

Ever since he had received Daniel's letter from North Courtlandt detailing how hastily the de Bourghs exited to pursue the coveted Mr

Carrington in Lyme, Mr Collins was fraught with ambiguity for the security of his future and livelihood at Rosings. He was sensible of the wrath of The Honorable Lady Catherine de Bourgh and has seen her give up her own nephew, Mr Darcy, at the drop of a hat—and they are related! What chance would he have as a mere cleric? His failure and disappointments were unacceptable. He had to reestablish his profound deference to her at the very first opportunity to promote her pity in him since he was determined to make amends for all his shortcomings from this point forward.

Mrs Collins was found hanging herbs in the larder when Rebecca came running excitedly saying, "Mrs Collins, ma'am. Mr Collins requests your most urgent presence by the front gate. The de Bourgh's carriage is about to pass the house."

"Thank you, Rebecca," she said as she swiftly placed her herbs on the counter and proceeded out the door. Charlotte ran to the front gate finding Mr Collins pacing about, not knowing where to look first. He was searching for both Charlotte and Lady Catherine, hoping Charlotte would approach before the latter. When Mrs Collins finally arrived at his side, they straightened their attire to look as attentive and indulging as possible.

For all their preparations, the barouche appeared and disappeared more rapidly than they could comprehend. To the Collins' mutual dissatisfaction, the shades were drawn and no one took the liberty to peer out of the windows, let alone slow down. This small act had the adverse effect of advancing an uncontrollable attack of nervous perspiration upon Mr Collins. He could only assume the worse or otherwise, the de Bourghs would have certainly stopped.

"Mrs Collins," he said hanging his head in defeat, "what are we to do now? Lady Catherine cannot tolerate incompetence and I am afraid that is precisely the classification she has placed me in. After all my years of servitude and allegiance! With Mr Bennet still in the peak of health, where are we to go now for we will be destitute? I must write Daniel who boasts of room enough for a family of six and inform him that we are now under his obligation. This is a melancholy paradox, is it not?"

"You must not cart away our furninshings just yet, Mr Collins," replied Charlotte trying to comfort her overwrought husband. "It is not the de Bourgh's custom to stop at our home after a long journey. Lady Catherine has many times gone directly to Rosings. They are true to their character, wouldn't you agree?" she said with a level head.

"That she is, but under these circumstances, after Daniel and I failed her with our clumsy arrangements in an assignment of such vital importance beholding the entire future of her only daughter, this snubbing takes on a whole new meaning! One would think that if all went well she would be agreeable to give me some recognition as she passed by. No Mrs Collins, we are done in for she has been put out by my relations once again." Feeling his energies drain, his body went limp.

"Do not relate it to your brother yet, Mr Collins as there is nothing to lose in waiting until it is evident that we are obligated to do so through some formal notification. In the meantime, the wisest thing to do is to carry on much as before. You will persevere and I will continue with hanging my herbs as I was doing prior to this trifling interruption." With that, Mrs Collins turned and walked diligently back to her work, leaving Mr Collins alone to deal with his own anguish and remorse.

*   *   *

The barouche finally came to rest at Rosings. Mr Carrington, who had not seen it before, noticed the neatly arranged beech trees as they rode down the main road. He viewed the beautiful combination of perinneals and shrubs that carpeted the front of the intimidating brown brick mansion which encompassed Miss de Bourgh's world. The furninshings inside were large, overstuffed and plush, suggesting comfort and richness in every room, very much to his liking.

That evening, Lady Catherine lost no time in instructing Anne on methods to increase and maintain Mr Carrington's interest in her. She suggested Anne carefully measure every word spoken and choreograph her movements to captivate Mr Carrington's curiosity since, as with most men, perception is reality. She progressed with detail, into the guiles a young lady may use to obtain the object of her affection. Only Lady Catherine's seriousness prevented Miss de Bourgh from denying her mother her say. Anne listened dutifully although she knew in her heart that she was already well established with Mr Carrington.

"Do not take his presence here for granted, Anne. You must continue to put full effort into winning him over. He has not committed himself to you as of yet, you know. You can be sure he shall be observing your every move to see how refine you are. Stay on your guard at all times. Men observe when you least expect it."

"Yes, Mother," replied Anne laconically, doubting he would judge her so harshly.

"Make him feel the importance of his presence. Give him your full attention and ask his opinion wherever possible."

"I will try, Mother."

"Don't just try, Anne. You have to do. And do not presume to be more clever than he. A man likes nothing better than to feel his convictions and notions have a place in his prospective's life. He will give his views and if they are tolerable, you should accept them for there should be no nonsense about you."

"I will, of course, take them into consideration, as he shall mine."

"Yes, of course that is true. Your opinion is just as valuable. I do not want you to think it isn't. He is no better than you but your intellect must not be a threat to him. Men have fragile egos. If they are not constantly supported and adulated, they will seek verification elsewhere."

"I should like to think Mr Carrington thinks more of himself than what anyone's opinion can afford," defended Miss de Bourgh knowing full well that Mr Carrington was entirely satisfied with life, despite her, or anyone else's say so.

"I am sorry if you feel my advice is not necessary. I am only trying to help you, Anne. He has been tampered with by two very aggressive, beguiling women and I fear he might be improperly influenced. We should not execute our own undoing at this late stage of the game by some neglect on our part."

Anne thought a little more about what was expected from her and appeased her mother with a verbal acknowledgment. She came to understand that her mother forgot that Mr Carrington must choose her for who she was and nothing less. Anne knew she and Mr Carrington were destined for one another and any façade would have little to do to alter the matter. In conclusion, she would not think of her mother's advice any longer but would concentrate on the exclusive time she would now have to spend with Mr Carrington at Rosings. Whether or not it would end in honoring their marriage contract, she would enjoy these next few days to her best capacity and not defile it with dishonest behavior.

The following days were filled with serene walks throughout the parks and the quiet scrutiny of books. It did not take long before Mr Carrington asked for Miss de Bourgh's hand in marriage. Anne happily obliged. Lady Catherine could not contain her joy as the alleviation of the vile business put her in the spirit of a small celebration.

That afternoon, in light of Anne's success, Lady Catherine sent her servant to the Collinses with the long anticipated summons to dinner. Mrs Collins took the invitation as encouraging news but Mr Collins would not allow his spirits to be bolstered.

"See here, Mrs Collins. The very invitation I have dreaded. Lady Catherine will, no doubt, use this opportunity to see us off. I should have written Daniel when I was first inclined. As it stands, we shall be at his doorstep without the slightest notice."

"Lady Catherine's servant has told our Rebecca that Her Ladyship is in the best of moods and wished to have us to dinner to join in a small celebration," assured Charlotte.

"What was said was that Lady Catherine wished us to come to dinner because she had an urgent notification, of a significant nature, to put on me, after which there shall be a small celebration. This message of such serious nature could only be our removal from the parsonage followed by their saying their adieus with a small celebration for my past services. I am entirely spent, Mrs Collins. Indeed, this is as grave as it gets."

"Dearest, I see no indication of eviction in the likes of remarks such as those. Something is amidst at Rosings and we are now recommended to be part of it. Everything is to be revealed in good time, Mr Collins. You should ease your mind in reference to losing your office here at Hunsford Parsonage. The worry can be doing you no good!" she said patting his hand in an attempt to comfort him.

"I must prepare a formal apology for Lady Catherine. I must ask for forgiveness in falling short of my services to her and her daughter, the delicate Miss de Bourgh. I shall pay her homage and vow to be her most humble servant, caring only for their fullest and complete happiness thoughout the rest of their lives, even before my own. She will be known for her generosity and altruistic abilities for clemency and absolution amidst the worst travesty that ever befell a household at the incompetent hands of their undeserving pastor. I will make mention of Lady Catherine's good graces and unselfish compassion for those beneath her at every sermon from this day forward," he promised. "But now I must go to my office to draft my plea and practice its oration, for only through constant rehearsal can it make the right impact."

"Mr Collins! You must take this time to compose yourself! You are not fit to be seen in the state of mind you are in. A few hours of rest will benefit you greatly, more so than writing a stringent apology," urged Mrs Collins. "You will see. This is much ado about nothing."

"I hope you are correct Mrs Collins, but this is not the time to rest. I will compose nonetheless," said Mr Collins refusing himself the benefit from the comfort of his wife's words. "For all we know, he shall be present at dinner and we will have to avow him of every article of furniture Lady Catherine has charitably allowed us to use. For the first time, I can empathize with Mrs Bennet's feelings of insecurity in losing the very home you had put your good faith and hard work in." Mr Collins staggered to his office while Mrs Collins used her time to sit in the garden to meditate.

At precisely six o'clock, Mr and Mrs Collins were led to Rosings' parlor. Mr Collins froze at the doorway when his eyes fell on a man sitting with his back to the door. His first thought was that the man was the parish's fateful substitute. They stood hearing the cheerful assembly chatting intensely before them about all the changes the near future would bring. It took all the strength he had to gather his wits about him to enter the door. "Mrs Collins, allow me to give you a word of encouragement for it may be too much to bear," he stressed solemnly. "We are not to think of Lady Catherine's words as disabling us but, instead, we should consider it a purification from all things belonging to the world." Mrs Collins nodded with quiet understanding and put her hand out to support her faltering husband.

"Come in Mr Collins! Why are you just standing there in the doorway? Come in and have a seat. We shall be dining very soon but until then you must join our conversations for it does involve you. I trust you have met Mr Carrington in Pemberley during your stay there for Lady Georgiana's wedding," said Lady Catherine motioning the Collinses in from her seat.

"Mr Collins," said Mr Carrington giving him recognition. "Mrs Collins."

The divine discovery of having Mr Carrington seated with the de Bourghs overpowered every feeling of mourning and regret. Mrs Collins smiled readily and expressed her delight in seeing him once more. Mr Collins quickly recovered and broke into his prepared speech trying hard to leave out any parts that dealt with deportations. He was determined to disperse only the passages that extolled Lady Catherine.

"Lady Catherine, allow me to . . ." he groveled.

Lady Catherine, forgiving all his trespasses, was interested only in what she had to say and interrupted him saying, "I have the greatest pleasure in sharing the most wonderful news of Miss de Bourgh's engagement to Mr Carrington. I have summoned you here today to appoint you to deliver their wedding vows the last Sunday of this October. It will be held in our parish as the Honorable Lord Carrington will not be present. Directly following the wedding, the happy couple will proceed to Greenfield Castle and present themselves as man and wife to the village, who will partake in an additional celebration which Lord Carrington shall provide. You will perform the ceremony won't you, Mr Collins?"

"It shall be a tremendous honor to provide the services of holy matrimony to this worthy couple. It is most agreeable for me to play whatever role I can to bring these two together in the eyes of our Lord for no two people were ever more deserving. And you are benevolence itself to allow me to take part in this sacred event, Your Generous Ladyship. I shall begin working on the vows tomorrow, bright and early in the morning. Nay, I shall stay up tonight for I am inspired by the happiness surrounding us this very moment."

Seeing that he would continue without letting up, Lady Catherine rang the dinner bell while he was in mid speech. Everyone went in to dinner where Mr Collins took the first opportunity to propose a toast to the blessed couple as his life, and that of his wife, fell back to their respective routines.

In the afternoon that followed, Mr Collins made a special trip to Rosings to thank Lady Catherine, once again, for involving him in the matrimonial liturgies. Upon his return he sighted Mr Carrington and Miss de Bourgh trying their hand at the bow. He paused for a moment to take in the consummate delight of two winsome lovers enjoying each others company.

Standing there, he noticed that neither one of them possessed any degree of skill in the sport as a stray arrow flew right to him landing just past his feet. He picked it up and took the liberty of returning it while they were still in the midst of their game.

"Here you are!" he shouted holding the arrow up high, waving it so he was sure to be seen running toward them.

"Mr Collins! Where did you come from? We did not see you! You might have been hurt," exclaimed Anne fearfully.

"It is rather foolish to approach a game in progress from the direction of the target, especially when Miss de Bourgh and I are just learning," added Mr Carrington.

"Please, do not mind me. I should prove to be of great assistance to you. In my youth I was very good with the bow. I shot arrows constantly. Please proceed and take aim. I shall advise you on improving your technique and form," volunteered Mr Collins. Miss de Bourgh took aim. "Bring the arrow back a bit more, at shoulder length. That's it. Now don't let go until I am clear of the target," he instructed standing in front of the bow for a better view. Unfortunately, Miss de Bourgh could not hold onto the arrow securely and inadvertently let go. It shot directly toward Mr Collins, scarcely missing his shoulder. "Very good, Miss de Bourgh," said Mr Collins with an uncontrollable twitch of the eye. He ran to collect the arrow and stuck it on the bull's eye of the target. "There you go! Bull's eye!" he said with joyful glee. Miss de Bourgh prepared herself for another shot as Mr Collins ran for cover behind a nearby bush. As expected, none of her arrows hit the target, flying mostly past Mr Collins into the shrubbery.

"Do not worry yourselves. I shall retrieve them," bid Mr Collins as he recaptured the arrows in the bushes. When he returned to the target, he found that he was quite alone with only the servants there to collect the parts as Mr Carrington and Miss de Bourgh declared archery a hopeless sport and ended the game abruptly. Nevertheless, Mr Collins did not mind at all. He felt fortunate to be of some use to them, however insignificant it might have been.

A fortnight at Rosings passed by more rapidly than anyone had anticipated. Miss de Bourgh slowly escorted Mr Carrington to his carriage as Lady Catherine asked to be remembered to Lord Carrington.

"Do tell him that I appreciated my visit with him so very much and I will go to see him again some time after the wedding. You must let him know how deeply pleased I am to have you as my future son in law," said Lady Catherine as she thought of the marriage contract she had secured from him in his own hand. She stepped aside to allow Anne a final word.

"I would tell you to hasten back but Mother says we will be extremely occupied with tying up the loose ends of our hastened wedding plans. However, I readily admit that my thoughts will always be with you," related Anne.

"I would not be leaving you at all if I did not have to return to my father. He should hear of the good news in person. Moreover, we too must make arrangements. Greenfield shall have a new Mistress to prepare for and the village shall have a celebration to launch. Everything must be supervised to perfection for your initial inspection. Yet, with all I must do, I anticipate these shall be the longest weeks in the history of time," he said kissing her hand, finally entering the carriage. He rode away glancing back at his true love, staring for as long as possible.

Exiting the gate, he sat back in his seat and drew the window shade for the solace of darkness, failing to notice Mr Colllins, who stood vigil all morning to wave good bye.

Chapter 12

The receipt of an invitation to Miss de Bourgh's ball put Mrs Bennet in the highest of spirits. The Bennets were not only asked to attend the ceremony but were invited to stay at Rosings as the particularly welcomed guests of the de Bourghs. Mrs Bennet wasted no time in making her rounds to relate the intelligence to Mrs Philips and her Meryton neighbors, joyfully complaining of the tight schedule she had to endure with the tiresome task of packing for the trip. She returned to Longbourn late in the day as vibrant and enthused as if it was one of her own daughter's wedding.

"Autumnal weddings are so rejuvenating," she said to Mr Bennet admiring the brilliant rustic red and orange leaves falling from the branches that marked the coming of winter. "It is all so stimulating. I can't understand why you are so unyielding when you can see that Lady Catherine honors us by having us to Rosings. We were invited as a family and you should go! I will need you to remain at hand," she scorned. "Above all, are you not curious to finally see the infamous Rosings Mr Collins endlessly gloated about?"

"Mr Collins' admiration of Rosings does little to impress me and I see no need to make any such effort as to travel more than half day's journey to be miserable somewhere else when I will be perfectly happy here alone. You may send my condolences to the groom," stated Mr Bennet disappearing into the library.

"Oh, Mr Bennet! You make it so frustrating for me!" cried Mrs Bennet exasperated with her husband. "And you Kitty, why do you walk so glum when you need not worry? I have told you, your Sir Jon will most certainly be there! His correspondence says he is looking forward to it. Surely that should be enough to fill you with high hopes. It certainly works to brighten my day! Now go upstairs and gather your finest gowns together. You shall naturally present yourself in your best at Rosings. I will send Hill up to assist you shortly but first I must find Mary and encourage her to prepare as well. This is her second chance at an exhibition and she must do it to perfection! Lady Catherine's recognition of us will be an additional asset for her. It will form a distinguishable estimation of the entire family and make Mary very much in demand. She makes me so proud of her now that she has a newly acquired respect for the institution of marriage!" she said flourishing as she glided outdoors in search of Mary.

Kitty was not impressed, nor was she especially anxious to see Sir Jon again. Rosings would mean mourning Dr Kindrel in an acutely uncomfortable way. 'I prefer to stay home, to lie in my bed and grieve over my loss,' she thought as she made her way upstairs to follow her mother's orders. She reached into her draw to pull out the most recent letter she received from Lydia to remind herself of her misery. It read:

Dear Kitty,

I have just met your Dr Kindrel. He was delicious in his uniform! The most handsome of men, excepting my Ensign Wickham. We used your name to introduce ourselves and he was very receptive to us. We liked him very much. My Wickham developed a keen friendship with him in a very short time and brought me back some unfortunate news. I hope you are sitting for you will be absolutely floored to know that Dr Kindrel has confessed to my Wickham of his leaving a loved one behind in London and is not in the market for a substitute for he has designs to return to her when his fortune is made. I am sure he had no idea my Wickham was fishing on your behalf as your name was never mentioned by him or the good doctor in that context. Either way, he has moved on now to another encampment preventing me from exploring further. I am afraid you must choose again. If only Papa would let you come here. You would have your pick from every available soldier as easily as going to a haberdashery to select the finest hat. I will see to it, as it is the duty of an old married sister, younger though I am. Do give Papa your most sincere effort. You will find it well worth the trouble. I am still trying to unpack and will write you again once settled. Say hello to Mary, Mama and Papa. Your's

Mrs Lydia Wickham

PS. Do tell Papa the removal produced unexpected expenses and we would appreciate any assistance he could muster.

*   *   *

The Bennet women arrived at Rosings one week prior to the commencement of the ball as was recommended by Lady Catherine. They were among the first to arrive and found Rosings to be every bit as magnificent as Mr Collins had communicated. Mrs Bennet shuddered as the prominence of the property unsettled her with its opulence and pageantry. Only Kitty found it too stuffy, comparing it to Pemberley's formidable yet elegant simplicity.

Lady Catherine received the ladies very cordially. Miss de Bourgh escorted Mary and Kitty for a stroll around the park as soon as they were settled. It provided Lady Catherine the opportunity she had hoped for to speak to Mrs Bennet in private. She escorted Mrs Bennet into her sitting room and spoke to her in a modified, less intimidating fashion than she had when they met once before. Mrs Bennet was overwhelmed by the tribute an exclusive interview offered and thought carefully before she spoke, censuring herself, fearful of her own vociferous ways before The Right Honorable Lady Catherine.

"Mrs Bennet, it has come to my attention that you were selfless in helping my Anne secure Mr Carrington. I must thank you for your swift and effective handling of the matter," began Lady Catherine after some consideration. "You may as well know that all would have been lost if not for your involvement and for that I wish to express my sincerest gratitude."

"It was my pleasure, Lady Catherine," extolled Mrs Bennet. "With five daughters of my own, I could not but have become proficient in the art," she answered as succinctly as she could.

"I just have my Anne, but I did do my best. I proceeded as my parents had done before me and their parents before them," shared Lady Catherine. "Apparently, I have erred in failing to keep up with the changing times. My methods are quickly becoming extinct as young ladies are forgetting themselves in the ceaseless pursuit of men. In my days, there was approbation in having a man make all the sacrifices for the woman."

"Of course you did your best. I trust in that immensely," said Mrs Bennet earnestly feeling a closeness developing between the two. "Our duties, as mothers, are the same as with any family—to care for our children by securing a sound and stable future for them. It is fundamental! We, you and I, have done well for ourselves, if I do say so myself," she said proudly.

"That we have," agreed Lady Catherine, "and it has been a difficult task."

"Yes. As the women of the house, we must keep our guard up at all times. It is an exhausting endeavor but it cannot be left to the men. We deserve all the credit since they know not what it means to be a singular woman in our society," offered Mrs Bennet quickly relaxing her reserve.

"Indeed. Yet, with our common goals, I'm afraid our philosophies and styles differ, and yours has proven to be superior when it comes to making a match," said Lady Catherine impressed with Mrs Bennet's comments. "What is your methodology? How do you conceive your plan? I must know for I shall not be denied the intelligence."

"Lady Catherine, it is my philosophy that men do not always come willingly, you know, but if a young lady aspires to know a man, he will naturally discover favor in her. Its only human nature! See how my Kitty has captured Sir Jon. He was desired by all the ladies at Pemberley's ball, which my Lizzy had successfully put together. Kitty captured his heart by being beautiful and aloof. She made sure she outshined the other girls then gave Sir Jon no regard by dancing with someone else first. She provided competition for him among the other guests, yet making certain she was available only for him. There is nothing a man likes better than a healthy chase, much like hunting!"

"Sir Jon, I'm afraid has always had that problem of needing to win at all costs. I remember him as a childhood friend of Lord Watney. He was recklessly selfish and irresponsible as a boy. I did not particularly care for him then and I find him to be no different now that he is fully grown. I hear he remains conceited and self indulgent. An undesirable type for marriage," warned Lady Catherine. "I feel I must caution you for it's the least I can do."

"But all people of fortune cannot see beyond themselves. It is the dynastic principle. The elite monopolize and indulge themselves while holding everyone else hostage to their whims. The upper classes, those with rank and breeding, have historically been proud with the option to discriminate. That is one of the privileges of being an aristocrat. I have never met one who behaved to the contrary. You do not notice because you are one of them." she said bluntly.

Lady Catherine rose from her seat. 'So you have humbled me once again, Mrs Bennet. This is more than one body can take,'she thought with indignation. "That is quite enough," she said giving Mrs Bennet the benefit of the doubt that she could not have understood the implications of what she just said. "We must join the others now. They must be wondering where we are. I have arranged for refreshments this afternoon and the Collinses are to join us," she said as they left the room in search of the others.

*   *   *

Guests continued to arrive day by day. The majority of these were elderly Baronets, Barons, Counts and their wives. Mrs Bennet concluded that this older group needed to be housed at Rosings a few days in advance of the ball in order to collect themselves from their travels. Whatever the case may be, Mrs Bennet was entrenched with their arrivals. She looked out of her window to watch them disembark, impressed with the fine barouches that transported coachmen and footmen dressed as dashing as their employers. 'It is unsporting of these guests to arrive without their sons. We should have had the advantage,' sighed Mrs Bennet. 'Well, never mind, they are sure to follow in good time since it is only days away and when they do it will be another productive evening—only this time for Mary."

Happily amongst the guests was Daniel, invited by Miss de Bourgh. The merry trio was now reassembled only to become an inseparable foursome as Mr Carrington joined the group. The itinerary in Rosings was far less physical than it had been in Pemberley with chamber music and recitals considered the distractions of choice. The quartet remained together as often as they could afford without being neglectful to the other guests. Kitty preferred Rosings' library professing an interest in an intriguing book, a ruse she learned from her father.

Mr Collins strongly desired to keep the company of his brother but continuously experienced difficulty in achieving it. Despite the fact that Daniel was housed in Hunsford Parsonage, he rose to visit Rosings early each morning and stayed until late after dinner every evening. Mr Collins found he had to stay up late to converse with his brother and did not appreciate the inconvenience of it at all.

"Mrs Collins, I am ecstatic that my brother had succeeded in his new position as pastor of Courtlandt Parsonage but I am certain he has need of my guidance in many matters that he is too preoccupied to concern himself with. I cannot be of help to him if he does not confide in me. When I try to speak to him he just says everything is going fine. I am afraid he may be blind to his own shortcomings for I myself have had a hard time of it with my very first commission. What do you think? Do you find it is too good to be true?"

"I think you have to accept that your brother is independent now and will conduct his parish the way he sees fit. I am sure he will come to you if he has need of advice. At the moment, he is preoccupied with the company of Miss Bennet. Why should he invest these precious moments on you when correspondence will do just as well where the parish is concerned?"

"What do you mean he is preoccupied with Miss Bennet? You must be mistaken for I have told him that before he thinks of his own desires, he must establish himself at his parish for an inestimable period of time. I have advocated that very good piece of advice when he was here with us this past spring. It was what Lady Catherine had advised me before she dispatched me to retrieve a bride. I worked for years to establish myself with the security a husband should provide a wife. You are mistaken, Mrs Collins. Daniel's interests are not what you think. He is merely overconfident. I assure you, he shall adhere to my advice or what would Lady Catherine think if my brother does not follow my example?"

"That should not be your concern now, dearest. He is under the influence of Lady Georgiana and takes advice from her as is rightfully his duty. Lady Catherine cannot but honor that as should we."

"I hope you are right, Mrs Collins. I don't want Lady Catherine displeased. She has exhibited her munificent generosity with forgiving us and the Bennets by having them stay at her estate. You know, I have never stayed there one single night," he said with a hint of envy. He turned his back on Mrs Collins, ashamed of his own feelings, saying beneath his breath, "The fortuity the Bennets have is unnatural!"

"It could not go to a kinder family, Mr Collins," enlightened Mrs Collins.

*　　*　　*

Rosings' ballroom was magnificent. Everything was on as grand a scale as was at all possible. The most distinguished of their class was in attendance. The aristocracy entered the ballroom dressed to the hilt, making a splendid show of the event. "A little overdone," Kitty would say, not at all taken by the glitter and gold.

Miss de Bourgh was jubilant in the arms of Mr Carrington. They, along with Lady Catherine, received their guests into the ballroom. Lady Catherine stood extremely proud and remarkably cheerful. She was wholly gratified by the sweet satisfying sight of her daughter and future son in a divine state of happiness. Lord and Lady Watney gave their well wishes as they entered the room. They exchanged numerous accounts of pre wedding bedlam with empathetic glee. The Watneys moved on into the ballroom assuring Miss de Bourgh and Mr Carrington that marriage was a perfect state of affairs, giving their final congratulations.

Mr and Mrs Bingley were as congenial as ever looking forward to the wedding as they entered conversing happily with the Darcys. They were elated at the news of the Carrington/de Bourgh engagement and would not miss the event for the world.

Mrs Bennet and her daughters followed next. Once again, Mrs Bennet had supervised Kitty's attire and dressed her as superbly as before. Mary looked especially elegant as well. This time she too allowed her mother to supervise her look. The Bennet ladies stood outside the ballroom to allow Mrs Bennet a final inspection of her daughters.

"Mary, you should have left your hair the way the hairdresser made it up! Sometimes I lose all hope for you!" scoffed Mrs Bennet. "I suppose I should be grateful you have kept on the gown we agreed on. It is exceptional, flattering you much more than any of your previous gowns, and my compliments to your fine selection of jewels. They are briliiant! We are fortunate with Jane. I must say, I am glad of that," she said as they stood in the doorway. Scouting the room she instructed, "Kitty, go to Sir Jon. I see him walking this way toward you. With such eagerness, it is a wonder that he did not come sooner to spend some extra time with you! Young men in love are usually hard pressed to be kept apart from their lady. Anyway, there he is. You should meet him half way so that everyone will know you reciprocate his feelings to some degree. A little assurance will do no harm." She watched Kitty enter the ballroom and concentrated on her until she was met by Sir Jon. Satisfied, she turned her attentions to Mary.

"Now Mary, I have high hopes for you," she said. She fussed with Mary's gown trying to control her excitement. "I can see the promise in you that I was long hoping for. Just point out the gentleman you want when you see him, my dear," instructed Mrs Bennet. "Do not fear to strive for the best. As you can see by your sister's example, they are here for the taking. Generally, I would suggest we should separate to cover more ground but today, I have come up with an alternate plan. We shall stand, immovable, just beyond the entrance where Lady Catherine and Miss de Bourgh greet their guests. This way we won't miss a single face as they stroll in. You can select the ones you like and I shall choose the ones I like. Then, just before the dancing starts, we shall waste no time arranging the proper introductions. It is a good thing we have many friends here to help us with these connections. Oh, this is so exhilarating! Quickly now, let us enter for we must choose the best vantage point inside!" she said with celerity.

They stood inside across the receiving line faithfully refusing to leave their post for fear of missing someone new. Pleasing her mother, Mary waited patiently for the entire party to file in. Mrs Bennet worked steadily as she judged the men and eliminated them one by one. As time went by, Mrs Bennet felt the weight of certain failure fall heavily upon her shoulders. She discovered, to her dismay, that all of Lady Catherine's guests were patriarchal or married. Many of them were escorted in by nurses, requiring special assistance to merely enter and be seated! Mrs Bennet was flustered as the room continued to fill with the aged and infirmed. As the antiquated wandered by, Mrs Bennet glanced at an elderly nobleman peering in their direction. He bowed his head in acknowledgment of their presence. Mrs Bennet acquiesced politely then, as the final guests entered the ballroom, pulled Mary aside to discuss their predicament.

"Is everyone above the age of five and forty? These are all Lady Catherine's friends. Doesn't Miss de Bourgh have friends of her own?" she asked Mary.

"Miss de Bourgh has no friends to call her own, Mama. She has always been in the company of her mother and her mother's associations," explained Mary. "Mr Carrington has no other friends to speak of either, claiming them all as mere acquaintances, except for the married couples you see before you." Mary was fully aware that all the guests were Lady Catherine's and Lord Carrington's peers when Miss de Bourgh and she reviewed the guest list a short time ago.

"I find this most upsetting, Mary! It was to be an evening of conquest for you. I cannot express my sorrowful discontentment," she said despondently, "After all the expense and trouble of dressing you so finely, and with you cooperating for the very first time! I am disheartened as I had such high expectations. The entire affair has been totally devalued. Go on Mary. Find your way through the evening and make the best of it if you can, but do not lose faith. I will mingle and make some inquiries to keep up the pursuit for my side of it," she said as compensation. "Believe me my only consolation is that Mr Bennet is not here to taunt me with his piercing remarks. I can hear him now saying, 'you have sent me to Rosings on another fool's errand, Mrs Bennet!' I would never live it down if he were here. Anyway, chin up, my dear. Remember your married sisters promise to do their duty by you," she said encouraging her daughter as she dismissed her from her side for the remainder of the evening.

Mr Carrington and Miss de Bourgh opened the dance floor as the orchestra played their first overture. The Watneys, Darcys and Bingleys followed. Kitty danced the first two sets with Sir Jon as expected and Mary danced mostly with Daniel, while Mrs Bennet surrendered her to her choice. The dance floor crowded quickly as the guests chose their partners. It was a befitting gathering, very much to everyone's satisfaction, excepting Mrs Bennet. Her only pleasure was in the praise these dignified gentlemen offered Kitty. Indeed, Kitty was elegant and charming, even in her melancholy state. Sir Jon was ennobled to be at her side, accepting her compliments as his own, thanking the issuer with pride. He became irretrievably intoxicated with Kitty anew and remained faithfully by her side once again.

Lady Catherine approached the Darcys when she noted a free moment. She appeared a bit apprehensive as she confronted them. "Mrs Darcy," she began, extending a conciliatory hand to Lizzy as Mr Darcy stood nearby. "I am so very happy you have accepted our invitation and decided to join us here at Rosings in celebration of Anne's engagement. It concerned me when you did not come to stay with us this week prior, as your mother and sisters have. You were required to share in our felicity as it was not complete without your presence and that of your husband," she said humbly. Mr Darcy listened intently as Lizzy accepted her comments with grace. Lady Georgiana was standing by and strayed even closer to listen in. "We have not seen each other for these past two years because of my own irrational pride for principle and intolerance toward your marriage. You are a full member of the family now. Mr Darcy would not have it any other way and neither would I. I want you to know you are welcomed to return to Rosings at your leisure when the occasion is less formal. I know Mrs Collins will be glad to have you visit more often as I shall take the liberty to tell her you have promised to do so straightaway."

"We are grateful for your warm welcome and generous invitation, Lady Catherine. Mr Darcy and I receive it with extreme happiness. We have not come sooner because we had guests of our own, among who were the Bingleys. Fortunately, we were able to make arrangements to arrive here tonight and remain from this point forward to see Miss de Bourgh married, as you have so amicably offered," related Lizzy.

"Yes, that will please me," said Lady Catherine as she patted Mr Darcy's arm in a tender loving manner.

"Please, allow me to add that I particularly appreciate your accepting me as a member of the family. It means a lot to us to move on from our pitiful beginning," confessed Lizzy as she looked at Mr Darcy for affirmation.

"For that I am solely to blame. I have long thought you the cause of Anne's unhappy solitary situation and had concluded that your family was offensive and inferior to mine in every way," began Lady Catherine as Mr and Mrs Darcy tensed up a bit hoping she would not recount the events. "But your family has shown themselves to be most honorable. They have proven themselves to be forgiving, sincere and extremely instrumental in the newly found happiness of my daughter's life. My Anne is very much in love with Mr Carrington and he reciprocates her feelings. They are a perfect match through personality as well as rank and birth. I have been blind to this prerequisite in my unrelenting desire for Mr Darcy to honor the marriage contract drawn between myself and his mother, my sister, Lady Anne. Mr Darcy was fortunate indeed to have met you and to have had the insight to determine that you were the only one for him. Neither of them, Anne or Fitzwilliam, would have been happy together. The union would have compromised them both. The role of Mrs Darcy was meant for you," she said movingly. "You, Mrs Darcy, are as gentile and valuable to me as any of my other family members. I admit I have given everyone grief from my fallacious shortsightedness, but I am not above asking for your forgiveness and do so now."

"There is no need for forgiveness. You have carefully watched over the Darcy family in the absence of their own parents and only sought their success and security. It has all worked out as part of a greater plan," said Lizzy grateful for the cohesion this generous exchange gave the families.

"I have extended an open invitation for the Bennet family to visit Rosings whenever they wish, as I have to you. Do take advantage of it, my dear," she said turning to walk away.

As Lady Georgiana heard what was said, she stopped Lady Catherine in her steps and hugged her planting a loving kiss on her cheek. Lady Catherine returned the hug and broke free, turning to smile at Mr Darcy. The Darcys hugged each other in exoneration. There has been a most welcomed amendment to their situation in life and it was accepted with celebration.

*   *   *

Mrs Bennet almost forfeited her search as her mingling failed to produce any possible prospects. In a final effort, she decided to scout around the card room to survey the players and listen in on conversations hoping a few would pertain to singular sons, nephews and the like. Observing a large number of gray heads, Mrs Bennet felt she had little to risk and overtly scrutinized them one by one calling upon her intuition to detect probable fathers or uncles of bachelor offspring. Absorbed in her mission, smiling politely as she moved from table to table, she was unaware that she, herself, was being observed. It took her by surprise when a stately looking gentleman said, "Madame, have you an interest in cards? I am sure we can find a seat for you somewhere?"

Recognizing him as the distinguished gentleman that acknowledged her presence at the door, she answered, "I thank you very much sir, but I am not inclined to play. I am merely taking a turn to acquaint myself with the company."

"I have tired of cards and am eager for companionship as well. Allow me to introduce myself. I am Your Grace, Lord Michael Krasdale, the Duke of Biddenden," he said with a slight bow of his head. Her eyes lit up as she heard him announce his very distinguished title. 'This nobleman will carry some influence over the others. He is certainly worth knowing,' she strategized.

"How do you do?" she asked with an implied curtsy. "It is an honor to meet you, Your Grace. I am Mrs Bennet."

"This room has taken on a stuffy nature, Mrs Bennet. The music playing in the ballroom is sedate and slowly paced, very much to my liking. I have waited all evening for the composition. Have you an escort with you tonight?" asked the Duke.

"No, indeed I do not. My Mr Bennet has abandoned me to myself for my entire stay," she said forgetting herself.

"Then I need only ask for your permission to share this dance with me. Would you bestow me the honor?" he asked charismatically.

"It will be a pleasure," she answered with a complaisant smile. Taking his elbow, she was escorted to the ballroom and joined in the dance.

"Mrs Bennet, I have been observing you from the start. Please do not think it overstepping my place if I compliment you on your dress and style for I shall not be prevented from doing so as you have captured the beauty of Venus herself tonight," he said as they danced steadily on.

"Thank you for saying so, Your Grace. Your compliment flatters me and is well received," she said with pride, feeling content with herself. "A gentleman should never be prevented from making such applications when they are well intended."

"Ah, I am glad to see we think alike. In my circles we are not accustomed to holding back from what we wish to say."

"I agree to that and admit I am guilty of speaking my mind as well," answered Mrs Bennet. "You may speak freely in my company if you wish, Duke, as I will not hold you to convention for, in this case, you have met your equal," she laughed.

"Dare I inquire then if you were standing by the door earlier this evening in order to judge the party for the possibility of sighting an eligible man? I confess, I have seen this practice before in my many years and found it most entertaining. It is a great device to provide an added advantage for those seeking connections," he said glancing at her for a reaction.

"You are a man of the world!" she said suddenly drawn in by the conversation, anxious to hear more.

"Be straight out with it Mrs Bennet, as I shall not be judgemental," he ordered pausing to judge her receptiveness. "You and I should not be about games you know and consume ourselves with futile preliminaries. It is a waste of time. Getting to the point of it is much more sophisticated and to my liking," he said freely.

"I admit, that was my business," she owned, hoping he would presume her as sophisticated as himself. "One must always be at the ready or lose her options. I believe in that wholeheartedly."

"Very true, Madame. I admire your forthrightness. It is remarkably refreshing for a woman to be so blunt. I, personally, find it stimulating!"

he said admiringly. "I don't get out much anymore but when I do, I like to seize the opportunity to enjoy myself to the fullest, like in the days of old."

Taking on his cue, she added, "I cannot agree with you more. There is a lot to say for seizing the opportunity. Precisely why I also meet the challenge to find a little personal amusement wherever I go as I would live life no other way."

"We have much in common, you and me. Our dance will soon come to an end, so I shall make use of this fine opportunity to convey my sincerest, deepest interest in you, my lady. From the first moment I saw you, sizing every man that crossed your path I knew you were the one for me. And now that you have confirmed your desire to make the most of it, without your husband, there should be nothing to hold you back from returning with me to my room tonight. I promise you shall take great delight in what I have to offer."

"Please, Duke. You mistake my meaning and take unwarranted liberties," she said in a fluster. "Allow me to correct you for I am a married woman and was seeking a companion, not for myself but for my daughter."

"Not in this assembly, you weren't," he said cooly. "Lady Catherine has no young companions of the proper age for your daughter. But I see I am mistaken. I should not have been so blunt as I am afraid you must play a little game before our tumble tonight. Very well then, proceed my darling and I shall play along for I embrace your spirit," he said gripping her hand tightly as they danced.

"I tell you, Duke, you have erred! If my Mr Bennet were here, you would not speak so foolishly," she said feeling her composure slipping away. "He would not hesitate to put you in your rightful place!"

"Well, now that does put a new light on it!" he said jesting. "If you wish for me to fight for your hand, it must be done with pistols at twenty paces. Wogdons to be exact as I cannot lift a sword for my own defense anymore, you know. I may look youthful, well preserved as I am, but I am one and eighty years now and I prefer to reserve my strength for a toss every now and then, when the opportunity arises! In any case, we need not involve your husband, even if he were here, now do we?" he asked as the music came to an end holding ever tighter to her hand. He escorted her off the floor with the intention of leading her to his room. Mrs Bennet pulled away, vigorously slapping his fragile hand while trying to avoid permanent injury.

"Unhand me Your Grace or I shall forget your age and discipline you as if you were a boy of five," she said attempting to defend herself.

"Would you?" he asked in adulation clapping his hands enthusiastically with the joyous glee a child would have when presented with a new toy. "Upstairs! Tonight! My word, I have chosen well!"

Mrs Bennet broke loose and turned to leave the duke behind but he followed devotedly. Coming upon the first in her family capable of supplying a rescue, she turned to the Darcys and spoke quickly with alarm.

"Lizzy! Lizzy! Come with me to the sitting room for I am relentlessly pursued by a sinister man who means to dishonor me, if given the chance. Make haste! We must run for he is hot on my trail," she said grabbing Lizzy away from Mr Darcy. She turned to point him out and took notice that he was not far behind. "He approaches!" she gasped as they ran. Mr Darcy, intent on defending Mrs Bennet's honor against the unruly cad, turned heroically only to confront the frail shell of a man he knew very well. Giving himself a chance to regain his composure, Mr Darcy quickly blocked the duke's view from the ladies' direction and asked, "Where do you go, Your Grace?"

"I am seeking my lady love who has just stolen away from me with your lovely wife. Are they to return anytime soon? We were playing a little game of cat and mouse. But if you don't know how long she will be I should like to take a seat and wait for her return as I am a great believer in the preservation of energy, you know," he said with honesty.

"Do sit down, Your Grace, as you and I should form a compromise that will suit us both," offered Mr Darcy taking control of the situation. "I shall tear my wife away from Mrs Bennet if you will take this seat here. When I have returned to the dance floor, with my wife in hand, you shall know that Mrs Bennet is free once more. Then you can continue to pursue her to your hearts content," he said taking his leave and in doing so, sacrificed Mrs Bennet for the return of his wife.

In the sitting room, he came upon the entire family, all of which were terribly concerned for Mrs Bennet's disgraceful predicament. "Here comes Mr Darcy now!" exclaimed Mrs Bennet. "What do you know about that scandalous remnant of a man?" she asked in an unsettled manner.

"He is My Lord the Duke of Biddenden, a good friend to my grandfather, on my mother's side. He is widowed three times, most recently, two years ago."

"I remember him," added Mr Bingley. "He must be very lonely these days, all alone in that big estate with nothing but servants surrounding him all day."

"He must be desperately lonely," added Mr Darcy earning him a severe look from the women.

"How could he be lonely with all that money? How much does he have? He must have more than you!" declared Mrs Bennet too curious for her own good. Everyone in the room stood aghast, thinking it inconceivable that she would even care at a time like this. "Well, of course he is wealthy," she answered herself, ignoring their reproachful look, "he is a duke!"

"Now Mama, would you be so inclined to marry such a miserable man for his wealth and title?" asked Kitty taking advantage of the similarity in circumstances.

"Kitty, don't be so vulgar. It is not for me that I ask but for Mary," clarified Mrs Bennet. "What would Mr Bennet say if he even knew of this?" she cried. Her concern was not so much for the brazen flirtation since she would use that bit of news to make Mr Bennet jealous some time in the future. Instead she was embarrassed the duke considered her comparable in age.

"Kitty, Mama is joking of course," said Jane trying to save face in front of the husbands. "Right now she has a bigger problem on her hands than satisfying your philosophical views."

"Mama, you must be direct, even if it hurts his feelings," suggested Lizzy hoping to end the discussion, "I can see no other way."

"I have already given it my best attempt. I told him he was a forward insufferable man and he simply lifted his brows and said, 'wonderful, wonderful'. He shook so contentedly that I thought he was going through a fit of spasms right before my eyes! I cannot be harder on him or he shall die and I would be to blame."

"Mr Darcy, you know him best. Is there any way to curb this man's actions?" asked Jane.

"I can only imagine that all of her shunning and verbal abuse is serving to whet his appetite as it makes him feel he is alive with the chase. As she said, I fear abusing him could be worse as he thinks it a game. I suggest she remove herself to her chamber for the rest of the evening. He might have a change of heart tomorrow."

"I can't very well stay locked up in my chambers the whole evening!" declined Mrs Bennet. "How shall I tell my friends and neighbors in Meryton that I spent the ball at Rosings locked away? That just won't do. And I can't very well return home before the wedding for it shall insult Lady Catherine. No, you must all do your duty by me and come to my aid when he is near by forming a ring around me to keep me hidden from his sight and that is the end of it," she said as she got up to rejoin the dance. "This is all your father's fault, you know! He should have come along as I told him to. Alas girls, observe the curse your endless beauty will bring."

*   *   *

The festivities continued as the family found His Grace napping in the very seat Mr Darcy had left him in. Tip toeing past him, they joined the other guests as they proceeded to the banquet hall. There, Sir Jon approached Mrs Bennet asking for the whereabouts of Mr Bennet. Informed that Mr Bennet could not come, he spoke with her instead.

"I desired to speak to Mr Bennet on a matter that only he could assist me with, but it should be no secret to you, Mrs Bennet. I propose to ask Mr Bennet for Miss Catherine's hand in marriage. I promise her all that a baronetage has to offer, title, fortune, a vast estate and various properties. I am sure Mr Bennet cannot disapprove of such a proposition for we shall be a glamorous couple," he said loudly with pretension and certainty.

"Disapprove! It is what my Kitty deserves. She is all beauty and dutiful besides. She will make you a wonderful wife and you will be the happiest of men," confirmed Mrs Bennet.

"I have not asked Miss Catherine yet. I am pressed with the inclination to wait to speak to Mr Bennet," he informed her, making a show of his proposal as the nearby guests listened freely.

"I assure you, you will have his approval. Please accept my invitation to call on him at Longbourn. You should return with us after the wedding to be done with it as Mr Bennet will give you his blessing directly!" she exclaimed with excitement as the evening proved to be rewarding after all. Those around her offered their congratulations and before long the entire party was privy to the fact.

The duke awoke from all the commotion and moved hastily toward the celebrated Mrs Bennet. The Darcys and Bingleys observed his approach and immediately dispersed themselves among the crowd, blending in with the assembly in attempt to prevent their share in a new scandal.

Kitty was shocked as the news of the engagement traveled quickly. 'This is all out of control! How could this have happened so hastily? If only he would have confided in me first I would have told him I was not ready. What am I to do now that he and Mama are accepting best wishes from everyone!?!'

Kitty ran out of the room to Rosing's library. 'How could everyone be so content when I am so miserable?' Kitty brooded the evening away resolving there was nothing she could do about it. 'If only Dr. Kindrel were here with me. He would approach Mama and settle the matter. She was fond of him and though he has no large fortune, I would be happily married and secured for the future just the same. But I mustn't forget that Lydia wrote he was returning to a girl he left behind in London. In all our sweet conversations, we never spoke of such things. We were the best of friends, that was all and for the rest of my life I will regret it,' she sighed. Her tears fell uncontrollably. 'Mama was right in arranging my marriage to Sir Jon. It shall be the only way to get over my beloved doctor.'

Miss de Bourgh's wedding was not for another week. Most of the guests who arrived for the ball had returned home, with the exception of a chosen few who were either invited or requested to stay for the wedding ceremony. The duke was one of the latter.

The days that followed were filled with tranquil tours of Rosings, book readings and poetry recitals. The evenings were composed of chamber music and concerts for the listening ear. The duke did his best to evoke Mrs. Bennet's interests, but failed consistently as he had no male heirs to attach Mary to. "He should sit still until rigor mortis sets in," she would tell Mary, fagged by his wearisome, futile attempts.

Sir Jon remained by Kitty's side for every event. He was terribly restless during the poetry reading and made Kitty miserable in return.

"Rosings has always lacked in its ability to entertain properly, but this is by far the most fatiguing and burdensome form of leisure any guest should be forced to endure. This is precisely why I choose to live my life beyond the confines of the countryside. If it were not for you, Miss Catherine, I would not spend another minute in this place," said Sir Jon with hardly a whisper.

"Shh!" admonished Kitty. "The de Bourghs enjoy these types of diversions and the others seem to enjoy it as well. You cannot mind it so much as to censure it for everyone. I take care to enjoy myself. If you try, you might find you can learn to favor it as well," coaxed Kitty. She was pleased that such entertainments did not involve any significant interactions with one another.

"I have tried," declared Sir Jon. "I have suffered it up to now, sitting still this past half hour. In fact, these have been the most agonizing four days in the history of my life! Where is the enthusiasm? What is there to stimulate the guests to stir themselves into exhilaration? It is inconceivable that there has not been so much as a spirited piccolo to provoke us. I know what I enjoy and what I do not enjoy," he said with disdain. "And this form of entertainment, I do not enjoy."

"They will hear you," warned Kitty disconcerted with his ill manners.

"I, for one, have had enough. I shall not endure such persecution any longer. I must make the proper excuses and take my leave tomorrow," he avowed.

"What could you possibly say to excuse you from the wedding ceremony? It is only a few days away now and there is no way you could leave without offending the de Bourghs who have cordially welcomed you with this extended stay after hearing about our proposed engagement. To leave now would be the height of arrogance and disrespect."

"Miss Catherine, I have established quite a knack for fabricating excuses to remove myself from uncomfortable and difficult circumstances. In this case, I shall tell them I received a letter informing me of a death in the family that requires my attendance. Mr Carrington, of all people, with his father on the brink and overcome with blindness, would understand and not stop me from leaving. They would even send me on my way with well wishes," he snickered. "I understand your worry. You fear you will not see me soon enough, but you must remember you are promised to me. I shall visit you at Longbourn to speak to your father when you have returned. I will send you notice. Then we will throw a ball where I will call the tunes. We will entertain as convention has never seen before. We shall invite the black arts with psalmists and mediums to entertain and we will be certain our future will be pulled in the right direction. Let us hope we conjure the proper ancestors," he said with enthusiasm. "That will only be the beginning for us. I promise your life with me shall not be near anything as dismal and dreary as this. You will be enamored with life beyond the confines of propriety once we are united."

"You are quite mistaken, Sir Jon. I would very much like for you to leave, if that is your wish. My only cause for alarm is the fabrication of a family death. It is beyond civility and I find it extremely distasteful," she said bluntly.

"They shall be none the wiser. Lady Catherine does not know all the members of my family. Some are quite distant. The only challenge will be in feigning sincerity. Once I have accomplished that, I have succeeded.

She would never find out and I submit, I have already decided it shall be done," he said ending the conversation.

Mrs. Collins noticed the couple conversing with subtle discomposure. "Something is really upsetting Miss Catherine. Have you observed how her youthful glow dissipates when she is beside Sir Jon? These are not very good signs," she shared with Mr. Collins.

"Mrs. Collins, please do not cause a disruption in the recital. Lady Catherine does not take it lightly. It is most improper," he admonished, quieting his wife with a hasty dismissal of her astute observation.

Early next morning, Sir Jon made his excuses. As foreseen, everyone understood and wished his family well as he left Rosings. Kitty felt relieved. She wanted time away from him and was appeased when he was gone. She never realized how much she enjoyed her singular status until then. Mrs Bennet, mistaking her moodiness as brooding for Sir Jon, thought it understandable that she not mingle excessively with the company.

Those days were sheer bliss for Kitty who spent them entirely in Rosing's library until the arrival of Col Fitzwilliam. Remembering the kind Colonel that befriended Dr. Kindrel at Pemberley, Kitty abandoned the library and exerted herself to greet him properly.

"So glad you have arrived Col Fitzwilliam. Why didn't you come in time for the ball?" she inquired when she shared a moment with him.

"I would have come for the week if I was able, but I could not contract the leave from the militia. I am fortunate I could only get away for a three day stay," he said politely. "It will, at a minimum, allow me to attend the wedding. It is, after all, why we are all here, isn't it?" said Col Fitzwilliam amicably.

"Then, I am pleased you were able to make it at all. Please Col. Fitzwilliam, tell me how Dr. Kindrel has been serving the milita. I have heard no recent news of him and am eager to learn all I can. I hope he is well."

"Dr. Kindrel has increased in reputation faster than we ever thought possible. The troops' patients are recovering in record number. He is most respected and is in the constant company of top ranking officials," informed Col. Fitzwilliam. "I daresay he made me praiseworthy as well, for he was my recommendation!"

"That is wonderful news. I could not have wished more for him. Would you, by chance, be fortunate enough to restore yourself to his good company upon your return to the encampment?" she inquired. Her manner was so anxious and the yearning was so clearly expressed by her face that she could not conceal her attachment.

"He has left my regiment some time ago and will more than likely not return my way. He has a great deal of work ahead of him. He is requested everywhere at once. However, if there is a message I can give him," offered Col Fitzwilliam, "I guarantee you, he shall receive it."

"No, thank you. Just let him know I remember him fondly and am elated with his success," said Kitty struggling to control her flagrant disappointment. She had hoped to have discovered Dr Kindrel's whereabouts and escape to him, if only in her dreams. Col Fitzwilliam was taken by her disappointment. It peaked his curiosity as he found himself compelled to hear more of what she had to say of his friend. He encouraged her to speak as he observed her closely. It was obvious to him that she missed the estranged Dr Kindrel and was grieved to be without him. He listened earnestly with compassion and by the close of the conversation, though she confessed nothing, everything had been said.

*   *   *

Our happy quartet had a wonderful time in each other's company. Just prior to the ceremony, they came together to secure plans for the future of their friendship.

"Miss Bennet," began Daniel, "your inspiration has been sadly lacking and the parish children long to see you again. Can I take the liberty to inform them of your hasty return to North Courtlandt?"

"I would like nothing more than to reacquaint myself with them as well, but the likelihood of it being in the near future is grim. It would be inappropriate for me to visit you alone at North Courtlandt Parsonage and the Watneys should pass their honeymoon unencumbered by me until they announce their return from Europe."

"Perhaps he would be inspired by visiting you at Longbourn," suggested Miss de Bourgh. "As for Mr Carrington and I, we would love to have you both as our guests at Greenfield Castle when we have properly settled, honeymoon or not."

"I thank you for your invitation but I fear I must decline. I cannot abandon the parish ceaselessly for my own selfish desires. There is too much work to be done there and I do not wish to be neglectful. We must wait patiently until the appropriate time reveals itself. Until then, correspondence must do," suggested Daniel responsibly.

The ceremony was performed brilliantly by Mr Collins. At its conclusion, everyone in attendance wished them well as the couple set off directly to Dover. Lady Catherine waved good bye with a joyful tear in her eye. The moment she had waited for had come and gone, making her and her daughter better people in the end.

The congregation soon dispersed as the major event was now over with everyone going their separate ways. The Darcys issued an invitation to Lady Catherine for a stay at Pemberley to ease the newness of her solitude. Their invitation was gratefully accepted.

Chapter 13

The Bennet women returned to Longbourn finding Mr Bennet waiting outside patiently for the carriage to arrive. Mrs Bennet was happy to see him standing there. She could not wait to inform him on the most current events concerning Kitty.

"Mr Bennet, there is news of tremendous proportions to relate to you! You can never guess it!" she cried out of the window as the carriage came to a full stop.

"I will not guess anything. I just want to see you have arrived safely. That is sufficient knowledge for me. When you are of a mind to brief me on your news, you may seek me out in the library," he said turning into the house with Mrs Bennet following directly.

"Mr Bennet, I shall appeal to your interest with the finest announcement yet," she insisted.

"Is another function calling you away so soon when you've just arrived?" he asked.

"Better than that! Sit down and I shall inform you," she said joyfully. "Sir Jon has announced to all of the party at Rosings that he has every determination to come to Longbourn and ask you for Kitty's hand in marriage! You should have heard the compliments he received on behalf of his 'magnificent choice'. I was so full of pride and happiness. I knew she would do it," she paused. "So, how do you like that, Mr Bennet!?! Doesn't that affect you in any way?"

"And so goes all discretion and decorum as with our honorable Mr Wickham. Has he no fear that I would not accept his proposal—though I would not deprive Kitty of such a marriage," he answered, peeved by his wife's declaration and that of his future son in law. He strolled into the library stopping at his desk. He would not sit for fear Mrs Bennet would follow his lead and make herself comfortable in his private space.

"He does not and should not fear your opposition!" she demanded. "There is no question that you shall accept Sir Jon. He is a Baronet and would secure an enviable future for our Kitty!" Annoyed with his lack of enthusiasm, Mrs Bennet quickly ended the conversation. "Well, there you have it. I have placed it before you to do with what you will. As for me, I must get out of my travel clothes to prepare for a fine dinner tonight since our closest neighbors will want to help celebrate our return."

"Do the proper thing, Mrs Bennet and advertise your feast for what it is—an opportunity for gossip and bragging." he said ushering her out of the library as she laughed at the veracity of his comments. "Call me when dinner is ready. I shall get all the details with the others as I need not hear it twice."

Mary stayed out on the grounds for a quiet walk about the park. She needed to stretch her legs after the long journey home. There were a lot of changes going on all around her and being home did not seem as comforting as it had in the past. She enjoyed being with her friends and most of all she enjoyed being with Daniel. Standing there alone in the park, she took solace in the effortless imagery of herself at North Courtlandt Parsonage, helping the children with their spiritual growth as she had done before, only this time it would be a little different as she would surely be Mrs Daniel Collins.

Kitty grew restless and increasingly uneasy as the time passed. The news of Sir Jon's intended arrival within the next few weeks drew her to distraction. At breakfast, she dropped her glass at the mention of his name.

"Kitty, if you do not compose yourself, Sir Jon may not think you fit for a wife. I understand you are anxious about doing well in a baronetage but it is not something to be afraid of, my dear. You must grasp it and make it your own," instructed Mrs Bennet. "Once you are in the proper environment and atmosphere, you will know what to do instinctively. Your sisters, Jane and Lizzy can help you when I am not available. You will do fine, rest assured of that. Sir Jon would have it no other way, but nothing will happen if you do not make it to the wedding itself!" she warned.

"Mama, you are right," said Kitty in a sudden burst of inspiration. "I am too tense and need to relax. I was thinking about my sister, Lizzy, hoping I could visit her for a fortnight so she can enlighten me as to how the change would most likely affect my life."

"How can you possibly leave for a fortnight? Sir Jon will have arrived by then! Why do you not go to Jane's instead?"

"Lizzy has married into the greatest fortune of all my sisters. I should like to have the benefit of her experience, with all the servants and demand for the proper air and etiquette. There are many questions I want answered. I must go to her. I am determined. I shall leave instantly, Mama, and return a day before Sir Jon's arrival," she said concealing her true desire to be as far away from Longbourn as possible.

"Do you think one day would be enough to rest after the long ride home? You must look your best, you know. Besides, winter is fast approaching and the roads may become impassable."

"Do not worry, Mama. If the roads are not satisfactory I shall return sooner."

"If it will settle your nerves Kitty, you may go. I daresay, you are all undone. I shall send notice to Lizzy and tell her of your going."

Kitty packed lightly and took off early the next morning. She found the sound of the leaves crumbling under the wheels to be very soothing and the cold, brisk air delightfully liberating. She made it to Pemberley with relative ease and was welcomed at the door by Lizzy herself.

"Kitty, you know you are always welcomed at Pemberley but I am surprised to see you here. Isn't Sir Jon expected at Longbourn before long?" she asked with great concern.

"That's the problem, Lizzy. Lets enter the house before I break down in tears right here," she said suddenly finding her sorrow could not be restrained.

*   *   *

Sir Jon arrived in Longbourn two weeks later as scheduled. The Bennets met him at the door a bit unnerved since Kitty failed to return from Pemberley as intended. They received a letter from Lizzy late yesterday explaining that Kitty was detained and would not return on time. Mrs Bennet provoked Mr Bennet to retrieve Kitty in spite of any detainment facing her, for nothing could have been more important than Sir Jon's application for her hand. Kitty had to be present for Sir Jon to propose to or her fate would not be sealed. Only the late hour saved Mr Bennet from making the long trek the night before. However, today, as Mrs Bennet fervently welcomed Sir Jon, Mr Bennet mounted his horse to take on the lone jaunt to Pemberley.

"Please, do come in, Sir Jon. We are delighted to see you. I hope your ride was an enjoyable one," started Mrs Bennet cheerfully rushing the stable hand to take his mount. Sir Jon took a swift glance around in search of Kitty. "Are the roads particularly crude this time of year?" she asked to distract him.

"They are entangled with twigs and fallen branches which make them taxing but not completely impassable. Is Miss Catherine far off?" asked Sir Jon.

"You must forgive us for I am sadly obliged to relate a most irksome circumstance. Kitty is not here at the present time as she had to revise her schedule to return unexpectedly," she said ushering him into the house. Sir Jon entered Longbourn agitated by the need to tolerate Kitty's absence when she was thoroughly informed to expect him. He did not care to associate with Mrs Bennet any more than necessary, interpreting her enthusiastic behavior as vulgar and extremely displeasing. He looked about their residence and judged it adequate for the Bennets, but quite inferior to what he was used to. "Actually, she is awaiting Mr Bennet's arrival at her sister's estate. He was to collect her yesterday but was ill prepared to do so then. That is why he has left as you arrived," said Mrs Bennet as she escorted Sir Jon into the parlor. "You must have missed luncheon to have traveled the distance in this perverse weather! I am sure you can use a drink and something hot to fill your stomach. Mary, offer Sir Jon any assistance he needs to make him comfortable and have Hill bring in the soup things with some hearty sandwiches," she said empathetically.

In short time, Sir Jon was sipping hot coffee with Mary sitting across from him in quiet repose. "You will be able to speak to Mr Bennet and ask for Kitty's hand as soon as they return. In the meantime, please accept my hospitality and remain here at Longbourn overnight. I promise you will be very comfortable and they should, by all means, arrive by late morning tomorrow if they get an early start," explained Mrs Bennet as she did not think he would be opposed to the idea.

"I will accept your hospitality since Miss Catherine is expected and you have given it so graciously," he said reluctantly. He was tired and cold from his long ride to Longbourn. He could only blame himself for taking his horse and not his coach in this insidious changing weather. Mrs Bennet was happily relieved.

"Dinner will be served at half pass five. We are to have a small party tonight. I am expecting my sister Mrs Philips, her husband and Sir William Lucas with his wife and daughter, Maria. The Lucases live only one quarter mile down the lane and are old friends of ours. Sir William was knighted in St James court yet remains a very amiable man. You may recall you have met their eldest daughter, Mrs Collins at Pemberely, then again at Rosings. Her husband Mr Collins performed the wedding nuptials for Mr and Mrs Carrington. You missed a lovely wedding—as all weddings are lovely. It is a shame you could not be there, but under the circumstances, it is understood. Mr Collins was at his best, though he does go on a little more than he should. I'm afraid he enjoys hearing his own voice with or without an audience. He is a distant cousin of my Mr Bennet, you know . . . ." said Mrs Bennet in attempt to entertain Sir Jon.

"I would think he was a distant cousin of yours. You seem to have a similar family trait," interrupted the irreverent Sir Jon cutting Mrs Bennet short as he began to realize what his evening was to entail. Mrs

Bennet continued to speak when Sir Jon brusquely requested to see his room.

"Oh, dear me! I did not mean to be so thoughtless. Of course you must be worn-out after your long journey. Follow me," she said leading him up the stairs. "You shall have one of my daughter's old rooms. Jane shared this room with Lizzy prior to their marriages. I had it redecorated as a guestroom since we did not have one before. You can see, the room is big enough for two and they were quite comfortable, as I'm sure you will be too," she said once in the room.

"Thank you. I shall remain upstairs until dinner," he said showing her the door.

"Please do come down in time to meet my guests as they will arrive prior to dinner. They are eager to make your acquaintance," reminded Mrs Bennet joyfully as she left his room. Mrs Bennet was in an exceptionally good humor as she supervised dinner. She had the cook prepare all her best dishes saying, "There shall be soup, partridges, venison and pudding with everything dressed to perfection!" Mrs Bennet prided herself on her domestic skills. Her meals were reputed for being the best in all of Meryton, as Mr Darcy himself would testify. When the Lucases arrived at five o'clock, anxious to meet the infamous Sir Jon, they found Mr and Mrs Philips already there anticipating Sir Jon's appearance as well. While they waited, they debated over Kitty's inconvenient disappearance with collective concern. It was an unfortunate set of circumstances, they all agreed, as they had expected to celebrate the good news of Kitty's engagement.

Instead they were asked to be charitable and ease Sir Jon's inconveniences through merriment and light conversation. United, they commited themselves to provide the best distractions they could until late into the night. Sir William vowed to keep him involved in conversations of St James' court and the aristocracy. Mrs Bennet was very pleased. She was grateful for the benevolence her family and friends displayed.

Incredibly, Sir Jon did not descend in time to mingle with the guests. Despite her attempts to call him, he repeatedly failed to appear. Mrs Bennet was bewildered as he had ample time to recover from his trip and had the intelligence of her program well in advance. She could not help but determine that, excepting illness, he was inexcusably rude, even if he did suffer a blow by the delay in seeing Kitty.

"Sir Jon was expected to come down prior to dinner but must have needed a greater respite than originally thought. He was deeply disappointed that his beloved Kitty was not here, although he should have made the best of it," she said apologetically, making his excuses. She wanted her friends to get the best impression of him as she had long boasted.

"That is strange behavior from someone entering the family," voiced Mrs Philips taking exception. "It should not matter to such a degree, that she is not here when her mother, sister and aunt are. One should think he would take the opportunity to get better acquainted with his future family." She was unforgiving and Mrs Bennet began to feel uneasy.

The Lucases tried to be a bit more condoning and optimistic. Sir William, who was by far the friendliest and most obliging of the entire assembly said, "We should only imagine that his journey here was more strenuous than he let on. The weather is becoming increasingly bitter. We too had a difficult time walking here and we are familiar with the roads. We cannot be so hard on him as he must be inclined to be at his best for dinner. I'm sure I would be too." He was not certain his comments appeased his hostess but was satisfied that he made the attempt.

"Not I. I would make myself available for my hostess and respect her home by putting my best foot forward no matter what the cost to me," stated Mrs Philips.

"Either way, he must be called down for dinner as we will not defer our mealtime," said Mrs Bennet hurt by the affront Sir Jon caused her in front of her guests. She went to knock on his door for the last time without success.

Sir Jon finally emerged from his accommodations forty five minutes late. By then, dinner had been served. He gave an exaggerated bow of apology to everyone. "Please forgive my tardiness as I was more indisposed than, I, myself had guessed." The company looked at each other approvingly, eager to let by gone be by gone.

Mrs Bennet felt redeemed enough to reinvest all her energies in her small reception. She wanted to show him off and did not want the occasion spoiled. Sir William was the first to engage him in conversation. He made repeated attempts to excite Sir Jon's amusement and intrigue but found himself quickly out of topics of interest as Sir Jon did not contribute at all. His responses were brief and to the point, never carrying the dialogue to the next level. Mrs Bennet took her turn by rekindling fond memories of the balls and distractions they shared urging him to recall amusing accounts as well, but again he did not use the appeal to extend the conversation. One by one, everyone tried to engage him. Against social protocol, he slighted them all and to Mrs Bennet's chagrin, he ate the carefully prepared menu without so much as a compliment to her or the cook. His disgraceful conduct made dinner painfully long and protracted as everyone retreated to eat in silence.

With the meal finally over, the party left the dining room. Mr Philips led the men into the library and Mrs Bennet showed the women into the parlor. Just as the women settled to discuss the dinner the men entered into the parlor as well. It seems there was no need to keep separate as Sir Jon did not approve of the brand of smoke or drink Mr Bennet supplied preferring a hot cup of tea instead, in anticipation of a good night's sleep. It was a quiet party with Sir Jon sitting separate from the rest and no one daring to speak since what they had on their minds was his distasteful, arrogant, antisocial behavior. By now they were fully aware that he had no intention of speaking or associating with them. Desperate to recover the evening, Mrs Bennet had the tea things put away offering a game of whist to fill the void, but Sir Jon would not participate.

"Card games are not to my fancy when the stakes are not worth the effort. It is quite a bore if you ask me. However, a good night's rest shall provide me with a much more enjoyable distraction," he said pompously, making a further nuisance of himself.

Mrs Bennet recalled that he did indeed wager large and thought that her party, falling short of his terms, were in fact the ones at fault. "Well then, Sir Jon," she said attempting to please him, "Mary can entertain us at the pianoforte. She is quite good you know especially since we had no musician to teach her. She took it up completely through her own effort."

She signaled for Mary to play. Mary rose dutifully, for her mother's sake, as the guests welcomed whatever form of entertainment Mrs Bennet provided. Mary played aggressively, eager to liven up the party. The company endured it well and sat back to be entertained. Sir Jon rose with impunity and went upstairs to his room without so much as a thank you or goodnight. Everyone was shocked at his brash behavior. Even the placating Sir William found his actions indefensible.

"He must be preoccupied with asking Mr Bennet for Kitty's hand. Things will be different tomorrow. You shall see," explained Mrs Bennet regretting that she made him the apex of the evening. "Shall we call it a night?"

Happily, the guests agreed it would be best to leave and wrapped themselves in their cloaks to return home. Huddled at the door, they observed the aftermath of an unexpected snowfall that prevented them from leaving.

"The snow covers the ground thickly, Mrs Bennet, and the fallen leaves make for a most slippery condition. I am afraid we do not live so close as to risk this hazardous journey in the dark. The Philipses must spend the night and so should we," surmised Sir William. He did not like causing Mrs Bennet any further undue hardship, especially when she was so obviously in need of her solitude but he and his wife did not want to risk falling and breaking a bone.

"Do not worry Sir William. There is room enough for all to stay the night. We just need a little cooperation from everyone," she quickly responded preventing any more offenses toward her cherished friends. "My sister, Mrs Philips may sleep in my room with me while you and Lady Lucas sleep in Mr Bennet's room. Maria can use Kitty's bed in Mary's room. Mr Philips, I regret, you must share with Sir Jon in Jane and Lizzy's old room." Those were the best accommodations Mrs Bennet could arrange with the amount of rooms she had in the house, supplying everyone with a bed to sleep on. Pleased with the arrangements and

Mrs Bennet's kindness, the Philipses and the Lucases accepted without hesitation. Unfortunately, the same could not be said of Sir Jon who was less than agreeable to it, for he would not share his room with anyone, let alone a mere solicitor.

"You cannot expect a man of my rank and stature to share a night with another whose society is so beneath him. Send them on their way! The weather cannot be as bad as all that," he responded as he closed the door preventing further negotiation. Mrs Bennet found her nerves severely challenged. She could not endure any more of his brazen lack of cooperation and determined him the most offensive and haughty of men. Under any other circumstances, she would have thrown him out on his ear but the thought of Kitty forced her to keep uncharacteristically composed. Mr Philips graciously offered to stay in a parlor chair by the fire with the addition of a blanket promising he would be the warmest of them all. Reluctantly, Mrs Bennet allowed him to do so, thanking him for the gallant sacrifice. Her guests went to their assigned rooms thanking Mrs Bennet for her generousity, bidding each other a good night.

In her bed, Mrs Bennet spent a most disturbing sleepless night. Her thoughts wandered from event to event. 'Today, here tonight, I gained a new prospective on Sir Jon. He has an unyielding air of self importance and remains above his company no matter what the circumstance. I have long accepted that behavior from the higher upper classes, as is their privilege, but his manner delivers that strong hubristic effect that Lady Catherine herself condemned when she warned me of him. She is a good friend to have given me such fine counsel. This behavior in a son in law is intolerable. His unscrupulous, apathetic attitude and disagreeable countenance make him sink down low like a stone in water. He even eclipses the old Mr Darcy, the one I loathed from the start for his grandeur. Yet, as disagreeable and horrid as Mr Darcy was, he came around admirably through his insatiable love for Lizzy. But, what if Kitty cannot shake this ill manner,' thought Mrs Bennet disconsolately tossing and turning. 'Many marriages are formed with the idea that happiness would evolve as time passes, even when the possibility was not evident from the start, however in this case there may be no hope at all! I would not do that to my Kitty for all the fortune in the world. Lizzy and Jane would just have to continue having balls until we could find her another rich and proper man. Alas, the way things stand Kitty is already wholeheartedly attached. The way she moped her days away at Rosings when he left her side. The way she went to Lizzy's to prepare for a new life. No, I must make the best of it if he is the target of her desires.'

She turned to get some benefit out of the rest of the night but discovered Mrs Philips's snoring would not allow her to drift away in quiet slumber. 'What if Mr Bennet and Kitty do not make it home in this weather? How can I keep Sir Jon distracted without an outburst on my part? They must make it home or I may not be able to hold true to my convictions,' she thought as she finally closed her eyes.

*   *   *

Meanwhile, at Pemberley in the very same evening, Mr Bennet was greeted by Lizzy. "Papa, I am surprised to see you here!" she exclaimed. "I never thought you would ride all this way on horseback!"

"What was I to do when Kitty had the coach? Mrs Bennet was beside herself when she did not return as promised and sent me to personally fetch her post haste. Sir Jon has arrived at Longbourn and sits in our parlor as we speak. The man himself saw me ride off earlier today. Now, where is Kitty? She must be told to be ready to leave by the crack of dawn for Mrs Bennet fears Sir Jon may come to his senses and flee before Kitty is properly contracted away," he said with his usual tact.

A servant took his outergarments and waited for further orders. "Papa, come and warm yourself by the fire. You could not have had dinner if you are just arriving. I will have something hot and nutritious prepared for you," she said sending the servant off to fulfill the task.

"Later. Right now I just want to see Kitty," he said again asserting to do his duty before he would relax.

"She is in the salon. I'll take you there if you want to see her right away," answered Lizzy.

"Indeed, I do. I would like to know why she was so unavoidably detained that she would leave her intended waiting, forcing me to come all this way."

"Papa, you should know, we have another guest with us who arrived earlier today as well. It was Mr Darcy and I who would not allow Kitty to leave until she met with him. Kitty is not at fault here for she was unaware of the arrangement we made and therefore could not inform you as to the nature of the delay. In reality, we too, were not sure of his accepting our invitation and would not cause undue stress to anyone by announcing him before actually achieving the gentleman's presence. I want you to be collected and in good spirits before you meet him. Would you like to sit with me in the family parlor before seeing them?"

"Lizzy, dear, I did not come prepared for a social call but if I am to meet someone of such significance, I will not procrastinate. I do not want to be conceived as pompous, you know."

"Never you, Papa," said Lizzy lovingly leading him to the salon.

Once there, they found Mr Darcy, Kitty and Dr Kindrel staring at Lizzy in deafening silence, trying to read her face for clues as to Mr Bennet's demeanor. Mr Darcy finally spoke up while walking over to greet his father in law.

"Mr Bennet, it is an unexpected pleasure to have you here with us tonight. You must be tired from your long excursion. Do sit by the fire and have a glass of Port with us. Perhaps you might enjoy taking it with brandy? It should help warm you quickly. You remember Dr Kindrel, don't you?" he said placing a drink in Mr Bennet's hand. Dr Kindrel bowed respectfully and stood to maintain the floor until Mr Bennet would sit. Mr Bennet spotted Kitty and began to address her after a brief greeting to the doctor.

"Kitty, you have worried your mother to distraction when you did not return. Have you forgotten the love smitten Sir Jon? Go up now and gather your things for we must depart at the very crack of dawn so that I may give your hand away and put your mother at ease by breakfast."

"Sir, . . ." said Dr Kindrel still trying to attain his attention.

"Papa, if I leave now, it would serve only to make me suffer the most unhappiest set of events that were ever set before me in my entire life!" cried Kitty in protest.

"Now Kitty, don't hold back. I can tell, through your self restraint, you mean to spare me but go on child. Be out with it," he said leaning back in his chair preparing himself to be overwhelmed.

"Papa," she began slowly gathering her thoughts, hoping to proceed with discretion in front of the others. "I almost don't know where to begin but I feel I must first tell you that I have met someone who I consider the most wonderful, considerate and honorable man I have ever had the privilege to know—only, it is not Sir Jon."

"You are the ambitious one! I can see that your mother has taught you well. But my excellent understanding tells me your good senses have escaped you. Let me remind you, you are already announced as promised to Sir Jon and, as society has it, you cannot have two. You must be generous and leave some of the men for the other single ladies. If you proceed in this fashion, no one will take you seriously," he said bracing himself for more. "As for your intended, he is waiting for you at Longbourn."

"I shall never marry Sir Jon, Papa when I am so determined to marry Dr Kindrel," she blurted forgetting the good doctor had not yet proposed. Turning to him she solemnly blurted, "Wonderful, loveliest, most handsome Dr Kindrel, I am not promised to Sir Jon as he has never asked me but only assumed it to be so. I could never accept anyone's proposal but your own and since it is only you I desire, please tell my father that we are to marry or I will never give myself to anyone for the rest of my life!"

"Miss Catherine, I can never tell your father any such thing," he said shaking his head to the mortification of everyone in the room. Mr Bennet, rescuing his daughter from her own humiliation, broke in swiftly with an apology to the doctor.

"Dr Kindrel, please forgive my capricious daughter for there is a strong trait of dementia in the family, on her mother's side of course, which passed directly to Kitty making her the most foolish of all my daughters, which, in this family, is no easy feat. You can see she displays no shortage of drama and imagination. I suggest that you can hardly take her, or any of them, seriously for they will drive you to celibacy!" Turning to admonish Kitty, he said, "Now child, I see no reason to linger. The coach shall light the lanterns and if we proceed slowly, we can make it home by dawn," he said changing his plans to leave right away. Kitty was visibly stricken by both her father's comments and Dr Kindrel's refusal. She moved in agonizing sorrow to her father's side but Dr Kindrel reached out to stop her in her tracks.

"Please do not mistake me Sir. I have not refused Miss Catherine's most welcomed sweet proposal and shall make no attempt to forget the application," he said addressing Mr Bennet. "I confess that your daughter, Miss Catherine, has completely filled my mind and heart ever since our first encounter in London where I had determined her my most excellent, settled purpose in life. I do not refuse her, because I shall never refuse her anything. I have not asked for her hand myself, knowing I could not, at present, provide her with all she deserves. Only my concern for her well being has made it impossible for me to deter her from her promised comfort and riches, but as destiny has brought us together one more time, calling on me to expose my truest, selfish sentiments, I find I can't be prudent. Indeed, if I am so fortunate to have her, as her father, I must first ask you to be wise on her behalf because I find I can no longer endure her torturous absence from my life and will no longer selflessly sacrifice my needs. I ask you please to consider my proposal of marriage to her instead of Sir Jon's. In deference to you, I will not take her away if you refuse. Yet know this, I have a successful practice and work hard. I have made a name for myself that should prove to honor her and provide for a secure honest living in our future. If you consent, I will indelibly cherish her for the rest of my life," he said holding Kitty's hand so she could acknowledge his sincerity.

All eyes fell on Mr Bennet who needed a moment or two to contemplate. Mr Bennet sat quietly, sipping on his Port before he finally answered. "My good man," he began, "there is something to be said for fair play, and although Sir Jon awaits Kitty at Longbourn, you were the first to honorably ask for her hand. Kitty," he said, "I would never allow you to sacrifice yourself for the sake of your mother if you cannot also be happy in the process and since she herself has often said, 'one man is as good as another,' you not only have my consent but my blessing and good wishes as well."

"Thank you, Papa," she exclaimed embracing him happily as the Darcys looked on feeling quite relieved. Mr Darcy rang for the servant and ordered, "There is champagne in the cellarette, Sarah. Bring it forth as we are to have a toast!"

"Yes Sir. Right away," she responded hurriedly.

"We will make a toast to the triumphant union of the future Dr and Mrs Kindrel!"

During the merrymaking, Lizzy commended her father for putting Kitty's contentment first as he had once done for her. "I knew you would not let Kitty down if it came to her happiness versus Mama's, or I myself would have been married to Mr Collins these past few years!" she laughed. "Papa, how will you tell Mama? You must stand fast for I fear she will not approve of Kitty's failing to marry Sir Jon. I suggest you try to console her with the knowledge that Kitty will achieve the life she has always dreamed of in finally getting her officer."

"Do not fear for me, Lizzy. I will take great pleasure in executing the deed. You know very well that I live for the very sport of keeping Mrs Bennet humble. I should like to see how she settles the matter with our friends and neighbors. It will prove quite the challenge for her as her flaunting of the illustrious Sir Jon was one of the most thorough operations I have ever seen," he jested as they rejoiced in what was to come.

*   *   *

The morning sun rose over Longbourn sooner than Mrs Bennet hoped. Executing her duties by her guests, she rose early to provide everyone with a lush and lavish breakfast. Sir Jon awoke to find the snow had not only prevented the guests from leaving but may also prevent Miss Catherine from returning. He promptly requested to take his breakfast in his room. Never allowing anyone the privilege, Mrs Bennet willfully declined the request. She was on edge from her lack of sleep and was not in the mood to endure his ostentatious grandeurs so early in the day. If Sir Jon wanted to breakfast, he had to come down for it or continue to fast.

"Hill, tell Sir Jon that it is not our custom to eat in our beds and there shall be no exceptions," instructed Mrs Bennet. "We will wait precisely five minutes more for him before we proceed." Sir William stood gazing out the window as the snow turned to rain. Sir Jon soon made his appearance and joined them for breakfast.

"Mrs Bennet, it has been most inconsiderate of Miss Catherine to keep me waiting like this. I am deeply offended and cannot believe you have brought her up to be so discourteous," he complained as he sat himself down for his meal without greeting the others.

Mrs Bennet did not want to ruin breakfast for her guests. "Please believe this has never happened before, has it Mrs Philips," she answered defending herself while motioning her guests to sit as well.

"No, of course not. Never! We came to celebrate the good news and were all caught by surprise that Miss Catherine was not here," commented Mrs Philips as the others nodded in agreement trying to console Sir Jon.

"I thank you for the reminder, Mrs Philips," he said sarcastically.

"In the light of day, the fallen snow seems less threatening. The rain will work to melt it even faster. I think the roads are much improved and should be passable now. We thank you for your gracious hospitality and your exquisite meals, Mrs Bennet but we will leave promptly after breakfast," proclaimed Sir William triumphantly. Mrs Bennet accepted his compliments with the deepest gratitude. It was nice to be appreciated for all her troubles and she began to recover her good graces.

"It is difficult for me to believe it impassable last night when it is not yet winter," challenged Sir Jon. "If there were any threat at all, I myself would not have made the trip. I should have waited for spring, but I suppose being put out is part of the obligation. I daresay it is rather a bothersome thing to ask Mr Bennet for his daughter's hand. How old fashioned is this useless protocol that demands respect for the family when none should be had. It has made an insensible demand on my time. Miss Catherine should agree to my proposal and that should be the end of it. I should have done this at Rosings when the mood was right. Now it is complete aggravation."

Those words were unforgivable. He had belittled Mr Bennet's rightful place to approve of his daughter's future and in doing so insulted the respectability his wife and entire household fully deserved.

"Sir Jon, you take unbridled liberties with that preposterous notion! I find it hard to believe that someone of your birth and station could have so little regard for convention and ceremony. It is of no small importance. That attitude is indecent. Do you not realize that, besides our breeding and individual fortunes, etiquette and custom is what separates the classes? It would be a dangerous sign of disrespect to us, and all people of society, for you to advocate such behavior," stated Sir William trying to protect the Bennets' honor. "Such a commentary can only be taken as an offense to your gentle hostess. I would ask that you refrain from the conversation in her presence, especially with the absence of Mr Bennet."

"Take it as you wish. I will not bend to tradition when it does not suit me and neither will Miss Catherine when she is my wife. She will do as I say when I alone am her lord and master." Sir William recoiled as Sir Jon spoke. He had put forth his best effort but having no true authority in Longbourn, he found there was nothing more he could do.

The other guests were equally astonished but remained respectful to their present situation in an effort to calm the distressful atmosphere, feeling pity for Mrs Bennet and most of all, Miss Catherine. Neither of them could understand how the Bennet family could possibly find contentment in such a man.

Mrs Bennet was greatly humiliated. She was ashamed that she brought Sir Jon into her home to insult her family and good friends. Furthermore, to publicly claim to be a lord and master over Kitty and recklessly bring her to her ruin was fundamentally unacceptable. She could not be restrained.

"Sir Jon, allow me to help you reach a certain reality. This is my home and I will suffer you no more. You are the most disagreeable, contemptible, distasteful excuse for a gentleman I have ever seen. Your antagonistic haughtiness is completely inappropriate here yet you have used your privilege to accost me and my guests in every way imaginable. You should have learned by now that superiority comes from more than just a title. It comes from civility and respect both of which you, Sir, have been found deficient. I will not allow your black heart to infect my innocent Kitty for you will be no relation of mine. You are undone in this house and I ask you to leave it right away for your arrogant self importance is nothing to me and mine!" she said as her blood ran high.

"Mrs Bennet, you have looked deep into a society you so obviously know nothing of. Nobility begins with a bold piece of land and rich blood. There is nothing more required of us. But I am not here to educate you for you seem to overlook the fact that I have come for one purpose only and that is Miss Catherine's hand. She will marry me despite your disapproval for she is irretrievably captivated by me. You will not be able to prohibit our marriage as she is of age to continue without your blessing or that of Mr Bennet. I shall leave only when Miss Catherine returns as we have made inexorable promises to each other. I remain steadfast in my proposal and when she arrives we will leave post haste never to distress your home again, as was my true intention. And since nothing more of significance can be said, I will await her upstairs," he said undermining Mrs Bennet's authority. Unruffled, he turned and went up to his room.

Sir Lucas and Mr Philips felt helpless as Sir Jon ascended the stairs. They were no physical match for him and he could not be otherwise persuaded. The women gathered around Mrs Bennet as she was near fainting from the impact of it all. She was filled with grief as her heart lay heavy for Kitty.

"Mary, you were right. There is no companion worth giving up all you are and all you have been taught in life. This man is incompatible for anyone but himself. It is beyond comprehension that I have given my approval to their marriage at Rosings. His coming to ask Mr Bennet for her hand puts us all in a bind for it is true that she loves him dearly," cried Mrs Bennet feeling disenchanted and totally defeated. She was escorted to a sofa in the parlor and wrapped with a blanket while her caring friends tried to console her. "I hope it rains heavily so Mr Bennet cannot return with Kitty," she said as a last resort.

No sooner did she complete her sentence when a faint breeze ushered Mr Bennet into the vestibule with heavily soaked garments. "Mr Bennet!" exclaimed Mrs Bennet rising from her seat to push him out the door. "You must leave this instant. Go back. You are not wanted here!" she exclaimed in a panic.

"Mrs Bennet! Have you lost your mind completely? Loosen your grip and let me go, woman! It is unbearable out there and I deserve no such treatment," he said forcing his way back in.

"Oh Mr Bennet," cried Mrs Bennet breaking down with the loss of all hope. "I must give you a full account of what has transpired here before you utter another word," she said crying so furiously, she could not continue. The others had to inform him of the day's occurrences while she sat moaning frantically at every mention of the affair. "He is a foul man who came only to pollute our doorstep and kidnap our Kitty!" she finally blurted out.

"Well, open the door, Mrs Bennet, and let the fresh air in, for if he offends, he must be put out," he said soothing his wife with unexpected composure. He took the time to remove his hat, gloves, and coat with complacency and said, "It is a good thing I traveled hard and fast. I thought I was coming to deliver a most foreboding message but under these circumstances, I find it will be my pleasure to speak to Sir Jon and present him with a note Kitty has entrusted me to deliver to him." He went up the stairs and knocked on Sir Jon's door.

"Mr Philips, you should have accompanied him for Sir Jon will surely abuse him with no physical constraint. He is so well built and my Mr Bennet is so fatigued and out of shape. Look at him! His entire body is the very essence of atrophy! He will surely be killed and I shall be out of Longbourn tomorrow!" she cried. " Sister," she said to Mrs Philips trying to collect herself, "there is a duke you know but I threw away his advances. He is a little more weathered than my Mr Bennet, yet, if I need him, he would come to my aid straightaway. You should have seen him, Sister," she said getting Mrs Philips' full attention, "I gave him one dance and he was undone. It just wasn't enough for him! I wish you could have seen the way he dressed. He was cloaked with elegant refinery. So dignified! But, oh, what a disaster it will be!" she said turning to Mary. "I will have to renew my relationship with that lovesick decaying duke for our mere survival," she said. "This has been an education for me. You will not marry into nobility, Mary, as I cannot go through this again," she claimed as she took Mary's hand while everyone wondered if Mrs Bennet had not lost her mind for the last time. Mary quickly nodded in acknowledgement, vowing never to marry nobility. Satisfied with Mary's agreement, Mrs Bennet returned to her conversation of the duke. "I have not mentioned my duke before for he was my surprise to Mr Bennet when he would provoke me next," she explained to Mrs Philips. "I wanted to make Mr Bennet delightfully jealous but now, facing the prospect of actually being with that man makes it all so disagreeable. How could I ever have planned to jest about it," she cried disconcertedly. "Oh, I cannot bear to see my poor defenseless Mr Bennet wounded."

The seriousness of her final comment redirected everyone's attention to Mr Bennet's plight. They heard the forceful movement of footsteps above as they stood gravely listening for the clamor of the rough and tumble physical violence would bring, each wondering how Mr Bennet would survive it.

But the clamor never came. Within a matter of minutes, Sir Jon took his leave to brave the cruel weather as singular as he arrived. He gave no thanks to Mrs Bennet and no good byes to her companions. Everyone stood breathless until Mr Bennet returned downstairs where he was rushed by them all at once as he entered the parlor. Gently pushing them aside he escorted Mrs Bennet back to the sofa where he quietly sat her down.

"Mr Bennet, what happened? What did you say? Did he assault you? How did you finally persuade him to leave without Kitty?" questioned Mrs Bennet while the others were held in equal suspense.

"I cannot own up to the credit myself, Mrs Bennet. That honor goes to Kitty who has managed it single handedly," he confessed as he sat down beside his wife.

"This is no time for riddles, Mr Bennet, and where is Kitty? For the sake of my nerves, be swift with your news," insisted Mrs Bennet.

"Kitty wrote him a letter which I promptly delivered at the door as I stepped inside the room," he began.

"What letter? What did it say? Is she meeting him elsewhere to elope in Gretna Green as Lydia had done? She did envy Lydia so." Her comment gave Mr Bennet cause for pause. The eager audience closed in on him so as to encourage him to continue.

"I did not read it but I knew full well that its content explained how she was attached to another and could not, in good faith, marry him." The company gasped in amazement.

"Whatever do you mean she loved another? She was enamored with Sir Jon. Who else was there for her to love?" questioned Mrs Bennet in complete shock.

"Dr Kindrel. Apparently she met him in London during Jane's fatal illness," he said to Mrs Bennet.

"Jane had no fatal illness, Mr Bennet. What are you talking about?" she asked frazzled by yet another development.

"Kitty watched over our Jane during her stay in London. Jane had pneumonia and could have died along with her blessed unborn. There is where Kitty first met Dr Kindrel, who brought our Jane back to perfect health. He became very attached to our Kitty and when they met again at Pemberley they did not come together thinking you would not approve." Mr Bennet gave Mrs Bennet a stern look of admonition forcing her to cower away.

"The poor dears," she said knowing full well she was to blame. "I was overcome by titles and vast fortunes. I only wanted a change of community for her," she admitted. "You know, Sister, every exertion on my part was only for the future happiness of my daughters."

"Colonel Fitzwilliam had known of Dr Kindrel's feelings for her as it was all the doctor would speak of when they traveled to join the regiment. He then learned of Kitty's true feelings at Rosings and related them to Mr Darcy that same night. It seems Dr Kindrel gave her up so she could benefit from a better life in a baronetage."

"How selfless," sobbed Mrs Bennet as all the ladies affections were won over. "I do love that man! He is wholesome, well mannered and all that is good," she said wiping a tear remembering how many times he sat with her to pass the time of day.

"Mr Darcy kept it to himself refusing to interfere with the courtship of Sir Jon and Kitty. It was not until Kitty visited Pemberley last week that he came to understand that Kitty abhorred Sir Jon and was just marrying him to please her mother." Mrs Bennet let out a wail forcing Mrs Philips to comfort her as the story continued to unfold. "Lizzy, the dear soul, contacted Dr Kindrel and asked him to pay them a visit on the premise of an emergency, as she fully considered it. By the time I arrived, Dr Kindrel was already there, and he and Kitty were sworn lovers. Kitty did not know how to break the news to me but Dr Kindrel handled it with the greatest of skill. Truthfully, he is a decent gentleman above the rest. I gave my permission, for any man who has saved the life of my Jane and would please Kitty was worth facing your wrath, Mrs Bennet. They were married at Pemberley by their parson as part of our celebration last night. I am glad to say Kitty was very happy as she rode off in our carriage with her uniformed husband back to the militia."

Mr Bennet rose to leave the room for his library. He turned back and added, "By the way, my dear Mrs Bennet, it was not for naught that Dr Kindrel visited the Darcys in any case. As fate would have it, our Lizzy became faint and was properly examined by him. Apparently she is with child," he said nonchalantly and exited the room hearing the cheers and glad tidings of his friends and family.

*   *   *

As winter turned to spring, Dr and Mrs Kindrel returned to Longbourn. Mrs Bennet embraced him lovingly. He was respectful and considerate and she loved him as her own son. She hosted a ball for them in Netherfield to honor their marriage and proudly showed him to her friends and neighbors. Mary extended an invitation to Daniel who graciously accepted, as his parishioners urged him to seek her out for their benefit. He took the opportunity to remain for an extended stay in Lucas Lodge as a member of their family. The festivities provided abundant pleasures for everyone as Dr Kindrel was well received by them all.

Soon after the ball, Mrs Bennet hosted an intimate gathering for her daughters, their respective husbands and children. She and Mr Bennet were swollen with pride for their family and wanted to see them collected together in Longbourn as they had not been in a long time.

Mrs Bennet was preparing the children to join their parents outside, as she was delighted to have charge of their care whenever they were present. Requiring Mr Bennet's assistance to usher them outdoors, they approached the library and knocked on his door. She was taken by surprise when she was confronted by Daniel promptly exiting the room. He gallantly held the door open to let them in as he walked out with a satisfying smile. Occupied with the children, Mrs Bennet promptly requested a helping hand from Mr Bennet who readily complied. As they started outdoors, Mrs Bennet was taken by a sudden distraction.

"Mr Bennet," she said as she held him back, "could I be observing what I think I am?"

Mr Bennet looked into the garden and observed Miss Mary Bennet in the company of Daniel holding hands. "We better not go out just now, Mrs Bennet," he suggested turning her around. "You would not want to interrupt a proper marriage proposal now, would you?" he asked as he closed the door. Mrs Bennet dragged him to the window which provided the best view of the charming new couple. She let out a shriek of bliss when she observed them steal a kiss. "Mr Bennet, we are the most fortunate people on the face of this earth!"

Mr Bennet lifted little Elizabeth up to Mrs Bennet's arms and lovingly patted the fair head of young Charles who stood nearby. "You may inform me when it's safe to go out," he said as he returned to the library, leaving Mrs Bennet standing guard, happily peering out the window.

Lightning Source UK Ltd.
Milton Keynes UK
173840UK00001B/29/P